# Maui out of Body

By

## Oliver Gold

D1311198

*"It's no wonder that truth is stranger than fiction.
Fiction has to make sense."*
**Mark Twain**

*"There's no fiction story worth telling
that can't be made stranger by mixing in the truth."*
**Oliver Gold**

**Maui Out of Body**

**Copyright © 2018 Oliver Gold / Aloha S T Entertainment
All rights reserved**

**Except for use in any review the reproduction or
utilization of this work in whole or in part in printed film
or electronic form is a violation of copyright laws and a
mortal sin.**

**Second Edition
ISBN-13: 978-1722709709
ISBN-10: 1722709707**

*My mind is bent to tell of bodies changed
into new forms, O gods,
for you yourselves have wrought the changes,
breathe on these my undertakings, and bring down my
song in unbroken strains from the world's very beginning
even unto the present time.*

**From, "The Metamorphoses"
written by the Roman poet, Ovid, circa, 8 C.E.**

## Books by Oliver Gold

**Maui on the Rocks**
**Maui Leis an' Lies**
**Maui out of Body**

**Available on Amazon.com**

## 1 Cosmic Blackjack

The dealer at the table was an unforgiving spook feared by all... 'Karma.' He looked like Mark Twain in a rumpled, white-linen dinner jacket. His bow tie hung untied. His whiskered face frowned at his cards like Twain's used to, after sipping plain water. He leaned back in his casino chair, blew smoke rings from his cigar, and waited for Oliver Gold's next mistake.

"Card?" Karma-Twain offered, 'Tom Sawyer-mischief' dancing in his ancient, little bloodshot eyes. He held the deck out in front of him. It wasn't a pack of Tarot cards like you might imagine. No, just regulation Hoyle playing cards stained from years of tears, sweat and spilled Coca-Cola.

Oliver added up the two cards already in his hand, a *seven and a six... makes thirteen, probably the worst hand in Blackjack.* He'd have to take a card. Ole looked across the table at the other two players. The 'Specter of Death' was hunched over with extreme arthritis from swinging his scythe since life began. For once begun, Death's career, was never ending. His eyeless face seemed to be staring into Oliver's future as he sharpened that long blade with a whetstone. The slow scrape, scrape... made Ole's teeth hurt. It was an annoying high-pitched squeal... like a security alarm on a rental car. Death glared out from under his hooded, black sweatshirt. He had a grin on his skull like he was posing for a new pirate flag. It was an unreadable poker-face grin, all teeth and bones. But they weren't playing poker. They never played poker. They always played Blackjack.

The other player at the table was, 'Eternal Re-birth.' She looked like a chubby, baby-faced cupid with a romance-arrow notched in her little bow. Her rapidly beating wings provided the only breeze in the riverboat casino of Oliver's mind.

Ole stalled for time. He had stranger things to consider than taking another hit from Karma. This morning's phone call of doom had hit him like a bowled 'Strike.' All his pins went flying and the rolling ball of his former life disappeared into the machine of time. Hours later, his body, mind and spirit were still disconnected. It was like that stun-buzz you get when you bang your elbow on something hard. His nervous system was still paralyzed or whatever that feeling is when it happens.

What he'd become after that phone call, would haunt him for the rest of his life. It was shocking, like he'd taken a high dive into the shallow end of the pool. Even worse, because this time, he had a body to hide. Oliver looked at his cards. They stared back with tattered indifference. He looked up at the three women painted high on the ceiling inside his mind. They were the darlings of a beautiful mural, kind of like the Sistine Chapel; only these three angels were naked:  His ex-wife, Tanya was depicted swinging a sword, battling imaginary enemies in the Salvador Dali clouds above her. A legion of evil, winged-attorneys surrounded her, urging her on and on forever into the divorce war she had wanted so badly. Her golden hair was swirling down her naked back, white as a dove.

*Yah brah, you plan your retirement in Hawaii with Tanya. She drives you to the Seattle airport, kisses you goodbye and hires divorce attorneys meaner than Charles Manson. (Ever since the divorce, new voices like this one,* haunt the casino.)

Painted alongside Tanya was Suki, the petite Japanese millionaire he'd met on Maui. She was depicted wearing only a leather tool belt around her slim naked waist. Bent over, cute, bare butt in the air, remodeling a circular stairway that led up into Tanya's clouds.

*Suki with the big crush on you. She has almost everything you ever wanted in a woman: the mansion, the Mercedes convertible and an insatiable mania for sex. She likes you so much, she lets you move in, to help her remodel her big house. When you get it almost done, she throws you out and lets a handsome finish carpenter move in.*

Next to Suki was Desiree, his glamorous booking agent with the tall, well-gifted body of an Italian fashion model. She's posing at the top of Suki's stairway like a naked Playboy bunny, throwing money into the clouds with wild abandon.

*Desiree gonna make you a rock star. Books you in Las Vegas! Face it brah you believe in everyone you meet, especially the pretty women.* That haunting voice was right, he was the epitome of the Fool card in the Tarot deck. A jester of a man, hiking in the mountains, his gaze on clouds of fanciful imaginations, while stepping off the edge of a cliff.

He would always remember those three women like that; beautiful, crazy, and naked. The mural was painted on clouds of imagination that encircled a turning wheel. This was the samsara wheel of Oliver's life. It looked like it was wobbling out of control. Maybe it'd blown a tire. He should 'a known better. Cause and effect, believing and heart break, are two sides of the same karma coin, inescapable.

His first mistake... believing in Tanya, was just youthful idealism. His second mistake with Suki... well okay, he's a slow learner. His third mistake? The big-money musical career promised by Desiree, had left him wondering where to hide a body.

*Yah where? Maui's a small island.* The voice in his head sounded dead serious. This was serious.

*Pray my son, pray from your heart.* Now, there was a sweet voice he recognized, his own mother's. *Mom's solution to everything, was prayer.* He considered this for a moment. *Why hadn't he taken her advice right away?*

He held his two cards in front of his forehead so his third eye could think about it. This hand of Blackjack was taking too long for Karma, Death and Re-birth. They got up from the table and headed for the casino's bar.

Oliver wrestled with the idea of prayer. *Was there even a God to pray to?* Ole was a retired chemistry teacher, skeptical but not an atheist. Being an atheist would be too much work, trying to defend a theory that claimed there were no other theories. He'd seen the photos from the Hubble telescope. Space had a lot more galaxies for a supreme God to rule over than previously thought. Uncountable galaxies; each with more stars than all the grains of sand on the earth. *How do we know that?* He wondered. *How big a number is that?* Ole would need more than a slide-rule to figure how exponential that must be; a number so large, that even his hand calculator couldn't calc it.

Skepticism is the back bone of the scientific method. He brought it with him to theology as well. He wanted to believe in God, but the scientist in him wasn't sure how or why he should. He grew up believing in Jesus. He still loved Jesus, whose only crime, was trying to teach compassion.

*Uh huh, all this sweet talk coming from a guy who needs to hide a body? Who you kidding? We know who you are. We are you.*

Oliver ignored the voices. The biggest headache for religion these days was science. Mankind's successful pursuit of knowledge had pushed disease, fear, and ignorance aside. The space age was pushing *religion* into a corner as well. In July 1969, the single most powerful blow to myth and religion happened. Neil Armstrong and Buzz Aldrin walked on earth's moon. Everyone on earth could see for themselves, on world-wide television. There were no pearly gates, no angels with golden slippers, no green or blue cheese, no cow jumping over. Just the moon, a dusty and a barren satellite of rock, circling a small water planet in space. This should have iced it for skeptical Oliver Gold, however, there was a disturbing flaw in his scientific mind. He still wanted to believe in Jesus. Sure, he wanted to find self-realization like the Buddha. But the hard, cold facts of life could now be found in the gospel of the Hubble Telescope. *How did Pascal's wager go?* He tried to remember. *Something about the value of believing or not?*

Oliver knew that 'believing,' was the root cause of all his disappointment and anger. Believing in stuff, believing in people, especially beautiful women, made his heart an easy target for Cupid's arrows and the heartbreak that follows. *Did Pascal win or lose his bet?* Ole tried to think. The answer was coming to him, bit by bit from a philosophy class at Drake University a long time ago.

*Thirty-seven years ago, old man.* That stubborn inner voice has a calendar and he's not afraid to use it.

No matter, the voice was right this time. It had been A while since he was in college. Ole remembered a little about Blaise Pascal. He was an accountant doing the basic adding and subtracting that accountant worker-bees do all day. Smarter than the average bee, he invented the first integer-based calculator. This made his work much easier, so he patented it. That invention from the mid-seventeenth century was the best mathematical machine of its kind for over two-hundred years.

Pascal's other inventions were stuck to the rim of Oliver's memory like burnt pizza on the edge of a pan. Hydraulic power and the syringe to name only two. The small bits of pizza crust he could remember of Pascal's theology, went something like this: *There is more value in believing in God than not believing.*

Drake University professor, Thom Landry explained it to his philosophy students in simpler terms:

"It's a safer bet, to believe in God. He will know you believe because He's keeping track of all your thoughts as well as ruling over all the monkeys, giraffes, ants, fish, clams, and every other creature on earth. Plus, he keeps track of every living thing on millions of planets all over the vastness of space. That's a lot of bad behavior to keep track of, but he's God, so he can get around faster than the speed of your puny imagination, which is really slow compared to His."

Ole remembered prof's logical conclusion. He could still hear the little old man's big baritone voice exaggerate each word:

"So... when... you... die... and... you... will... die," he explained, in case his students had any doubt. "If... you're a believer and you're good in this life, you have a chance of getting into Heaven. Bingo! You win.

"But… if… you… don't… believe… in… God… when… you… die, and by some unlucky chance you were right, there is no god. Ta dah! Congratulations! You win! But what did you win? No God, no Heaven, no nothing. So, what did you gain by not believing? Nothing." Prof Landry stopped for a moment, wiped off his eye glasses with a handkerchief, then dramatically placed them back on his unshaven, old face. He slid his glasses down his nose with one hand and looked over the tops of the lenses. This was his, *'I'm serious here, so pay attention,'* teacher pose. Maybe that's why Oliver remembered him, so many years later.

"But… if…you… did… not… believe… in… God, and there *is* a God. Surprise! There's a God! Then just because you didn't believe in Him, and He will know because he's been keeping track of you… because He loves you… and wants you to change your mind before you die, but you don't. So, when you die, you lose Pascal's wager. Now, you're totally out of luck. Because, the moment your dead, God's vengeance awaits you. You don't get an attorney, you don't get to plea bargain. You don't even get a trial. Your head is shaved, your identity is checked in the big judgment book, you get knocked around a bit by the good angels and then you're dropped down the trash chute into Hell." Prof Landry paused, sipped a glass of water, smiled wickedly and continued, "I'm sure you've heard of Hell; a place of fiery anguish and eternal torture that God built for the billions of his beloved people and angels that choose not to believe or do believe, and disobey any of his rules. Being dropped into Hell is bad, really... really, bad. You will burn to death forever without dying, so God can watch you suffer." Professor Landry paused here, to let that egg boil in their minds, then went on.

"This of course implies that God, who created the immense vastness of space and all the butterflies and rain-bows and beautiful women and pigeons and everything else, is so insecure and vain that he uses the threat of torture, even actual real, sadistic torture to advance his own, 'I am greater than everybody else' value. Oh, and he's been doing this in almost every religion since the dawn (?) of mankind.

"There is no good or bad in the minds of tigers, chipmunks, vampire bats or any other animal. Right or wrong, Heaven or Hell exist *only* in the minds of people. Only the human mind explains the unknowable, with wonderful and scary conceptualizations like these."

As a young undergraduate student, Oliver had tried to apply the tools of algebra to this kind of theology, trying to shake out the logic from the nonsense. When he was done with the math, the formula was so outlandish, he feared he would be burned at the stake for sounding blasphemous. So, he never published his results.

Tonight, back in the noisy casino of his mind, Oliver glanced over at Re-birth and Death. They each looked bored, having tossed in their hands totaling over twenty-one. Busted by the dealer, they'd left a lot of chips on the table. Ole didn't make eye contact, his thoughts, still on his college days.

In 'Introduction to Eastern Religions.' he learned the law of karma. It made so much sense, cause and effect. No matter if you believed in God or not, karma was the real boss. Bad actions... bad future. Good actions...

wonderful future. It was just like the Buddha basket of sutras (words strung together like flower *lei, making a fragrance of beauty in the mind).* Oliver had memorized a few of these orchids:

*"What we are today, comes from our thoughts of yesterday and our present thoughts build our life of tomorrow: Our life is the creation of our mind."*

'Introduction to Western Religions,' was an eye-opener also. Christianity was old, mysterious, filled with hope and torture, as well as beautiful traditions. Believing was good, not believing was dangerous to your eternal health, lesson learned.

Oliver opened one eye ever so slightly and peered under the lid like a kid peeking under a garage door. Across the green felt of the casino table, frumpy old Mark Twain looked drunk out of his hair. You'd think Karma would have a bit more self-respect. But Karma doesn't care what we think of *him.* He's only concerned with what we intend, say or do. That's what makes the chips fall toward our merit or punishment.

Once we think, say or do, or have a body to hide, we leave the perfection of Zen. Once we name things good or bad, Heaven or Hell, we put karma into play.

On the other side of the Blackjack table, Death started in again, scraping his whetstone on the well-worn edges of his scythe. It was monotonous as a pendulum clock. Time slowed down... fast.

The cupid of Re-birth had stopped her neurotic fanning around and was slumped in a casino chair sound asleep. Her fat little beer belly rising and falling with every breath.

"Hit me!" Oliver finally broke the silence.

Cupid awoke... she sat up straight as her pudgy little body would allow and rubbed her eyes. Death stopped sharpening his scythe. Karma set his cigar down on the edge of the table, rolled up the wrinkled sleeves of his dinner jacket and dealt Oliver a new card. Ole carefully studied his cards... *Seven of Hearts...plus thirteen... makes twenty. That 'll play.* With his best Blackjack face, he hid his delight. *Hearts and sevens are both symbols of good luck,* he hoped it was...

"You've got mail!" His computer hollered at him from the bedroom.

## 2  A Suspicious Child

Ole opened his eyes, he was on his knees in the seventh-floor condo he shared with a married couple at the Sands of Kahana. He was holding imaginary cards up to his forehead with his right hand. If he'd kept his eyes closed just a few more seconds, he'd have seen the fat little Cupid of Re-birth shoot a 'Love Arrow' right into his heart. Ole didn't feel it. There were so many lost love shafts stuck there already, it felt like a full quiver. He ignored his computer and stayed on his knees. He'd promised his mom he'd pray when things got tough. Things were mafia tough today. His mom had more Christian faith than the current pope. He'd call her right now, but he was too messed up to talk to anyone, that shocking phone call.

Mom always worried about her son, now a fifty-something retired teacher. She didn't know it yet, but there was a lot more to worry about this morning. Ole stayed, knees to the floor, wondering how to begin again, without ending up back at the Blackjack table. His forehead interrupted him.

*Why do you believe in people? They just let you down.*

Same old question he'd wondered for years... it must have started when he was a kid. He could remember believing everything his first-grade teacher, Sister Mary Magdalene told him. She was wise as well as beautiful. At least what he could see of her smooth face and hands. They were pale, almost as white as the stiff cardboard that covered her forehead down to her lovely eyebrows. She had piercing, clear brown eyes with crescents of gold in them that sent love, light and kindness in all directions. Oliver fell in love with her the first day of school. She was a celestial being. She was like an angel must be: brilliant, holy and a little scary. When Sister Mary walked into the classroom, she brought with her a presence of blessedness and unquestionable authority. All the children sat up straight and gave her their full attention. Each was required to stand when speaking to her. She taught her children how to wait in line politely at lunch time. She introduced them to Dick, Jane and Spot. From these three very believable animated characters, Ole learned how to better observe the world around him.

"Look Jane! Look, look, look," said Dick. Ole didn't want to look, see or think about what he had to do today. That phone call had thrown him out of body, out of mind, and driven him to pray for his soul. His knees hurt. Worry was twisting his neck muscles into steel cables. He counted to five, then ten, then his memories took him back in time again.

Sister Mary told stories of living in Hawaii where she'd worked at the leper colony on Molokai. Her sad tales of the lepers there at Kaluapapa, would keep Ole washing his hands three times a day for the rest of his life. All the first-graders dropped their pennies and nickels from their left-over lunch money, into a milk bottle that Sister Mary kept on her desk. Giving a nickel to charity was very hard to do. That five cents could buy a whole Snickers bar in those days. But young Oliver often gave up a nickel, because Sister Mary said the money would help Father

Damian in caring for the suffering invalids that lived there and could never leave.

Under Sister Mary Magdalene's scary-looking black robe and white cardboard, Oliver could imagine a beautiful, naked woman. He, of course, had no idea at six-years-old what to do with a naked woman, but he was sure it had something to do with the kind of love he was feeling for her.

One day with their heads resting on wood desks, Sister Mary told them the story of Jesus. It was a wonderful story, full of miracles. Ole had never heard of miracles. He'd heard of Jesus of course. All the students at Saint John's School walked in solemn single file from the school to the church every morning for mass. Plus, Oliver's family attended church every Sunday, however, the mass was in Latin and the sermon came out too loud over the speaker system in the church, so he ignored it and knocked around with his brother. Usually, it wasn't long before their dad separated the boys. So, Ole slept through most of the sermons, like any kid would.

Attending first grade, wearing a pressed blue shirt and tie every day to school, young Oliver was starting to feel smart. He was swept away, believing the story about the birth of Jesus in a poor manger. Not so much with the Santa Claus story. He recognized some serious problems. Santa lived at the North Pole. *Only Polar bears and seals live at the North Pole.* Santa had a sleigh pulled by flying Reindeer. *Uh huh.* Ole was pretty sure that cows, horses, giraffes and other creatures without wings could not fly.

That is, until pretty Sister Mary taught him the power of 'miracles.' Jesus could walk on water, he was famous for bringing dead people back to life and other miracles, so why couldn't reindeer fly? The Santa story wasn't so confusing any more. It was a 'miracle.'

Ole's mother was a beautiful young woman. He loved her more than anyone else and never pictured her naked. This was a nicer kind of love than he felt for Sister Mary which continued to make him itch.

When his pretty mom looked into his eyes and re-read the 'Night Before Christmas,' he hung on every magic word. She said Santa made toys for all the good girls and boys. However, he gave only raw onions to bad kids on Christmas eve. That appealed to Oliver's sense of fairness. But even though mom said so, he wondered about the part where Santa delivers toys and onions all over the world in one night? *Could reindeer fly that fast? How many onions and toys can you fit into one sleigh anyway? There were several hundred kids at his school alone. Santa's sleigh would have to be ginormous to carry enough onions for Saint John's students, let alone all the children in all the countries of the world.* Ole's mom was wonderful, and pretty, and made it all so exciting that it had to be true. His mother would never, never lie to him.

Oliver managed to figure it out on his own. That toy and onion delivery deadline was the same night as Jesus' birthday, so if Santa and baby Jesus were working together on Christmas eve, making 'miracles,' then of course it was possible to deliver toys and onions around the world in one magic night. A night with a special star, and three wise kings, and angels singing the sweetest songs, and poor shepherds and cows. It was all so holy and beautiful.

On Christmas morning that year, Ole, his sister, Judy and his brother, Walter were thrilled to find three wooden snow sleds under the family Christmas tree. Each had a tag that said, "From Santa." Ole wasn't surprised at his good fortune. Judy had been good all year too. He was surprised, that his ornery little brother got a sled. If anybody deserved an onion, it was Walter.

That conflicted morning of three snow sleds was one of those rare Christmas mornings in Iowa, without a trace of snow. Something was very wrong with the Jesus / Santa / weather and onion delivery system.

So, the seeds of doubt were growing into the, 'facts of life,' sprouting in Oliver's young mind. Hiding his thoughts carefully, he made an outward show of thankfulness to Santa, attended mass with his family, prayed to Jesus and kept his mouth shut. Believing in both, seemed like the smart thing to do. Oliver learned at six-years-old that you can overcome doubt, if you close your eyes to reality. He would have to wait until he reached college before this theory was supported by a famous philosopher. Freidrick Nietzsche said it better, "Faith is not wanting to know what is true."

It was a few months later, almost Easter, when Sister Mary told her students how Jesus was killed. This was a terrible story. He'd seen the statue of Jesus nailed to the big cross up in the front of the church, however, he just never got it until Sister Mary shocked her first-grade children with the detailed, graphic, horrible torture and murder of Jesus. Oliver broke into tears. Why would such a nice man, an innocent man, a magic man who could make miracles, be put to death so cruelly?

Ole thought about the Santa story that parents love to tell. Harmless right? No, it's not harmless. They don't seem to realize how their parental credit score drops from the high 800's to the low 600's after the whole Santa deception begins to unfold. What makes it worse, is that Santa is fully supported by schools and shopping malls. So much so, that even suspicious kids like young Oliver, fail to see the truth for several years; years when they are developing their own sense of honesty. Parents should know better. When they tell their children that Santa Claus *never dies,* they spill the beans. Young Oliver caught those beans right away. His mom told him that Santa will be delivering toys and onions forever because Santa never dies. But Jesus died. Sister Mary said so. She knew everything about everything and she was scary beautiful. She was a first-grade teacher for God's sake, bestowed with authority and a black dress from the church. Plus, she had the most honest-looking, adorable, dreamy brown eyes. Oliver knew that nuns devote their entire lives to Jesus. It would be impossible for Sister M to lie.

A long time before this, way back almost two years ago, when Oliver was four-years-old, his grandpa had died. Ole went to the funeral. Death was real. Grandpa's dead body was put in a fancy, heavy box and buried in a hole in the ground with a tent over it. Grandpa never returned to hug him again. The whole family cried. The magic Jesus also died, so the Jesus story had to be real.

The saddest part of the story came out when Sister Mary told her students that Jesus did all this suffering for him, little Ole Gold and of course for all the other children in the world. He even died for all the grown-ups in the world. Some, she admitted, didn't deserve the sacrifice that Jesus made for them. Ole didn't know how to spell sacrifice or what it meant, but it sounded so important when pretty, Sister Mary talked about it with those lovely, sad eyes, young Oliver believed it with all his heart. She told her students that Jesus knew ahead of time he was going to be killed. He had time to get out of town, but he knew his job was to die, to save everyone from the Devil and all the bad stuff in the world. That was very confusing then, and still is today. But Ole appreciated how brave it was of Jesus to die for him and everybody else. He remembered praying directly to Jesus a prayer that went something like this:

*"Uh um… Dear Jesus, Sister Mary Magdalene says my heart is like a dirty little cottage in the woods. She said I should sweep it clean and put some flowers on the table and make some tea and invite you in. I love you, please come in. I'm so sorry they killed you. But it wasn't me that did it. I wasn't even born yet. So, don't blame me okay?*

*Oh, and thanks for the sled and protecting me and everybody else from the Devil. Amen."*

As for the game-changing story about Santa, living forever? Oliver figured this was impossible *unless,* Santa was more powerful than Jesus. Ah, but that couldn't be... no way. No one prayed to Santa Claus. There was a huge cathedral built just for Jesus to live in right next door to his school. Everyone in his family prayed to Jesus. Nobody built a cathedral to Santa Claus. Sure, it made sense to believe in him for all the obvious, 'toy' reasons. But the Jesus suffering and dying story, that was so mean and awful it had to be true. Nobody could lie that much. However, young Oliver had never met anyone like his someday booking agent, Desiree Scarlioni.

Maybe, he'd finally solved the equation of why he believed in pretty women. Mom and Sister Mary Magdalene had set him up. *They,* were the reason he was so gullible to this day. Oliver ran his hands through his hair. Now, all he had left were some new voices in his head, a broken heart, sore knees and a body to hide.

*Pascal believed in Jesus,* Oliver thought to himself, a*nd he was a very smart guy, an inventor and an accountant. Maybe I should I pray to Jesus?*

*Mom does,* whispered a voice in his forehead. Prayer was something skeptics avoid like malaria. His knees were begging him to avoid any more of it today, but his situation had become desperate.

*Just what do you hope to gain by praying? Forgiveness? Some place to hide the body? How about a new girlfriend?* Sarcasm is asking all the right questions.

Ole began the only prayer he could remember, one his mom had taught him as a child.

*"Our Father, who art in Heaven..."* he started, then jumped to the middle part... *"Forgive us this day... that I have to hide a body... any ideas about where, would be greatly appreciated. And, give us this day... a normal girlfriend... someone kind, who doesn't smoke, cuss or chew tobacco, isn't mentally ill, hooked on drugs or wine... a woman who wants to be married and uses deodorant..."*

"You've got mail!" His computer announced again.

*Two messages in five minutes? Were done here.*

## 3 Lyka from the Philippines

Oliver staggered toward the computer in his room. He hadn't been drinking. His knees hurt from all that praying plus, hardball-Blackjack with Death had worn down his nerves. Oliver lined himself up with the computer's running lights, kept his nose up, throttled down steady and landed rather unprofessionally on his Office Max, faux-leather desk chair.

Once safely down, Ole started digging for his portable keyboard. He carefully removed the most recent layer of cereal bowls, banana peels and dry tea bags off the top of his desk. Below that, was a secondary layer of robotics journals and chemistry periodicals. Retired from teaching didn't mean retired from learning. Below these, were yellow legal pads filled with chemical diagrams and molecular combinations. Further down, were sketch books filled with his drawings of robots. Lots of kids have imaginary friends when they're little. Oliver had a very special invisible friend. He called him, 'Robo I' to distinguish his first robot from the other robots he would invent and build someday. Robo I, was his best pal until mom and dad bought him a puppy.

There was never a 'Robo II.' You can't take an imaginary friend to grade school. Then high school, college, marriage, children, and career pushed his robot dreams aside. Only now, fifty years later, retired with more time to himself, had he started to tinker with, and draw designs for, 'Robo II.'

He finally uncovered the keyboard way down below a carboniferous layer of petrified orange peels. Ole typed in his secret password, 1234567 and waited for AOL to open his little gray mailbox. It had its red flag in the 'up' position. While he waited, he looked at his hands lying on his desk. They were a musician's hands. The left one had close-trimmed nails and finger calluses for playing chords. The right hand had longer fingernails for picking out the melodies. There was no dirt or grease under those nails. He'd quit gardening and fixing his own car years ago. But today, there was something about his hands he'd never noticed. His left hand looked like his mother's hand, smooth skin with graceful fingers and thumb. His right hand looked like his father's hand, stronger and rougher in general. The fingernails on the dad side were older looking and cracked in places.

*You should call your parents more often.* The suggestion came rippling over the intercom inside Oliver's mental casino.

"I call mom twice a week. I call dad every Tuesday." He answered out loud. Talking to himself helped drown out the voices in his head.

*You are such a loser brah.* One of the voices refused to be drowned. Ole shrugged his shoulders and winced. The left arm hurt something awful. Turning fifty-five-years-old had kind of snuck up and surprised him.

AOL mail finally opened. News tragedies scrolled past from right to left. Each horrible event had a ten-second lifespan. Another US drone attack in Pakistan had killed a car full of suspected terrorists and their children. Twenty-six African elephants were found shot and left to die, their tusks sawed off by poachers. Some blonde actress he didn't recognize had shocked the media with a low-cut dress at a celebrity party he didn't get invited to. The world seemed as messed up as he was.

A weak signal was coming in on his mind's dharma long-wave. He could tell it was one of the Buddha sutras, but it was all broken-up.

*The world is suffering because of, 'crackle... snap... pop'... the human condition. Only when mankind finds true compassion within, 'snap... crackle... pop'... will the outer world begin to heal.*

Buddha must be broadcasting through a cosmic storm of Rice Krispies somewhere between India and Oliver's bed-room.

*Yah, India is far away brah. Maybe you should go there and get enlightened like Dr. Richard Alpert did. He changed his name to Ram Dass. You could call yourself, "Rama-Rama-Ding-Dong."*

Oliver fondly remembered past meditations at the Buddhist temple over in Paia with Ram Dass. Since his stroke, Ram Dass didn't appear in public very often. When he did, people saw a white aura of Zen bliss surrounding him. Ram's aura reminded Oliver of renaissance paintings. Radiant halos circled the heads of apostles and saints as they were being stoned to death or shot full of arrows. Christianity with its never-ending string of martyrs and its crucifixion symbol of suffering and death, somehow appealed to the masses. 'Holy' images like this, recur again and again throughout the liturgical church calendar lest anyone try to forget.

Ole rubbed his sore left arm with his 'dad' hand, anxious to open his new e mail. With his 'mom' hand, he scrolled to the top of his two-thousand and twenty-six unopened emails. He knew they were spam-mail, but he kept them anyway. They made him feel less lonely. He'd been on Maui for over a year and still no steady girlfriend to laugh with and take care of. Thousands of emails meant at least some one was trying to reach out to him. He was lonely. Desiree Scarlioni was out of his life forever. Maybe, he'd build a robot that looked as beautiful as she had been... before this morning. A woman who wouldn't lie to him.

*Boohoo, poor miserable you. That's just sick brah.*

He read the first new message. It was from a Nigerian princess. She needed his help to transfer her 'inheritance' to a US bank account. She trusted him and would generously share her five-hundred-thousand dollars if he would just send his bank's routing and checking account number to her by return email. There was a photo of the princess herself, a gorgeous ebony doll with a diamond necklace and wearing a gold turban and a flowing, gold, see-through dress that revealed her matching gold bikini. The believer-flaw in his personality wanted to help her.

Fortunately, his dad's skeptic hand was on the mouse now. He hit right click and delete.

Oliver's eyes lit up like two coast guard search lights when he saw the second message was from 'Lyka,' his recent pen-pal in the Philippines. Oliver opened her attached photo.

"So cute..." he whispered. She was much more than cute. She had a beautiful, familiar, smile. Lyka had light brown skin, like a perfect tan. She could be seventeen-years-old or thirty-five. Asian women have some sort of DNA, miracle, youth-chemistry working for them.

*Pick her for your lab partner!* Both inner voices agreed.

One of her tan shoulders was bare because her pink blouse was fashionably cut that way. She was tall and lean and young and beautiful. Behind her on a bare concrete block wall, hung a picture of Jesus pointing to his flaming heart. There were swords stuck in it. Oliver had always wondered about that image. *Did the way humans tortured and misunderstood Jesus keep his heart in eternal pain? Was this the image that first inspired the term, 'heart burn' for the all the antacid commercials? Could Jesus ever, really forgive human mortals for killing him?*

Standing in front of that picture seemed to give Lyka more sincerity than the glamour-shot photos he received from other women online. Was she sending a subliminal message? *"I believe in Jesus and I would believe in you."*

Lyka claimed she was twenty-six-years old. She'd seen Oliver's dating profile on Asianeuro.com a few months ago and started writing to him. He'd pretty much ignored her all this time because he was dating Desiree back then. When he did answer Lyka's messages, it was with typed one-line replies like, "why don't you look for someone your own age?"

She had answered, "I'm looking for an older man who is serious about marriage, not a young playboy."

"Well, I'm a playboy these days, but it's not by choice. I'd rather be married again. However, I'm too old for you. Do you have an older sister?"

"Yes, but she married an American man and you are not too old for me, don't worry," she wrote back. "You are handsome to me."

"You should marry a young man and have a bunch of kids. I'm fifty-five years old. I have three grown daughters. I don't want any more children. Thanks for writing to me, but find someone your own age, good-bye." "Neither do I," she typed back.
"I'm the next to the oldest of seven children.
I feel like I helped my parents raise them. I don't want to have children."

This made her more interesting but even so, corresponding with someone so young and far away felt like a waste of time. Lyka didn't stop writing week after week, sometimes three times a week.

*She doesn't want kids, she believes in Jesus, she's way cute and the second oldest child, so she's the nurturing type. Face it brah, she's too good for you.*

Ole couldn't afford to fly to the Philippines and Lyka didn't have the money to fly to Maui. She would remain locked out Oliver's life by the padlocks of age, distance and cash. Three practical tumblers, all scrambled; and he didn't have the combination. Sarcasm started speaking in 'pidgin,' listing the reasons Oliver should forget Lyka:

*She too young fo' you brah. She too fah away. She no got house on Maui, no Mercedes kah. An' look, she poor brah. See 'da house what she live in. She has nah' ting.*

Then, the other voice in his head spoke in proper English. *Yes, however, she is beautiful and she thinks you're handsome.*

He looked in his bedroom mirror. Maybe he could still pass for handsome, even at his age. He was six foot, one. Well, he *used* to be six-one. Now as he aged, he was closer to five-eleven. But he still had a solid build, same weight and same thirty-two-inch waist he had in high school, thanks to a lifetime of yoga and ayurvedic diet. Yah, if you didn't look too close around the eyes or noticed the wrinkles on his forehead, Lyka was right. He looked quite dashing.

*Oh brah... don't forget humble.* Sarcasm is always waiting.

Ole thought about his criteria for his perfect girlfriend, a.k.a. someday wife: *She should own a home on Maui, drive a Mercedes convertible and be way cute with a flaming crush on him. Oh, and she should own a liquor store.*

Suki, the Japanese millionaire, fit the template in every detail except the liquor store part. But she did own her own retail clothing store in Kihei. Too bad she threw him out. That still hurt. This pretty Lyka didn't even come close to his someday, wife requirements. However, she *was* way cute and writing to him a lot. He opened her email.

Hi Oliver,
You asked if I have sister on Maui. Yes, Lacey is my sister. She married to your friend Captain Billy Bones. She tell me about you many months ago. When I see your handsome picture in your profile, is when I write you. I am working in bookstore. It's hot today in Philippines, but then it's raining so, okay for now. I am so bored. I wonder what you're doing. Do you think of me? Take care, your friend, Lyka

Ole's mind was smiling as big as his face. *No wonder she looked so familiar. She's the captain's wife's... sister. She looks a lot like Lacey, and Lacey's one, smokin'-hot Filipina.*
*Careful brah. She's your best friend's wife.*
"Just sayin'," he continued talking to himself. "I'm an appreciator of beautiful music, women, surf waves, classic cars, robots, sailboats, flowers and chemistry, in that order." It gave him a brief sense of normalcy to think of these material treasures. For a moment or two, he even forgot about hiding a body. He was just happy that somebody was emailing something to him, besides offers to buy lake-front home sites in Arizona. His mind went all

blank and peaceful. A haiku for Lyka came sauntering into his mind one word at a time. Ole counted out the syllables, it fit. Finding his notebook marked, 'song dust,' he carefully wrote,

*Her lips wet and warm*
*small teacup too hot to touch*
*impatient, I wait*

*How much would it cost to fly to the Philippines?* He'd have to save the money from his tip jar for a long time to taste those lips. It made him sad to think of her. They would never meet in person. He was having trouble keeping his eyes open. Without answering Lyka's message he stood up, stretched his arms high in the air and passed out. Somehow, he missed the floor and fell on his bed like a meteorite that at least one beautiful woman sees, as it falls from lonesome space.

## 4  Mind's Eye

Oliver woke up way past supper time. It didn't matter, he wasn't hungry, he was desperate. It would be easier to hide a body at night. The sun had set, leaving a few clouds above the island of Molokai. These red puff balls glowed with the last colors of the day, Strata-nimbus, hibiscus flowers. Ole didn't notice them. He got in his old Cadillac and just started driving around. He needed to find a remote spot.

"Card?" Karma asked.

Without thinking, Oliver nodded toward Mark Twain. Karma dropped his cigar in his haste to deal him a new card. The cigar began burning into the casino carpet of Ole's mind. He didn't notice this either. He was trying to concentrate on his driving.

Karma is always happiest when he's bestowing well-deserved punishment. Ole picked up his new card... *Three of Spades; that makes... twenty-three!*

*Why did you take another card, stupid? Now you're busted. Fate wins*... again.

*Where can you hide from your own foul deeds, brah?*

Oliver pointed his twenty-year-old Cadillac toward Lahaina trying to decide, *where? How?*

"New deck, new game!" Karma demanded triumphantly. It was a woman's voice this time. It sounded familiar. Mark Twain was gone. Karma had morphed himself into Ole's ex-wife, Tanya! Blonde, beautiful and cold as an Iowa blizzard. she pulled cards off the deck, dealing politely to Death and Re-Birth. Then, she growled and threw two cards at Oliver. Ducking his head and with his 'mom' hand still on the steering wheel, he picked his new cards up off the front seat and peeked, *Two of Spades... Nine of Diamonds... makes eleven, the second worst hand in Blackjack.*

He put the cards face up on the wide expanse of the car's white leather. He needed a plan. His foot came off the gas-pedal. He needed to slow down and think. Hiding a body was not what he'd planned to do this weekend.

He shut his eyes. They scraped down his eyeballs like six-grit sandpaper. Ole knew driving with his eyes closed was a bad idea. Maybe his mind's eye would take over.

Some Hindu adults, children and babies wear a painted white or red dot, a 'bindi' between their eyebrows as an outward expression of the meditative third eye. This is a symbol of the inner celestial cosmos in its unmanifested state that dwells within each person. Raised in a Western religion, Oliver's baby-forehead had been baptized clean of all the filthy sin that comes with just being born as a helpless human baby. Think of baptism water as Soft-Scrub for the bath tile of your newborn soul. As he grew older, his forehead was smudged black every year on Ash Wednesday. He received a thumbprint in the rough shape of a cross; a symbol of death to remind him he was dirt. So, Ole had no 'bindi dot' on his forehead to light his way back to peacefulness. In fact, the inside of his mind was dark as the back-side of the moon. Feeling his way around in there, he tripped on the edge of a sinus crater and tumbled down some stairs, all the way to the basement of his sub-conscious. It was even darker down here: a dank root-cellar where he'd been stashing the blame for all the things he'd done wrong in his life. If it wasn't so dark, he'd see stacks of his mistakes piled high, like years of old newspapers; a lifetime collection of what he could have done better.

Most people avoid such dark places in their minds. Oliver had been down here too many times to count. Most of his *recent* mistakes, traced the same template. Find a beautiful bat-do-do crazy woman, believe in her, fall in love with her… crash and burn. He'd done it again, only this time it ended badly. One phone call and he'd gone psycho.

*Where you gonna hide the body?*

Ole was bumping around in the 'blame cellar,' still confused by what he'd done, when he found a cave entrance he hadn't noticed in a long time. It was tight, but he squeezed his way in, and re-discovered the bubbling spring of his Hypo-Thalamus. A bamboo dipper was lying on a mossy slope under some ferns at the edge of the pool. He dipped himself some water and poured it in his hand to drink. It tasted like the Alka-Seltzer fizz of compassion. One sip led to a moment of temporary relief bringing forgiveness for himself and for her. At the same time, the garage door of his third eye began to slowly open.

Instead of seeing *in* this time, his mind's eye shone *out* into the darkness with a soft yellow light. Not much light, kind of like one of those small electric candles you can buy at Costco. The warm feeling of compassion smoothed his disappointment in himself. He sighed, spilling all the carbon dioxide out of his lungs. That always made him feel better. One of his favorite poems by the Buddhist monk, Ryokan, came glowing out as light waves but he heard the words in his third ear.

*"The thief left it behind… the moon at the window."*

That was exactly how it felt, Ole had been robbed of his future by a beautiful Italian booking agent. But the excitement of life continues… on and…

*Who's driving the car brah?* Sarcasm interrupted any further optimism.

Oliver had forgotten about the car. He forced his eyes open to have a look. That hurt; his sandpaper lids dug a few more scratches across his eyeballs. It was little help, he could barely see the interior of the car. There was white leather, the radio light and the speedometer light reading less than two-miles-per-hour. Oliver rubbed his eyes… two dusty saloons in a dried-up ghost town. He hadn't cried one tear over that woman.

## 5  Crazy is as Crazy Does

*Cold brah. Tha'z just cold. Where's the sensitive song-writer guy who once loved his booking agent?*

Oliver shrugged his shoulders. The left one screamed back at him. Maybe one of Cupid's arrows had missed his heart and hit him in the arm.

*Crazy is as crazy does.* That voice in his forehead smirked.

*Oh cool. Did you learn that from Forest Gump?* Sarcasm snapped back.

Ole needed a plan, if he could only think, which he couldn't because both halves of his brain were fighting over a fictitious movie character named, Forest. He realized his third eye must still be driving, but he could feel his angry hands gripping the steering wheel so tight, that it should snap in pieces. The next minute, his disappointment was stabbing him so deep that he slumped over the wheel wishing anger could win just so the heartache would go away.

*Whine, whine, whine, blah, blah, blah. Where you going, cold heart? What's the plan?*

Ole waited for an answer. Nothing. Blank screen. Absolutely nothing echoed back with a plan.

"Hit me," he said without enthusiasm.

Tanya hauled off and slugged him in the jaw. If he hadn't been buckled into the driver's seat, he would have been knocked clear over to the passenger-side window.

He shook the pain from his face. Surprised as he was by the punch, it was nothing compared to why she hadn't moved to Hawaii with him last year. That still hurt more than a big red welt on his chin. He heard Death laughing out loud in the back seat. Death always gets a kick out of domestic violence. He knows it can lead to murder. He didn't laugh long. He bowed his head, as if in solemn prayer. Of course, he wasn't praying, he was studying the two new Blackjack cards in his hand.

Re-birth was fluttering around on the casino ceiling of Ole's mind, shooting love arrows in every direction just for practice. Somehow, they all seemed to miss Tanya. Ole looked at his new card, *Two of Hearts…makes thirteen… the worst hand in Blackjack.* Karma-Tanya smiled with vengeful satisfaction as she lit another cigar. Ole blinked his eyes trying to see out the windshield. Everything was so dark. His eyes rolled around in his head like marbles, dry marbles. He caught a glimpse of his face in the rear-view mirror. He looked like a movie zombie. *Are you dead brah?* The voice was coming from somewhere between his bushy eyebrows, where the death ashes had been annually smudged across his third eye like mud on a windshield.

*No! I'm not dead. Confused… yes, disappointed… yes, dead… no.* Ole could feel his heart pumping out of control. Death reached a boney hand over Ole's shoulder to feel his throat for a pulse. He knocked Death's hand away and shook his head. It was loose and wobbly. Maybe he could spin it all the way around like that girl in the 'Exorcist.'

*Don't do it brah,* warned his forehead.

Oliver wasn't possessed, more like deeply dispossessed. Not a good time to be driving a car. He tried harder to see out the windshield. Lahaina had been his home for over a year. It should look familiar to him even at night. He tried to focus on signs with Hawaiian street names. The words were burning in flames with too many K's and M's and a lot of a'a's in the middle. Worse, the letters were all mixed up like Alphabet cereal on fire, instead of floating peacefully in milk. Other than the burning street signs, all he saw was a mysterious darkness.

*Turn on your headlights, stupid.*

Ole pulled the headlight knob all the way out. Two bedazzling white wings of light lit up the street ahead. He was kind of surprised to see he was on the right side of the road. It hurt to look, so he quickly shut his eyes again. His third eye took over. Ole needed to think. He needed a plan, a very clever plan. His mind's eye could guide him in the dark, even if he wasn't a practicing Hindu.

*Forget Hindu's. What's the plan brah?*

The old Cadillac sniffed along from curb to curb like a great, white bloodhound searching for a body. Only tonight Oliver needed a place to *hide* one.

*It must be almost midnight brah. Where? How?*

If he'd owned a watch, it would be wringing its hands instead of measuring time. He took another peek out the windshield. He was still okay. There was no traffic and no one out for a walk this late on a hot winter's night.

He was looking out the driver's side window when a Hawaiian youth skate boarded past his car. The young man seemed to glow in the dark as he floated down the street in sweeping curves. Even through blurry eyes, Ole noticed the tall, proud bearing of the bare-chested Hawaiian. He had a net bag slung over one of his tattooed shoulders. Other than that glowing guy, the town was quiet as a graveyard, lonely and haunted as Ole felt inside.

*You'll always have me,* snickered Death.

*Take a hit or fold and show y'er hand,* Re-birth groused.

Ole tried to ignore them. He knew he couldn't for very long. They were inescapable boors. Once he got this whole, 'body hiding' thing over with, things would go back to normal. He'd blend back in with the rest of Lahaina's local 'characters.' He was Oliver Gold, almost famous musician at the Pioneer Inn and on dinner boats. No one would remember what happened this weekend.

As guilty as he was, he felt sort of proud of himself. He wasn't living on food stamps. He picked up litter. Desiree, on the other hand, was from California. The only family she had, was her brother, and tragically, Manny had died in car wreck just two weeks ago. No one would miss Desiree Scarlioni, no one.

## 6 Let's Celebrate!

A week after Manny's funeral, Desiree called from California. In between fits of anguish and tears, she assured Ole that they were still going to make it big; with Oliver Gold filling Manny's empty shoes. Desi would have the band booked in Las Vegas and on cruise ships and maybe Europe, by next Summer. The remaining members of Manny's band were already working up arrangements of Oliver's music. But first, she was gonna take a break for a month or two, in her Maui home on the Pukalani golf course. She promised him that's where the two of them would chase each other from bedroom to bedroom as soon as the deal closed. It was a four-bedroom house.

Ole was with her last month at Maui Escrow, where she signed and initialed every one of the fifteen-pages in the purchase agreement. He remembered how carefully she went through the contract line by line. Booking agents are detail oriented. They make their money in the fine print. Ole wondering how many guitars you could buy with the seven-hundred and fifty-thousand dollars she was spending on a house. It took over an hour for her to finish reading and signing. He watched her write out a ten-thousand-dollar earnest money check, kiss it right on its face and hand it to the closer. He stapled the check to the real estate palapala (legal documents) and there were happy high-fives and handshakes all around. Desi pushed Ole up against a wall in the escrow office and kissed him like they were just married. Her public display of passion was such a turn on that wild fire raged up his back. It felt like the wall was reflecting Desi's hot body, broiling an Oliver sandwich. The closer coughed a small embarrassing cough and when the kissing stopped, he smiled his best, 'I just made a ton of money' smile, and gave Desiree a complimentary Maui Escrow pen.

What a thrill it was to be with a beautiful woman who had just bought a home on Maui. She drove Ole's Cadillac to her new house on the sixth fairway. It didn't look like anybody was home, so she parked in the driveway and they made out in the big front seat like they were teenagers. She wanted to go peek in the windows, but with serious effort, Oliver kissed her out of that idea.

"Let's celebrate!" She was bursting with excitement, so, she took him to lunch at the Pukalani Golf Club Restaurant. Her effervescence bubbled over like the hundred-dollar champagne she paid for. Three toasts of champagne and Ole could see the pain of losing her favorite brother in her eyes. Was she trying to drown her sorrow by buying a home on Maui? He wondered if spending seven-hundred-thousand-dollars would be enough.

A few nights after that celebration lunch, two teenagers rolled a golf cart out of the Pukalani maintenance shed and just for kicks, set it on fire. The fire jumped to the pro shop, then devoured the restaurant. By morning nothing remained but the sad faces of the thirty-four employees that were now out of a job.

## 7 Speed Bumps of the Past

His car was slowly rounding the town's famous Banyan tree and courthouse. At the stop sign, while Ole was wondering which direction to turn, the car turned left and prowled north on Front Street. He shut his eyes again. They hurt, way too dry. So was his throat. Hiding a body was gonna take some thinking and that might require some drinking.

Ole wasn't seeing it, but the town's street lights dimly lit the empty sidewalks and closed restaurants. The few bars that were open this late, rocked with loud happy tourists; not the kind place he needed tonight.

"How about a drink?" Ole muttered under his breath.

*How about another card?* Tanya was gone. A hookah-smoking caterpillar had taken her place and was blowing cigar smoke-rings of many colors through the wonderland of his mind.

"Not yet," he shot back.

*Thought you quit drinking, Mr. Yoga / Tai chi guy.*

He hadn't been drinking much these days. Paying the rent and buying a few groceries took most of his cash. Alcohol was a luxury item way back on page three of his budget spread sheet. Plus, it was yoga, not booze that had saved him from death by asthma, drawn him to the contemplative side of life, and taught him the joy of being a minimalist, the only lifestyle he could afford in Hawaii.

Besides yoga, he'd found a cleaner, less problem-based

addiction than booze. Her name was, 'Music.' He ate and slept with her. He wrote music, recorded it, sold it on i-tunes, performed it live, and she brought him enough easy coin that even if he wasn't famous, (yet), he was getting by.

As Ole's car sniffed along in the dark, he could feel the 'monkey-muse' on his back, her arms around his neck, squeezing him by the throat with her long musician's fingers. She was a demanding mistress, but he loved her with what was left of his heart after Desiree.

*Pay attention, will you? Find a place!*

One drink was sounding more reasonable every time one of the voices tried to boss him around. He'd learned the hard way, that booze does not make you happy. But then, Desiree Scarlioni had come along, now there were dozens of new reasons to be unhappy.

The car came to a sudden stop. Ole opened his eyes, he was at a red light. His mind's eye was on the ball. He shut his eyes, still drowning in the shallow end of his memory pool.

*Why do you hang on to your own pain like this?*

Well, Desi had done all the rich-girl stuff. She put gas in his car took him out to dinner, bought him drinks, bought him clothes, drove a convertible rental car (not a Mercedes). She was 'kiss me' gorgeous. Ole's shoulders started to shake just thinking about her. His grip tightened on the steering wheel as if it were Desi's throat.

*Stop it brah!*

Memories are the speed bumps of the past. That's why

we remember them. He'd kept track of all the major bumps in his life with journals. He'd filled forty-one books with the good, the bad and the bizarre events of his life. So, he wasn't trying to think about Desiree, she was just right there, always on the next page of his thinker.

*Maybe, you should look where you're going.*

He took another peek. His car turned right without its turn signal on. Then right again, down a long street that started with a flaming 'W.' He couldn't see the whole word. Two miles an hour was too fast. It was like riding the city bus, except he was all alone, on a comfortable white leather seat and the air-conditioning worked.

*Focus brah.*

The Cadillac turned a corner so tight one of the car's rear wheels rubbed hard then rode up on the cement curb. It slid off with a sharp scraping sound. The Pizza Hut and Taco Bell on that corner, were both closed. Metal warehouses looked down on him like superior court judges, dark and foreboding. He knew they were about to hand down a life-sentence. Ole's heart pounded in his chest as one judge pounded a gavel, *"Guilty as charged!"*

"You're wrong. You're wrong!" Oliver shouted back at his windshield. He wasn't innocent, but he wasn't Jimmy Buffet. This whole damn thing was, *her* fault.

## 8  E=MMC²

Oliver's third eye shut down completely. Perhaps it was retiring behind that 'bindi dot,' to a quiet Zen garden where Hindus do whatever Hindus do. So, Ole had to drive the car the old-fashioned way, with his eyes open. His hands took up a nervous drum staccato on the steering wheel. He tried pointing the Cadillac down the middle of the street. It was rolling in the wrong direction, straight toward a little tavern he knew of. The car seemed too wide to fit between all the cars parked on either side of the street.

*Ya betta park 'dis boat soon brah, before you run aground or hit something.*

The parked cars looked restless, huddling together, plotting their next move; like they might jump out and ambush him at any moment. So, as soon as he saw a long empty spot on his side of the road, he slowly rubbed his tires along the curb until his big chrome bumper mushed harmlessly against the plastic rear end of a newish looking BMW. He'd come to a halt within a block of the tavern. Ole shoved the gear shift into 'Park' and sat there wondering, *why his rather normal life had come to this?*

It's not that surprising that believing can let you down. But Oliver's philosophy flaw was trying to believe every point of view. A retired chemistry teacher can be a musician and a philosopher. Chemists search for the fundamental facts of life from the tiniest particles to the galactic. Ole had learned that every life, human, animal or plant, shares the same set of DNA Legos. But chemists, like theologians, want to know who manufactured the Legos. More interesting to the musician in his soul, the Lego neurons of all living things are held together with something called, 'string theory.' Nano-size fibers a million times thinner than a human hair were vibrating like violin strings in complex symphonies holding every atom together.

Einstein almost got it right. Oliver had improvised on Uncle Albert's formula. When you added music to the equation, the theory of relativity read like this: $E = MMC^2$ where Energy = Mass x Music x the Speed of Light, squared. Ole had worked out some of the supporting math in his spare time. It wasn't ready to be published in the American Scientific Journal quite yet.

*You are clearly a work in progress brah.*

Ole figured that if each life equals one verse in the continuing song of living, and Death is the resounding chorus waiting at the end of every life's, last page. Then moving from verse to chorus, should be a predictable amount of time, based on the tempo and the quality of the music each life aspires to. Plus, he should be able to predict the number of lives yet to be lived.

Lives that soar like 'The Lark Ascending' by Ralph Vaughn Williams, are obviously near Nirvana. Lives that jive along rudderless, filled with anger or hate, like some rap music, probably have a million lives ahead of them.

*Oh, my stars! Did you dive into the shallow end of the*

*lake and crack your head?*

Ole thought about that. *Nothing seemed quite right anymore.*

Buddhists believe multiple lives are necessary. It takes time to develop compassion. All sentient beings, even ants, mosquitoes and other undesirables, like ticks can do it. But, they must have enough lives ahead of them to evolve far enough to find compassion, and thus win a homestead claim to the Pure Land of Nirvana. Then, they are free at last from the samsara wheel of reincarnation.

Dharma means 'a path of duty or responsibility.' Each life responsively lived, makes us wiser. Yet life after life, all beings must sing their way to the bottom of that last page. There, Death, Karma and Re-birth wait by the cash register to make sure you pay for all you've done wrong and get merits (think Gold Bond stamps) for all your righteous intentions, words and deeds.

There is something strangely invigorating that happens after a loved one comes to the bottom of their last page. You grieve of course, but you also want to quickly turn to the next page of your own life. You want to dance and drink and skydive and run a marathon to prove that *you,* can keep on turning pages for a long time to come.

## 9 The Omen

Ole could see the dimly lit bar where nobody knew his name. It was just up the street. He got out of the car with his left arm and shoulder complaining about moving in any direction. Ole closed the heavy car door and forced one foot in front of the other. Walking was probably safer than riding the Cadillac-bloodhound-bus, however it was like wading through imaginary, deep water, slow going.

It wasn't parked cars that ambushed his thoughts it was that crazy Desiree Scarlioni. Desiree's sexy, happy smile and those perfect teeth were still stuck in Oliver's memory like dead bugs on fly paper.

As he got closer to the tavern's front door, a black cat ran past then stopped. It turned back and deliberately crossed Ole's path to the darker side of the sidewalk. *Of course, it would. It's an omen brah. Drinking is not the answer, you know this. Let's get out 'a here.*

Ole ignored the wise voice and the black cat. He kept wading through memories. The night he met Desi, she fell in love with his music which gave him an excuse to sit inappropriately close to her as often as possible. Their Jo-Jo juices were simmering nicely. By the full moon a week after meeting her, the soup was boiling over.

Oliver had driven her to a remote and very hidden beach on the north shore. He'd parked in an abandoned cane field and they'd run for the deeper seclusion of the beach. Their lips did not touch lightly or quiver with the timidity of a romantic first kiss. No, this was a frantic tour-des-France of unbridled hunger. It was a full blown, Grand Carpe Diem Delicious; a pent-up sexual seizing of intimate body parts. That first kiss sent them biting and scratching like tigers. They fell onto his beach towel with arms and legs entwined like experienced teenagers.

Desi led Oliver's hands to her vending machine of earthly delights. Every selection he pressed brought him a surprising reward. His beach towel changed into a flying carpet. Desiree became his personal Genie-slave right out of the magic-lantern of his naughty dreams. She granted all Ole's wishes and promised more to come. Flying that beach towel on a hidden beach that night completely disproved his first impression of her. She wasn't as innocent, as she looked.

*Mmmmm! There's a memory that doesn't hurt brah.*

Within days of that first kiss, Desi had booked Oliver Gold to headline a Las Vegas show backed by her brother Manny's rock and roll band. The big money gigs were set for next month, February, at the MGM Grand. This was very BIG MONEY. His share would be seven-hundred dollars per show, eight shows fifty-six-hundred bucks plus a room at the hotel for five nights, meals and airfare included. Desi said he'd have to share a room with her. He assured her it would be a pleasure. She'd laughed like an Arctic Loon ready for mating.

## 10  Sex and Cars

As he struggled toward the tavern, he could not stop
flipping episodes of former romance on the, 'Desiree
History Channel.' There was that crazy afternoon up in
Desi's hotel room. He was tearing a purple bikini off her
slim waist with his teeth. Every selection he touched on
her pyrotechnic vending machine of a body, lit a fast
burning fuse to a colorful display of sexual fireworks. At
the very peak of the *grand finale,* just when his Roman-
Candle was about to burst, Desi started talking loudly
about cars.

"I'M GONNA BUY A CONVERTIBLE," she shouted! "YOU
KNOW… ooooooh, ooooooh, TO DRIVE… WHEN I…
aaaaah, aaaaaaheeee, ooo… FOR WHEN WHEN… WHEN…
I- AYEEEE… STAY HERE ON MAUI-Weeee-EEE!"

It was an odd time to talk about *anything,* but she was
a rich girl and Ole was a driven kind of guy.

"If you buy a convertible… buy a Mercedes," he panted.
His lips and hands were hot as flaming matches. Ole knew
he'd found the 'perfect' girlfriend. She was a sports-
model, forty-year-old Mercedes and even an old
Mercedes is fun to drive.

## 11  It's Maui's Fault?

The tavern seemed further away. Ole squeezed his eyes down tight. Still no tears, but some good-ole Maui sweat slowly seeped under his eyelids. It gave him enough moisture to clearly see the small beer sign in the tavern's window. As he neared it, his thoughts bounced back and forth and fifth to Desiree. She said she loved him. She said she believed in him. She was delicious bait. He'd swallowed it. Now, even though she was out of his life forever, the hooks of loving her were tearing out his insides. Even the extremely painful and expensive divorce from Tanya had never hurt like this. He'd loved his wife for a long time. It'd been a good marriage. There had been no other woman involved, unless you consider Maui Island to be a brazen hooker of irresistible seduction, which she is.

*It's Maui's fault?*

*Uh huh, stole y'er heart, made you leave Seattle, and come live with her,* Sarcasm razzed on; *loving Hawaii too much cost you your marriage. And Oh, you'll never forget how, 'winning' your divorce war with Tanya left you owing your attorney forty-eight-thousand bucks. Congratulations! Do you see a pattern here, stupid?*

*You're the stupid half, Maui's a guy. Ha, ha, you were seduced by a guy island.*

*You're the stupid lobe, Islands don't have gender.*

That's when the fist fight started. His forehead voice punched Sarcasm right in the mouth. Sarcasm howled with pain and threw the forehead voice out the front window of the casino in Ole's mind. His forehead rolled across the busted glass and rushed back into the fight like a cowboy in a movie.

*You think I could resist her? You're the one who wanted to be famous!* Forehead broke a chair over Sarcasm's shoulder.

*You'll believe anything!* Sarcasm karate-kicked the forehead voice right between Oliver's eyes. Oliver's head flew back. This made it hard to stay on the sidewalk leading to the bar. He went sideways. It was near midnight, so there was no one on the street to see some haole guy stagger into a parked   car. Being broken by a woman makes you feel drunk, invisible, cast aside, dizzy and caught in a down shaft of vertigo... falling... falling right through the sidewalk, like your riding some ghostly elevator down and down, dropping through never-ending department store levels of sadness.

*Women that beautiful, all lie, you know that.* Sarcasm followed that kick with both fists hammering Oliver in the stomach.

*Why don't you look for a normal girlfriend?* Hollered his forehead as it tossed Sarcasm to the floor and kicked him in that sore arm. Ole winced from the pain. He thought of the only normal girlfriend he'd met since the divorce, his pen pal in the Philippines.

*Lacey thinks I'm handsome,* he tried to convince himself.

*What? That's Captain Billy's wife. What's wrong with you? That was Lyka that wrote you were handsome!* Sarcasm yelled back throwing a knife.

Both halves must have ducked just in time cause the blade stuck in Oliver's heart with another sharp pain and quivered. A tear fell from his good eye. Not over Desi... no way. This was a tear of anger or something tough and manly like... falling in love with his best friend's wife.

*You are such a fool,* both voices echoed. He could see them leaning on each other after the fight; granting him a temporary peace accord.

Oliver liked the captain and his wife from the first moment they'd met. They lived next door at the Valley Isle Resort, so he spent a lot of time playing ukuleles and worshiping sunsets with them. *It wasn't love at first sight with Lacey or anything like that,* he tried to reassure himself. He was fond of both; they were the best friends he had on Maui.

*Uh huh.* Sarcasm isn't buying it.

As for Desiree, his booking agent, he wanted to care for her and be in her band and travel the world and sleep next to her exciting vending machine. But, there was something deeply troubling about Desiree. She was a booking agent, a predator. She swam with music-industry sharks. Booking agents are always hungry. He figured someday she would she shake him by the neck and toss him off to Davey Jones' Locker and go after fresh tuna.

However, that was a risk he'd gladly taken; "hook, line, money and sinker," as Dad used to say. Shark, that she may be, Ole had considered asking Desi to marry him, wondering if he could afford a diamond large enough for her to say yes.

*Can you forget all 'dis story brah? What's the plan with the body?"*

The tavern was closer now; looked like just another mile or two from what he could see through his sweat tears.

"Hit me again."

Karma had changed into an African Hyena. She hunched her shaggy fore-shoulders up in mad laughter as she dealt Ole the card that would take him to Hell and back... *Ace of Clubs; adds up to twenty-three... no good. He'd have to take it as a one... so that makes, 'lucky fourteen?'*

## 12  The Phone Call of Awakening

The tavern shimmered like a water oasis up ahead of him. Ole was getting thirstier with every step, while his mind was sinking in the quicksand of random distractions: All those big money gigs Desi had planned for him in Las Vegas, Lyka the Philippine cutie, his mom and dad back in Iowa. However, the deepest mire of them all, was the shock of Manny's fatal car crash. Desi and the rest of the band were now in a paralyzed state of loss.

As he walked, his mind went back to that phone call this morning. He'd been leaning on the kitchen counter at the beach condo eating a bowl of cereal with water instead of milk. Milk in Hawaii costs more than champagne. Water is better for you. You get used to it, and the snap crackle pop sounds almost the same. Anyway, he was living the watered-down version of his retirement dreams. No more nine to five. A musician has every day off, surfing is free and playing music isn't really work if y'er good at it. So, Ole had felt good this morning. He was comfortable in his own skin. He would get by okay until the band got around this terrible bend in the river of grief, and Desi booked them some new gigs.

He ate a spoonful of cereal and gazed at the ocean view from the kitchen. The sliding glass door leading to the lanai was always open. There was no sliding screen, the weather was the same every day, sunny and warm with no chance of mosquitoes. The beach was right outside, framed by palm trees. He'd found a great place to live, sharing a condo at Sands of Kahana with Art and Sandy, who needed a room-mate to help them with their high monthly mortgage payments.

He himself would never need to carry a mortgage, because Desi was buying the house on the golf course. He knew he wasn't in love with her, but he was falling in love with the idea of marrying her. *She's amazing, rich, funny, rich, a musician, crazy sexy, rich and a song-writer like me.* He added up the good stuff. *We'll rebuild Manny's band; a band that has radio play in the US, Canada and Europe. We'll make a ton of money. I'll pay off my evil divorce attorney. She'll buy a Mercedes convertible*.

Desiree made him feel like he was a celebrity already. He wished he'd been able to fly to California to comfort her at Manny's funeral. He was laying his spoon down on the counter next to the watery cereal bowl, when his cell phone sang softly then, a little louder, "Tuuuues-day, affter-nooon." Hoping it was Desi he almost dropped the phone in his haste to flip it open.

"Hello?"

"Is this Oliver Gold?"

"This is Ole, who's callin'?"

"This is Manny... Manny Scarlioni."

Ole heard boards busting in his head; like the hull of a speedboat had just run hard onto a reef.

"Manny, you're dead."

"What? I'm not dead. Do I sound dead to you?"

Heavy surf was beating across Ole's brain coral; it was getting hard to breathe. Ole replied in a very suspicious whisper, "Who is this really? I've talked to Manny; this voice is different. Don't mess with me. Who is this?"

"It's me Manny Scarlioni. I don't know who you talked to. I'm not dead. Did my sister tell you I was dead?"

"Uh huh…"

"My sister's a liar. You've met her. You should know that by now."

"Your sister had to go to the morgue to identify your body. You gotta be dead."

"How did I die?"

"You fell asleep at the wheel after staying up all night at a hospital with your father. You hit a concrete bridge support on the freeway at over sixty miles an hour. There were no skid marks. She figured you fell asleep at the wheel."

"Christ aw' mighty"

"She sounded like she really loved you. She told me how she broke down while choosing your casket at the funeral home: the deluxe model, *The New Age Pharaoh,* all 100% recycled materials, mostly plastic milk bottles, but with real oak handles and a hand sewn white silk liner. I remember how she was sobbing when she told me how nice it contrasted with your once handsome face."

"That's just sick dude."

"She said there were over a hundred cars in your procession to the cemetery, if that makes your spirit feel any better. Can you still feel stuff when y'er dead?"

"Shut up about dead... I'm *not* dead! I don't know why I even called you. Desi gave me your card while we were getting drunk at Papa's wake. We were trying to get along. She said you're a famous musician over there in Hawaii?"

"Not as famous as you. I've got a few Cd's on i-tunes and some steady gigs."

"How much did she take you for?" Manny asked.

"Wha'da ya mean? Nuthin' brah; she's been puttin' gas in my car. She was always payin' for dinner... and drinks... and stuff. I figured she's rich. Desi never conned me out of a dime. I was falling in love with her. What's not to love? She's gorgeous and funny... and seems to have an amazing career. She called me from New York just a few weeks ago, said her hotel suite was so deluxe it had a fireplace and one of those fancy doormen who stand out in the snow to hail you a cab."

"New York?"

"Yah, she was there for a guest appearance on the David Letterman show."

"Say what? Dude! She's a beautician in three-chair beauty parlor in Oakland."

Ole gasped for air. That Ace of Clubs card was beating a fierce reality into him, pounding the tender, red meat of his heart. He spit out a rebuttal. "She's buying a home on a golf course on Maui. I saw her sign the papers!"

"Hah! She's being evicted from her house in Oakland. She's never saved a dime in her life. While we were drinking away our sorrows, she complained about how deep in debt she was from flying her credit-cards over to Hawaii all 'a time. She's always claiming she's frickin' fabulous. I bet she told you that she does fashion shows in Paris."

Oliver doubled over from the five-hundred-pound reality gorilla sucker punching him in the stomach with the Ace of Clubs. Ole struggled to breathe. All he could do was gasp.

"Ooow... you really are her brother." He heard his voice crack with emotion. "Desi told me she does fashion shows in Paris and all over Europe. I believed her. Your sister is gorgeous like world-class... stunning."

"Yah, she's a lemon tree all right... 'very pretty and the lemon flower...' you know the rest. It's a song written about psycho-liars like her. I hate that song and I hate her. She was always world-class lying to me when we were kids. I've stayed as far away from her as I could for over twenty years, until... papa's funeral."

"Sorry about your father Manny." Oliver offered. "I heard your brother and sister who recently passed away..." He began to offer further condolences.

"Who?" Manny shot back. "Bro, it's just Desi and me. We don't have any siblings. That's why I can't stand her. She's making crap like that up all 'a time."

*She invented a sister and then an extra brother? Then, she killed them? Julie by knife attack, Angelo by a stroke? Her favorite brother, her only brother, falls asleep and drives into a bridge at sixty-miles-per-hour?*

Oliver's brain was flashing warning lights on its dashboard, 'DANGER! GULLIBLE SENSOR OVERLOAD! STOP ENGINE!' All three flashed like strobe lights behind his third eye. The car alarm of stupidity, had been tripped and was assaulting his ears. He was choking on too much reality to swallow.

"Manny, if she invented imaginary siblings and then she made them die… made you die too, is that still murder?"

"She's a freaking nut case. Papa and I weren't that close, but I'm gonna miss him. I don't know what more I can say about my sister except, I ain't dead. When she told me, she'd been dating you over there in Hawaii for the last three months I figured you must like lemonade."

"She was so good to me brah. My friends loved her too. She told me Chubby Checker was her piano teacher when she was a kid and he gave her the piano she still plays today. I believed it… why not? Why'd she do like 'dis, brah?"

"Oliver, I don't know. Maybe people like us, who aren't liars think everybody else is honest too. It's a big, mean world out there bro, and it's full of liars. Wise up."

Oliver wasn't saying anything. His 'stun button' had been hit so many times he was speechless, so Manny went on.

"Take some advice from a musician brother. If you ever see her coming around again, head for the hills. She's a certifiable, crazy, half-box of cornflakes."

The line went dead, but Manny wasn't. He hated his sister so he wouldn't miss her. Nobody would miss her. Ole looked up, he was finally standing in front of the tavern staring at the beer sign in the window. In foot high neon-blue letters it read, 'BEER.'

Time slowed almost to a stop... fast. He tried to step forward, but he'd become a still-life painting titled, 'Broken Man Enters a Tavern.' It was so real, it looked like a photograph. His good arm was extended... reaching, but just short of touching the front door of the Sly Mongoose.

## 13  Godzilla In the Kitchen

Manny was alive! Oliver couldn't take another spoonful of watery cereal. His jaw had clamped shut. He squeezed his cell phone like it was Desiree's throat. He felt like a Godzilla, monstrously outraged, monstrously betrayed, disappointed and terribly sad. Oliver struggled against the high-power transmission lines of emotional reality. He'd become the lead Godzilla in some black and white movie. He yanked at the power lines around his bow-legged monster knees. The refrigerator and stove were pulled out into the center of the kitchen. The fridge fell forward and landed on its front doors. Sparks of anger were flying all over the walls and ceiling.

Manny's words were electrocuting him, small fighter planes were strafing him, armored tanks were advancing across the kitchen floor shooting at him. He struggled to rip free from the burning shock, so he could go stomp on the rest of the city. He reared up as high as his dinosaur legs could stretch and let out a terrible roar… the kind Godzilla is famous for. It came out like a silent scream, one that only the neighborhood dogs could hear. Godzilla tried to shoot flames out his nostrils, but only water and Rice Krispies flew across the room. The wires of reality held tight. All he could do was fry and silently scream. Oliver doesn't get calls from dead people very often. White-lightening arced across his giant lizard feet with an evil power surge, sending pulses of too much voltage up his spine. His seven chakras exploded like cherry bombs, one at a time: *Boom! Boom! Boom! Boom! Boom! Boom! Boom!*

When he was done exploding, he inhaled and began

imploding. His Godzilla jaw fell open exposing rows of sharp teeth. Oliver had lost his grip. There was a sonic crashing noise like shattering plastic, expensive plastic. Looking down he saw his webbed reptilian front claws had let go of his cellphone. It lay there busted on the hard-tiles of the kitchen floor.

*It's over brah. She's just another strangler-vine from the swamp forest where you find all your girlfriends. Oh, and you're gonna need a new phone, Godzilla.*

## 14  Winged Monkey

Uncle Oliver leaned his ridged back of horny Godzilla spikes on the kitchen counter and shrugged his shoulders. To his great surprise a pair of eagle-sized wings unfolded from the center of his back! This was a new twist in his now ruined life. The wings were magnificent, pumping up and down in a frightening display.

He'd always wondered how it would feel to stretch one's wings. Well, it felt powerful! Maybe he'd died and turned into an angel? Out of the round-circle corners of his eyes, he saw dirty, molted feathers come floating down. Maybe, he was a fallen angel?

He turned and saw his reflection in one of the kitchen windows.

"Noooooo!" He screeched, shaking his furry monkey head. The strap of that stupid-looking little bellhop cap was cutting into the meat under his chin. He was a winged-monkey from the land of Oz. The nose on his monkey-face was flat, his mouth hung agape showing pointed, little white teeth. He looked angry; a flying monkey that had just been screwed over by the wicked witch of North Oakland.

Ever since Oliver was a child and first saw 'The Wizard of Oz' in a movie theater, he'd been terrified of winged monkeys. Yet deep down, he'd always wanted to be one. Not the mean Kine, slave to an evil witch. No, he just wanted to fly and swoop and land like one. It looked so fun. It wasn't fun today.

He shut both eyes and shook his wings to make them go away. He stole another quick glance at his reflection.

"I AM NOT A WINGED MONKEY!" he shouted as he involuntarily flapped his new wings. They swept out over the kitchen counter knocking the empty cereal bowl and glass water pitcher off the counter. Both shattered on the floor tiles next to the carcass of his cell phone. He lifted his small monkey feet off the floor. He was flying! Ole's new wings carried him over broken glass of many colors.

*Just look at you! Mirror, mirror of the kitchen window who's the craziest chemistry teacher you know?*

"Hit me!" He cried out to the Fates. Instantly, Karma-hyena slapped down a new card... *Three of Spades seventeen... not close enough.*

Ole felt a strong lift under his wings and knew immediately it must be the evil memory of Desiree pushing him like a monkey-hang-glider across the living room. He ducked his head in time to miss the ceiling fan in the living room. He pumped his awesome wings heading for the great outdoors, but a split second before impact he realized the glass slider door was closed!

"KA-BLAM!" His left wing hit first, then his head smashed into the glass door. Apparently, condo sliding glass is tough enough to withstand high winds and flying monkeys because he didn't break through. He bounced back onto the living room floor with a whip-lashing crash, flat on his back.

Unfortunately, he wasn't knocked out, so everything hurt. Ole wanted to scream, not from the pain more from the bizarre Godzilla / monkey matrix he was in. Okay, not true. It was the pain, too much of it. His normal easy-going, positive Chi was all mashed together into a seven-chakra pile-up. Rush hour traffic on his spinal highway had stopped rushing. He lay there until the pain ambulance took an off-ramp and he could stand up again.

"Ouch," he hollered, then yelled, "WHO CLOSED THE SLIDER DOOR?" No answer, his roommates apparently weren't home or they'd have heard the crash. He was a little disappointed. He wanted to blame somebody besides himself.

*Good luck with that brah.*

The monkey wings were gone. Ole looked in the living room mirror above the Hawaiian print couch. He looked like he'd been mugged. *Bet'ta sit down before I pass out,* was the last thing he thought, as he passed out.

## 15 Prison?

When he awoke, he was naked, soaking wet, and sitting on a cheap plastic chair that seemed to be struggling to hold him up. The once red chair now faded to a dull pink, was under an ice-cold shower of water thinly spraying down on him from a rusty shower head. The water was painfully cold, and the shower room was a dank water closet that looked so rough he figured he'd died and gone to Hell.

*No brah, not Hell, there's no cold water in Hell,* his forehead reminds him.

Maybe this was a prison. He cranked the dial on the wall-mounted water heater all the way over to 'Hot.' Colder water sprayed even thinner, as he quickly showered soap off himself. The toilet next to him was a yellowed porcelain bowl with no toilet seat. The cinder block walls showed years of pink paint layered over years of green paint or maybe that was mildew.

*Must be prison brah. Must 'a been a fun night. What chu' do this time monkey-man?*

He couldn't remember getting in any trouble last night. He couldn't remember anything about last night. He shut off the cold water. The orange light on the water heater went off. He was shivering and his shoulder hurt somethin' awful.

There was a clean rag of a towel hanging on a wall rack made from a galvanized pipe. The towel was stiff as sandpaper, prison issue. He rubbed it around on his face wondering how many years he'd be incarcerated. Ole scraped the towel down his torso, then cleared a circle of reflection in the haze of a full-length mirror unprofessionally screwed onto the bathroom door. The top of his head was wrapped in clean white gauze and his shoulder was purple as an eggplant. It was swollen to the size of a softball. That shoulder throbbed. This couldn't be a dream. Being Godzilla is a dream. Flying like a monkey is a dream. The blotchy purple swelling of his shoulder ran all the way to his wrist which didn't move when he told it to.

*Your arm's broke, brah.*

Oliver wrapped the rough towel around his waist. He pushed open the door with the mirror and stepped over a two-inch high sill that had been chiseled out of what was once a wall. A floor of smooth cement met his feet in the next room. It was a warm floor, almost hot as the room. He stood there, out of place, out of body maybe? No, this was his body all right, broken arm, cracked head and all.

He'd never been in such a dreary room. It wasn't a prison, no bars on the windows. More like a cheap motel? Daylight was struggling to get in through dusty window slats. Dogs were barking outside and a rooster crowed. Then another rooster crowed, then another, then another one, louder this time.

*This is a third World nightmare, brah.*

As his eyes adjusted to the dim light in the room, his face went slack-jaw. There was a naked woman on the room's only bed. She wasn't moving, just lying there face down. She had attractive long legs leading up to a sheet that covered the slight hump of her butt. Her long black hair lay lifeless across the faded sheets. Her skin was a soft brown color like a perfect tan. She was a young Filipina, maybe fifteen-years-old. One arm hung down over the side of the bed. She wasn't moving.

*Is she dead?* The thought stole through his head chased

by a worse one. *Was there a fight? Did you kill her? Let's get out of here,* the paranoid side of his brain pleaded.

*Y'er a poet an' a lover brah. You didn't start killing people today... ah... did you?*

Ole wasn't sure. He didn't see any blood, so he moved toward the bed and reached out both hands to feel for a pulse. Only his right arm moved, the left sent him so much pain he let it hang. Then he heard her breathe. She was just sleeping. He relaxed a little and studied her nakedness. The girl looked familiar from the backside. He scanned the rough scene around him. Those were his clothes hung on a rope stretched from two big iron nails hammered into the concrete-block wall. There was a noisy refrigerator in one corner that looked like it was out of a vintage movie. Another pink plastic chair sat by a weathered desk. His suitcase and sandals sat neatly arranged at the foot of the bed. His attention circled back to the young woman.

*You been sleepin' with her brah,* accused his mind.

*No way,* he thought back at himself. *I neva' slept with a Filipina, not that I wouldn't like to.*

*Those are your clothes on the rope brah. You're naked in her room. You slept with her. Let's hope she's at least eighteen years-old.*

Ole touched the sleeping beauty on her bare shoulder. "Hey?" He whispered. She spun her head around so fast that Ole stepped back a pace; his towel began to slip off. He tried to grab it with both hands, but the left stopped short and hurt all the way to his teeth. "Ouch!" he winced as most of the towel fell to the floor.

"Oh, darling come back to bed. I'll put another ice-pack on your shoulder." It was Lacey, the captain's wife!

## 16  Myna Birds and Penny whistle

The shock of seeing Lacey with him in a cheap motel room brought him back to his still-life moment outside the front door of the Sly Mongoose. He blushed a deep purple shade of shame. The captain was his best friend. They liked the same kinds of things: guitars, sunsets, sailing, Hawaii...

*And Lacey,* one of the voices in his head slapped.

Oliver didn't want to be attracted to Lacey, he just couldn't help it. She turned him on in ways that decency should switch off. Lacey felt it too, Ole was sure of that.

He finally gripped the metal handle on the dented door that opens into the Sly Mongoose Bar. This tavern on the bottom floor of a steel warehouse is a dive no tourist would ever find or dare to enter. Ole, himself, had avoided the place until the night Tanya filed for a divorce.

*That still hurts brah, maybe we should have a drink; just one.* One of the voices in his head was starting to get it. Turning the door handle at exactly the stroke of midnight, he entered another world, one he didn't deserve. It was a world of normal, happy people with nothing to hide. He closed the door and looked about to see if anyone recognized him. Only the bartender, Auntie Donna, glanced his way with a welcoming smile. If you needed a place to get away from tourists, the Sly was an air-conditioned oasis on hot nights in late December. It had comfortable vibe, chairs with arms (safer, less chance of falling to the floor), dark corners and cheap drinks. You can meet new friends or be left alone at the Sly, the tavern of choice, for local folks on West Maui.

After a short que at the bar, Ole sipped his rum and Coke and kept his head down as he sort of humbled his way through the crowd. He found a small table back by the fire exit. The rum and Coke tasted more like Coke and water, weak as his resolve for the task ahead of him.

*The body brah...where?*

He should have ordered a double. He sat there in the dark figuring he looked as normal as anyone else in the place.

*What would you know about normal? Talking to mom on da' phone, hearing her smile, that's normal. You should call her. It's 6:00 AM back in Iowa. She's already making dad's coffee.*

Calling his parents in his current state of weird from a noisy bar was not gonna happen. Just thinking of phones made his shoulders tremble, like those monkey wings could pop out at any moment. The 'phone call' was still banging away in his head like one of those annoying, battery-operated monkey toys that clash cymbals together and won't stop. Ole took a long pull at the oars. The booze wasn't working fast enough to muffle the cymbals. He needed a stronger drink and a plan.

*Where? How?*

He curled his parent's hands into angry fists. *How could this happen to him? Oliver Gold, Mr. Law-abiding, retired chemistry teacher, father of three grown daughters, past commodore of the Seattle Yacht Club, re-inventing himself in Hawaii as a surf bum and local musician was now... a man on the run?* His thoughts were his own for a few moments until that 'know it all' voice broke in again.

*Why did you believe everything Desi said? And Manny what about him? He was dead for two weeks, dead and buried; that's dead brah.*

Ole gulped down the rest of the liquid sugar in his tumbler and walked to the bar for a double. The Sly was jumping on a... he tried to think. It hurt to think... Saturday night?

*How would you know what day of the week it is? You don't even know where to hide a body.*

"I've never done this before, alright?" He shouted back at his forehead. The bar was so loud nobody noticed. He was just another local guy talking to himself in a bar.

Ole got a double rum this time and circumvented the crowd as he wound his way back to his table. He slumped into the same upholstered chair and placed the drink in front of him like it was a votive candle. As he stared at the reflections of bar lights flickering on the side of the plastic glass, he was swept away again by the big-bad broom of Desiree memories.

Two nights a week, for over a year now, he'd played his music at the famous Pioneer Inn. He had discovered that every night, there was a very magic, Maui moment right after sunset. Across the street from the PI, stands the even more famous, one-hundred and forty-year old

Banyan forest. Well, it looks like a forest, but everyone knows it's only one tree with dozens of tree trunks and long horizontal limbs that have ambitions of over-taking the whole town someday. The myna birds will like that.

During every sunset, eighty-thousand myna birds fly into the banyan tree and start fighting over sleeping arrangements. (No one has ever actually counted them, so this number could be under-exaggerated.) Their raucous screeching starts way up in the top of the tree, the penthouse branches. The losers of round one, drop down a level and fight for the ocean-view branches. Then, the myna's fight for the garden view, street view and on down, all the way to dumpster view, where the last bird in the pecking order must roost, usually alone. The moment that last bird finally shuts up, the magic moment happens. There is a sudden burst of... 'quiet.' That's the magic. You sigh with relief. You go full Zen. It's like closing the door on a noisy room. It's that sudden... the sound of silence. Maybe this is where Paul Simon got the idea for his famous song... maybe not. The magic doesn't last long, a few fleeting seconds of marvelous peace and then the town crescendos back up to its normal, touristy buzz.

Oliver Gold knew all about this magic moment. Every time he set up his sound system, his mind wandered back to when he first got this gig, and how the birds quickly put him in his place. He used to turn up the volume on his mic and try to power-sing over that hour of shrieking cacophony. The birds won every time. Even when he juiced his amp all the way up, all two-hundred watts, not his voice, nor his guitar, nor his ukulele could be heard above the nightly bird war across the street. The mynas were louder than when the motorcycles rumbled by.

Often, way too often, there would be a full parade of these guys on big Harley Davidsons, snorting and fuming slowly through town in double lines of reverberating, bullshit noise. They were local guys who should know better. But they always acted like teenagers trying to out-fart each other with their loud bike exhaust and stink-shooting it all over the innocent pedestrians on the sidewalks.

The effect is gut wrenching. The blasts from their mufflers scare little children and everyone else with sudden SNORTS, GROWLS, and concussive motorcycle EXPLETIVES! Children drop their ice cream cones on the side walk and hide behind their parents. Old folks pull their hearing aids out of their ears to stop the pain from the muffler cannons. Diners in the restaurants can't hear each other talking. Waitresses can't hear the diners order drinks or food. Musician's stop playing, grit their teeth and wait while the rumbling, window-rattling noise avalanches rudely past.

When the good-old, Harley-boys have ruined the touristy ambiance on Front Street, you can hear them in the distance as they terrorize the side streets of the town. The little old plantation houses are the homes of senior citizens and young families. Pregnant mothers awaken from their well-deserved nap. Invalids and recovering sick people, night-shift service industry workers trying to get some sleep, hundreds or maybe thousands of innocent people awakened or annoyed by these clueless jerks.

'Look at me! Listen to me roar' they seem to brag. "It's the "Sound of Freedom!" they shout, to justify their selfishness.

*Fo' shame on 'dem guys brah.*

One night, just before Halloween, he was setting up his amps and so far, no bikers had rumbled past the Pioneer Inn. Of course, they always wait until he starts singing. He hit the power button on his sound board and whispered into his voice mic.

"Shazam," then a little louder, "Tarzan," then a little louder with the puff "P," "Peter Pan." The mix sounded right, no 'pop' through the speakers. He ran his hand through his unruly brown hair and made that Elvis snarl with his lips. He was Oliver Gold, local legend at the PI. He would empower his soul, chase enlightenment and sing his songs better than ever, right after a sip of ice tea. The crowd was looking his way, nearly every table filled. The Myna birds would start fighting any minute now. It was almost six pm.

*Bet'ta sing while can brah.*

So, Ole began with one of his new songs.

*"Another perfect day in Hawaii, a little rain, a lot 'ta sunshine… an' all I really wanna do, is surf all day… party all night… an' live a-lo-ha with you…"*

He was just starting the second verse when the myna birds started bickering. It began small then grew louder and louder. It sounded like a dozen dump trucks emptying loads of broken glass bottles down a hillside. There'd be no more singing for a while. However, Ole did have one small instrument that could be heard over the birds, an Irish penny whistle. With this, he began to pipe bright, lilting notes that rose high above all the fighting in the forest. That penny whistle had kept Oliver employed where other musicians had packed up and gone home. He even dedicated a few melodies to the mynas: 'Yellow

Bird,' 'Rubber Ducky,' and 'Fly like an Eagle.' The eagle song loses a lot of weight played solo on a penny whistle, but the mynas seemed to like that one the best.

It had been his fancy to imagine as he dreamed and piped away, how his penny whistle tunes could slip into the ears of people dining and drinking at the inn. He would send his music into the ears of tourists staggering off the dinner boats, into the ears of the homeless guys sleeping under the banyan tree, even into the ears of dogs and cats prowling the waterfront.

Ole played that pipe with expert passion, especially into the ears of beautiful women. This became his naughty, musical voyeurism. He would focus his aim at the ears of the unmarried and cutest-looking women nearby. He'd send subliminal messages along with the innocent melodies.

*Would you like to take me home with you? I'm available tonight. Come on in and buy me a drink.*

It never seemed to work until that one night in late October. He was piping the theme song from the movie, 'Titanic.' As he played, a very attractive, long-legged brunette came model-walking down the sidewalk. He intensified his sexy message and piped it like microwaves directly at her ears. She stopped, leaned on the restaurant's sidewalk railing and listened for a while. His sexy musical telegram seemed to be getting through. She lingered, not looking directly at him, but listening. She was gorgeous, thirty-something in age, a little on the classy side and a little on the trashy side. That's just what a lonely musician needs after sleeping with his guitar for months. He thought up a naughtier message, piping as romantically as the sad Irish tune allowed: *I want you...*

*yes you, leaning on the railing. Hear my wanton desire. You're in my power now. You want me too. You want me so bad.*

The tall woman turned and smiled at him. She walked into the restaurant and sat at a table near the stage. Oh, the power of music! Oliver played that penny whistle like he was an Irish snake-charmer with a white bindi-dot dabbed on the center of his forehead. He ramped up his inviting message:

*Let's fly away and make some magic tonight!*

She listened intently. Ole had her under his spell. He wouldn't be surprised if she stood up and belly-danced. She looked so hot and yet kind of innocent. He wished on all his lucky stars as he piped his desire into her ears at two-hundred and forty volts. It was after seven, the sun was down; the myna birds had finally gone to sleep, 'the magic moment' had arrived. He stopped piping. Everything was quiet.

"Hit me!" He microwaved out into the universe. Karma dropped down from the rafters on a long strand of silk. She was a black-widow spider about the size of a muddy softball, a perfect disguise for Halloween week on Maui. Karma-spider held up his new card, a Joker. Joker cards are never used in Blackjack, so Oliver wasn't sure what to do with it. The spider of karma laughed wickedly in his face and slowly climbed back up into the rafters of the restaurant.

*It's another omen, brah, watch out.*

*Yah, I wonder what...?* He got distracted by miss Long legs sitting there at the first table. She tossed her beautiful hair to one side and gazed straight at him. Her dark innocent eyes seemed to be pleading with him. *Come over here and kiss me.* That's what Ole imagined, anyway. His lips felt dry, his tongue felt hungry. Her steady gaze made his toes and knees shake. He tried playing the Irish pipe again, but faltered over a few notes and turned away from those inviting eyes. After a few missed beats, he recovered, found the melody once more and finished the song. He gasped for air, embarrassed over his flusterpation.

With the myna birds quiet at last, he set down the penny whistle and looked over at her. She was crossing her gorgeous legs this way and that, a mannerism that women do when they want to look available. Oliver could tell she wasn't a local girl. She wore a very expensive-looking Hawaiian, tourist blouse and a pleated mini-skirt. On her table for all to see, was a purse made by Gucci or Bubba Vuitton or somebody famous. It probably cost more than his fifteen-hundred-dollar Cadillac. She wasn't wearing any jewelry or a wedding ring. Her black hair was all messy giving her a trailer-trash run-away kind of scared, innocent look. She had a crazy gaze in her eyes, which made her even more interesting. She was the type of woman that just makes a man feel instantly horny. It's hard to explain. She was applauding politely with the rest of the crowd.

Ole was about to walk over to meet her when she stood up and walked right up to meet him. 'Chicken skin' started stampeding up and down his arms. It was a powerful moment.

"Hey handsome, you sure can penny whistle." She said, tossing her forest of gorgeous black hair over one bare shoulder. He knew this is how women behave when they want a guy, he'd read it in a magazine. Her lovely face had a smile of perfect white teeth, very kissable-looking lips and those innocent eyes. He looked back down at her lips and down her graceful neckline. Her round breasts were playing 'hide and seek,' trying to pop out of her Hawaiian-print top. She had a slim waist he wanted to squeeze, and those devastating long legs. He was so busy enjoying the scenery, he missed seeing the hand she held out for him to shake.

"Ahem," she cleared her throat.

He reached out to shake, but she grabbed his hand and pulled him into a big hug. It had been a long time since a woman held him that tight. He squeezed her back just as strong. She smelled nice, kind of like Carnauba car wax.

"I heard those naughty words you piped into my head," she whispered in his ear. "You want some magic tonight?"

Oliver let go the hug and stepped back a pace. *It worked?*

"Yeah doll, I want some magic with you. I'm Oliver Gold, local music legend and surf bum."

"Desiree Scarlioni," she said, blinking her innocent eyes.

## 17  Two Demons Walk into a Bar

Back in the Sly Mongoose, someone dropped or threw a beer bottle and the explosion of smashing glass brought Ole out of his memories. He picked up the votive candle and sipped his rum and Coke.

*Where brah, how?* His forehead insisted. *You've got your drink, now think!*

Oliver shoveled more coal into the furnace of his thinker. Instead of someplace to hide a body he thought of Lyka. *She is so darn cute.* He leaned his chair back against the wall of the tavern and closed his eyes. *Maybe Lyka will fall in love with me and we'll get married in a little Hawaiian church like Captain Billy and his beautiful Lacey did.*

*Lyka too young fo' you brah. Wake up to reality. She's twenty-six, you're what, ninety-something?* The voice was right. He was fifty-five. It sounded like, 'grandpa-land.' *Too late for another chance at romance?* He wondered with a sigh.

Ole sat there in the darkest corner of the bar wandering his desert of lost dreams. So, he didn't notice when the dented door of the tavern opened and two very sunburned demons crawled in. They drug their sweaty tails along behind them, slimming the cement floor like a pair of tired slugs. Their snake-like skins had peeled badly, leaving blotchy white spots on their otherwise reddish, crocodile faces. With long green, forked-tongues they licked their reptilian eyes to adjust to the dim interior of the bar and heaved collective sighs. Slobbering acidic demon drool, they stood up on their hind legs swaying for a moment, adjusting to the dim light.

When Oliver did notice them, what he and everyone else in the bar saw were two gorgeous teenage models standing there by the dented door. They seemed to be basking in the glow of an antique 'Kona Long Board' beer sign. They posed for the crowd like they were auditioning for acting roles in a porn movie. The noisy buzz of the bar went quiet as a church covered with snow at midnight, on the night after Christmas.

The two dolls were dressed to score, with matching black mini-skirts and white tank tops showing perky nipple bumps right where they should be. At first glance, Ole gave them high marks: somewhere between 7.5 and 8 on the babe 1 to 10 scale.

The whiskey-scented, air-conditioned tavern felt like Heaven to the two she-devils. Or perhaps as close to Heaven as these two might ever get. They even liked the Garth Brooks melancholy that dripped like rain from the sound system up in the high rafters of the ceiling.

In a far corner a pool game was in progress. The table surrounded by a mix of surf bums, homeless time-share salesmen, tour-boat skippers and other bottom feeders.

Oliver, like every guy in the place began wondering how he could introduce himself to these two over-sexed dolls. Then his angry depression and guilt overcame his lust; and he went back to watching memories reflect off the side of his votive rum glass.

*Lacey in a motel room with you? Had to be a dream,*

*brah. Even your life isn't that strange.* His forehead tries to help.

*Sure, it is, S*arcasm kicked in. *Remember Desi, the world-class psycho-liar-beautician? Her dead brother called from California. We went Godzilla and flying monkey, remember?*

*You don't handle shock very well do you? Or maybe some anthrax blew in the window and took you down.*

*No way... that never happens,* answered another voice. *It wasn't just a dream. It was a dream of epic, 'Paradise Lost,' stoned on marijuana, proportions.*

*Nah,* he thought to himself. *He hadn't smoked grass since college, a long time ago.*
*Thirty-seven...*

"Shut up brain," he shouted out into the tavern. Nobody appeared to notice.

*Why the flying monkey?* He wondered.

*Don't ask me, it was your dream.*

"You're my brain, I want some answers!" Ole shouted again. This time the guys playing pool turned and stared at him. He waved back with a shy grin and took another deep gulp from his votive candle.

*You've lost your center, your Zen presence. Try some yoga brah.*

*Screw yoga, I need another drink,* he thought back at his mind.

*Bad idea my son, you know bet'ta. Your problems are bigger than you think. Did you hate your father?*

"No! I love my father. Shut... up!" He was shouting again. The pool game stopped and four players looked over at Ole, shook their heads, laughed and went back to the game.

*You're the one asking questions,* his mind reminded him.

*Sometimes, we wonder just how much stupider you can get,* Sarcasm added.

"That makes three of us," Ole said quietly into his drink.

*Actually... there are more of us,* another voice in his head quipped.

*Who was that?* The first two voices echoed. No answer.

"Okay, who else is in there?" Ole growled. There was a long silence then the same old questions came swimming up from the swamp, *where? How?*

Both sides of his black and blue brain started hammering him.

*You don't have a clue, do you? You've got deep serious stuff here brah and instead of go fix, you're in a bar getting mashed.*

*Yah, no wonder you don't have any friends.*

"Oh yeah?" He fired back, but not so loud this time. "Manny called me an' told me the truth about his sister, so he's a real friend. And Captain Billy's a friend.

*After what you did? I don't think so.*

"I didn't do it. That was a dream!"

*And what's this*? Asked that mysterious new voice.

Ole shut up. Moving to Maui was a dream come true, but it was kind of like dying and going to Heaven ahead of all your family and friends. They're still back there on earth (the mainland) and you miss them terribly. Over a lifetime, Oliver had cared for them, saved and kept track of them like he would his favorite books. He missed his ex-wife and his grown daughters. Ole studied the ice cubes at rest now, in the two plastic votive candles sitting in front of him, dark and empty as his future.

## 18  Mary Beth Johnson

Oliver still had his past. He thought of his very first girlfriend, Mary Beth Johnson. She was the coconut-cream pie of his young dreams. He chased her around on the playground during every recess. That's how boys in first grade show their romantic intentions. He never caught her. She was fast, skinny and cute. Ole was still attracted to that kind of woman. Lacey's slim figure came to mind.

*Stop it brah. Only get you nah 'ting but trouble.*

*Bet'ta count your dollars, Mr. Thirsty, y'er about out 'ta money.*

The Sly Mongoose crowd was getting louder. He shut out the racket and dove back into his past. *Was there a first love before Mary Beth?* It took him a while to remember because he was thinking of girls. Then it hit him like a sack of dog food. It wasn't a girl. It was a boy. His first love was Snorty, a little brown and white puppy that his parents surprised him with, right after grandpa died.

His heart belonged to Snorty, until he met Mary Beth. She was the prettiest girl in the whole school; probably in the whole world. He was a fast runner, but all he ever touched was the back of her snow-covered winter coat. Snorty, however, would wiggle free, run a few steps ahead, then turn and smile his wide toothy grin. Snorty would stand there quivering with anticipation until Oliver caught him again. His little brown eyes loved Oliver with the kind of devotion he would never forget. He couldn't remember what color Mary Beth's eyes were because he never caught her.

Snorty and Ole tumbled around together like brothers. They watched dog shows like, 'Rin-Tin-Tin' and 'Lassie' on the family's six-inch wide, black and white TV. Snorty would lay on Ole's lap and watch upside down while Oliver scratched his tummy. Ole could remember laying like his puppy, upside down, with his head hanging over the front edge of the davenport. He would pretend he was walking on the ceiling as if it were the floor. He imagined hopping over the door tops and looking at all the living room furniture stuck up there on the floor.

Of course, Oliver loved his parents, but it was so different from the love he had for Snorty. Puppy love was funny, but it was so different from the kind of love he felt for Mary Beth and Sister Mary Magdalene.

Sister Mary had a nice voice and it softened even sweeter when she told stories of her life in Hawaii. Surfing close on every word, Ole would pretend he was in Hawaii, not Iowa. The oak floor ocean around his island desk smelled of dust mops and floor polish with the scent of flowers and spices from far-away places called, Kauai and Lanai and Oahu.

It was okay with Sister Mary if you fell asleep during story time but Oliver never closed his eyes. He watched Mary Beth sleep. She made drums beat in the jungle of his heart. He wanted to hold her and scratch her tummy.

## 19 Soul Trappers

Demons are always in a bad mood, but these two standing there by the Kona beer sign, were especially miserable. It had been a slow week in Hawaii. They were hot, thirsty and behind in their quest for souls. Everyone knows that human souls are quite valuable on the cosmic market. Think of souls as mink, beaver or muskrat pelts. As a child Oliver had been terrified by Sister Mary's stories of fallen angels lurking around, setting their trap lines and taking naughty souls to Hell. Of course, young Ole had believed every word of it.

With only nine pelts between them, these two devils were behind on their demonic team goal for the week. If they could trap just one more human soul before sunrise, they'd be eligible for the coveted Lucifer Achievement Award and go on to the Hawaii state finals for a chance to win a one-week, all-expenses-paid, vacation to refreshing, frozen Antarctica.

The Sly Mongoose wasn't the most likely bar to hunt for souls, but the demons were tired of crawling all over Lahaina. The yacht club was empty tonight. The Pioneer Inn was closed by ten o'clock. Cool Cat was full of happy young tourists. Same at Longhi's, where Marty Dread had everyone up dancing to his joyful reggae songs. The Dirty Monkey was up a whole flight of stairs, so the weary demons didn't bother. They were exhausted and desperate. They wanted that ice-cold, week-long vacation in Antarctica. They had pushed into the Sly Mongoose as a last resort. They knew it was usually filled with honest, service industry workers and other happy locals. It was almost impossible to trap a soul at the Sly Mongoose.

They scanned the dark interior of the tavern with their Inferno, thermo-vision looking for a victim. Their gazes locked immediately on a hunk of meat sitting alone back by the fire exit. To their membrane-lidded eyes, he looked like a lump of road kill. A faint blue color pulsed from his heart, by far... the loneliest guy in the place.

*That one,* they silently vibed to each other with a nod. They bumped their horned fists together and slimmed slowly over to his table.

## 20  A Child's Plan

Even years later, sitting in a bar, Ole could still see Mary Beth or at least her reflection on the side of his votive rum glass. He saw her long brown hair flying wild, as she ran away from him. She must have felt his passion, because one day while standing in line out in the hall, she leaned in close and kissed him on the cheek. That did it. He would grow up, marry Mary, and move to Hawaii.

In his childhood bed at night he would drown out the howling winter winds by turning up the volume on his small bedside radio. A scientist at heart, he had taken the plastic cover off the Philco radio so he could track the flow of electricity through the glowing tubes and sound wires to the black cone of paper that vibrated with the music. He made elaborate robot diagrams of 'Robo I,' with tubes and wires connecting along similar paths.

He snuggled under thick blankets and sang along with the radio thinking of his warm Hawaiian future with Mary Beth. Ole had no idea how this would happen, but he knew that someday somehow, it would. One night, he caught a 'Blues' station broadcasting all the way from Chicago. That, was over five-hundred miles away. Radio waves were like ray-guns and robots, the amazing science of the tomorrow land. That night, he planned out his future. He would grow up, become a scientist, build robots, play music in a Blues band, marry Mary Beth and move to Hawaii.

No one should be surprised when their dreams come true, or at least, *some* of their dreams, because they were *their* dreams from the very start. You own your dreams. That's why they come true. But you can't just wish upon a star, you must chase them, block all the other stuff that gets in the way, and tackle them. In the early morning buzz of the Sly Mongoose, Oliver's dreams had almost all come true: retired scientist, moving to Hawaii, becoming a local musician, all but the *Mary Beth* part.

*And how about the body, dreamer guy? Where? How?*

Yes, that was the problem. Ole took another long slurp of his drink. Rum drinkers are not wine snobs carefully sniffing the bouquet, guessing the vintage, quoting critiques memorized off the labels of fifty-dollar bottles of Merlot. Rum was sugar cane, distilled like moonshine and meant for sailors to pour down the hatch after a hard day of beating into the wind, plain and simple. Thinking of rum, made him thirsty again. That made his memory channel light up with more bad stuff.

Second grade was the worst year of Oliver's life. His dog Snorty bit a neighbor kid named, Mike Habberman. Mike was a mean son-of-a-bitch who liked to kick dogs and throw rocks at cars. Habberman punched Ole right in the stomach one morning on the way to school. Snorty saw the punch and bit Mike on his kicking leg. Mike cried like a baby yelling how he was gonna tell his daddy, who was someone called, 'a lawyer.' His family lived in the biggest house in Ole's neighborhood. His mom drove a brand new, light green nineteen-fifty-five Cadillac with electric windows that went up and down with the push of a button. All other cars in those days had cranks that rolled the windows up and down.

Mr. Habberman called the police. The police must have known the lawyer cause they sped to Ole's house with their siren screaming and both red lights flashing. There were two cops. They had guns. The police officers took Snorty out of Oliver's arms and put him in a cage in the back seat of their patrol car. Oliver's mom didn't have a gun and neither did he, so they couldn't put up a fight like Roy Rodgers and Dale Evans would have. They both just sat on the front porch steps and cried. It broke Oliver's heart almost as bad as when grandpa died.

Later that evening, during supper, dad said the police had Snorty, 'put to sleep.' When Ole pressed for more information, like when would Snorty be waking up and coming home? He was told that his puppy had been killed down at the pound. He was never coming home.

He decided right then, as a child, the police would never take him to the pound. So, he never ever bit anyone. And he never did trust the police for the rest of his life. Snorty had the happiest, big, brown eyes.

To make everything in his young world even worse, *all* his first love affairs ended in second grade. Mary Beth was assigned to a different class room. And of course, Sister Mary was a first-grade teacher, so he lost her as well. His love for Santa had faded fast when he learned the Jolly old onion farmer could never die. So, he was just sad from time to time, realizing that the human heart could take a lot of breaking. But, if you prayed real hard to Jesus, your heart could survive... to be broken again.

## 21  Darker Things on His Mind

To the suddenly quiet crowd in the Sly Mongoose, the
young hotties by the Kona beer sign were adorable. They
had that chic world-class look that was seldom seen (like
never), among the middle-age crowd in the Sly
Mongoose.

The taller girl looked a bit Irish, kind of devilish. She
had short wavy red hair and perfect legs that went almost
up to her chin. The petite girl was a brunette with her
long hair tied up high on the back of her head in a
youthful pony tail. She looked seventeen-years old.
Oliver's under-age caution alarm was buzzing along with
the clanging monkey-cymbals. He ignored the noise and
like everyone else enjoyed the view.

*This is a tavern. They got 'a be twenty-one to get in.*
The wild man voice in his brain tried to convince him.

He's weighing the odds of getting arrested for merely
talking to them. As young as they looked, he quickly
convinced himself that they were at least eighteen, out
bar-hopping with fake IDs.

Oliver had darker things on his mind than cute women.
But, due to his weakness for cute women, he stared at the
two out-of-place dolls. To his surprise, the girls stared
right back at him. They nodded to each other, bumped
their hands together and model-walked their sexy heat
directly toward him. He sat up straight, wiped the Coca-
Cola off his chin, and pushed his messy brown hair off his
forehead.

*Ah, now I can see bet'ta,* whispered his mind's eye.

"Hit me!" Ole sent a silent plea out to the cosmos. Karma swam into view. He was a serpent now with a shiny red apple in his mouth instead of a cigar. He produced a card from somewhere, flipped it at Oliver and dove back into the deepest darkest place on earth; the root cellar of Oliver's bad thoughts. Everyone has a place like this in their mind, where their wildest personality runs around naked looking for thrills, sex and adventure. Sigmund Freud called this uninhibited extreme of mind… the 'Id.' Ole hadn't worried about his own Id, until this morning's phone call. He looked at his new Blackjack card.

*Ace of Diamonds… that makes sixteen, way too low. Plus, a Joker card still makes sixteen.* Oliver's Ego was adding up the cards. In Freud's dissertation, the Ego is like a man or woman trying to rein in the powerful horse of wild desires… the Id. Oliver wanted to continue with the psychology, but the two young women were leaning on the outer edge of Ole's sticky table staring at him in an inviting way.

Ole couldn't think of two words to put together, so he just stared back. His Id was doing jumping jacks for joy on the casino table in his mind. Oliver's eyes, even his third eye, traveled down to their stiletto heels, then back up the girl's nicely shaped legs, smooth thighs, short-short skirts, flat, bare tummies, each navel pierced with a painful-looking, silver ring. They had regulation-size baseball boobs, graceful necks, pouty wet lips, too much eye makeup and wonderful hair. Up close, their scores jumped to 9.9 on his seismic chick meter. Overwhelmed, by their trashy gorgeousness, he still couldn't speak, so he gave them his best James Bond grin with a trembling Elvis snarl. Tall, fresh-looking Irish smiled back at him.

"Lonely?" She asked, loud enough to be heard over Garth Brooks and his, 'low places.'

"Nah," Ole lied. His bar-cool, guy-confidence came rushing back to him. "I'm waiting for a couple of good-looking-blondes; s'posed to meet me here tonight."

"Okay, I... ah... um... do you want us to leave?"

"Aw, they're late. So, buy me a drink and you can stay."

The brunette demon flashed a vibe at Irish... *this might be harder than we thought.*

The two girls looked around for a waitress. Busy as the place was, the only waitress was sitting on some guy's lap making out with him like they were all alone at a drive-in movie. So, the two dolls held hands and swayed over to the bar to order drinks.

"We'll start a tab." Irish told the busy lady barkeep. Auntie Donna knew almost everybody in lower Lahaina, but these two were not frequent fliers in her blue-collar club. As the girls returned with the drinks, Oliver could see Auntie Donna sending him not-so-subtle warnings. She shook her head at him in a crazy way, rolled her eyes and made like she had a noose around her neck. She hung her tongue out one side of her mouth like she was dead. Ole ignored her and smiled at the pretty young girls approaching his table with a tray of drinks.

"Here you go Ole," the brunette teenager offered with a smile from her candy-coated luscious lips. He wanted to kiss those lips and throw caution out the fire exit, into the alley.

*They look like double-trouble,* his ego-eye warned him with an inner boil and bubble.

He took the drink and wasn't surprised that the petite brunette knew his name. He was almost famous in Lahaina town. He was a local musician.

The brunette pulled a chair closer to him and sat down to his right. Irish sat to his left, one of her long legs lightly touching his under the table. It felt hot.

"What 're we drinking to?" Oliver raised his glass.

"I'll drink to that," toasted Irish.

"Get it in ya," saluted candy lips.

The conversation ended as they all slaked a thirst.

"Well, I was just a' leavin,'" Ole said, as he started to get up from the table... The girls' vibed panic at each other. Irish spoke first.

"No wait! I ah...I thought you were meeting some blondes?"

"Yah, it's a let-down all right, but that's life in this town. Some nights you get lucky, some nights you don't. Hey, I'll see ya around and thanks for the drink."

He stood up to leave. Both demons grabbed his arms and pulled him back down in his soft chair.

"Stay awhile Olivvve,er," the brunette whispered. She leaned closer and tickled his ear with her long, green tongue. It was a very, very hot tongue.

"Ah, I can't sugar. I gotta go hide a body."

*Did you really, just say that? You think it's funny? Y'er sicker than we thought,* grumbled his forehead's 'Super Ego' the one in charge of morality and social responsibility.

Ole tried to get up again. The girls held on.

"Let's have some more drinks!" Irish decided.

"Not thirsty," said Oliver.

"One more," the brunette insisted and blinked one eye. The flirt was more than it seemed, for it dried Ole's throat like a desert. He had never felt so thirsty in his entire life.

Ole looked side to side at the determined looks on each of their pretty faces. They still had him by both arms. "Are you two cops? Are you detaining me without the Miranda speech?"

"No-o way Ole me' boy" Irish said with a laugh, "we jus' wanna have a bit o' fu'in, wi' ye. What'z it you'eeed be wantin' meee handsome lad?"

Ole relaxed a bit. *They're either drunken tourists out for wild night or they're hookers.* Either way he was enjoying the attention.

*You're hiding out at a back table brah, no need get attention. Rememba' da' body?*

*Shut up brain,* he ordered himself. "What do I want? Ladies I want a glass of water! And a rum and Coke chaser… no, a double rum and a double water."

The little brunette jumped up and samba-walked

through the crowded tables. She looked dangerous as jail bait, maybe fifteen or sixteen...very far on the underbelly-side of legal.

"How old is she Irish?" Ole asked the redhead. He couldn't take his eyes off the way the brunette moved. It was hypnotic. Everyone else in the bar was watching her too. She looked like a high-class, under-age, Las Vegas escort.

"Do ye want 'er Ole?" Irish asked.

"Uh huh... I mean... I'm just... I mean, how old is she?"

"Do yee like 'er skirt?"

"How old is she?" He growled impatiently.

"Yeee can 'ave 'er ta' night, Oliver Gold," whispered Irish.

*Why tonight of all nights?* One of his inner horny voices complains.

## 22  The Cue Ball Fight

The teenage brunette sauntered back with six more drinks on a tray. As she passed the pool table, she vibed a quick demon-message to her Irish pal. *'Watch this, eight ball in the corner... no... the side pocket.'*

Staring at her legs and mini-skirt, one of the guys playing pool missed his easy eight-ball shot. His cue tip tore a new rip in the stained table felt. The white cue ball launched off the green like the space shuttle. Every face turned up to watch it rocket toward the fire-extinguishing nozzles high in the warehouse ceiling. The cue ball reached its zenith, arched beautifully, and came plummeting back to gravity, splashing down in a plastic basket of French fries and ketchup. The fat man sitting at that table was splattered bloody red like a scene from a horror movie. Wiping ketchup off his face, he jumped up and threw the cue ball back as hard as he could. It was a fast ball, hitting the pool player right in the gut. He doubled over, the cue ball fell onto the pool table with a thud. It spun slowly, having lost its space travel inertia. It looked like a ketchup-stained red and white ball of Christmas candy rolling in a wide circle heading for a corner pocket at the far end of the green. But suddenly, it made an impossible ninety-degree turn. The cue ball rolled sideways and kissed the eight-ball right on the side of its bald, black head. The eight was knocked left, in slow-motion, it dove like a prairie dog into the side pocket with a loud, "KA-PLUNK" heard around the room.

All the neon beer signs in the place began to blink off and on, like slot machines.

"I won!" the pool player cheered in breathless surprise, still holding his stomach.

"No way brah, that don' count," argued his buddy.

Irish winked back at the brunette and vibed, *'nice shot sista!'*

The fat guy covered with ketchup stormed over and punched the 'winner' in the face. His buddies jumped in to defend him and the fight was on. If Oliver had been in a better mood he might have smiled; just another fun night at the Sly Mongoose.

The cute brunette brought the drink tray to Ole's table. She slid two pints of beer over to Irish, kept two for herself and passed two glasses of water to Oliver. Then, she gracefully presented the double rum to him like he was the King of Siam. Her lovely hands caressed the scratched plastic tumbler as if it were the most priceless jewel in the world. She was mesmerizing, but he grabbed one of the tall glasses of water first, drained it dry and reached for the other.

"How old are you?" Ole demanded. He wasn't going to jail in some underage sting operation. He gulped down the second glass of water as fast as he could swallow.

"Let's just say... I'm old enough," she answered with her beer-frothed candy lips curling into a wicked smile.

Irish snickered back at her with a silent vibe, *Aye lassie you're older than the Garden of Eden.*

"What do you want ta' do tonight, Ole?" Candy-lips asked.

*Two beautiful girls show up out of nowhere and start buying you drinks.* His forehead is adding up the facts. *This is better than seeing those leprechauns last March. Soooooo... what do you want, Gullible Oliver?* Sarcasm wondered.

Ole thought about it. *What time was it anyway, maybe one o'clock in the morning? What do I want? I want my normal, impoverished life back as a local musician. I want to move closer to enlightenment. I want to stop all this drinking and get out 'a here. I wanna hide the body before the sun comes up.*

But, just in case they *were* leprechauns, he answered truthfully, "I want a big pot o' gold, and a Mercedes convertible and a home on a golf course on Maui... *and* another glass of water!"

Candy Lips sat down and pulled her chair closer to him. Oliver caught a whiff of her perfume. It was a heady mix of spilled beer, love-potion-number-nine, gasoline and burning tires. He was all guy, he liked it. But he had this figured out by now. They were hookers and there was no way he was going with them. He'd never paid for sex, preferring marriage. He'd been happily married to Tanya for a long time.

Oliver had met one, real hooker during his first year on Maui. Nami was her name, and she was a petite thirty-year-old Japanese doll. But he didn't do it. No way. He'd never done that. Not even a 'meet and greet,' one-night stand. He had his standards for sex; preferring romantic relationships where he liked the woman and she liked him so much, that the sex was a bonus: fun and caring and *free*.

*You've had enough booze for one night,* his forehead decided. *It's time we go... take care of things.*

Ole raised one of his drinks without toasting and drank it down. His throat was still a dry tunnel of sand. He lifted the other double rum.

"Thanks girls, it's been fun, gotta go." He tossed it back and stood up with a bit more wobble than expected.

Irish and the brunette gulped down their beers and slammed their empty mugs on the table.

*Let's bag this loser,* Candy vibed with sudden desperation.

"Oliver sweetie, we can' na 'ae pay the tab. We don' 'ave any money at 'all." Irish looked up at him with that bleary, helpless pleading, that lassies give you when they've had too much to drink.

"Wha'?" He hadn't seen this coming. He checked his pockets and found no bills, but he did have a wallet. He was in a hurry to leave and four or five rum and Cokes was four over his speed-limit. So, he tacked his way port and starboard through the crowd over to Auntie Donna at the bar. When he got her attention, he waved the rhinestone-studded wallet at her. She was still wearing her concerned face, shaking her head from side to side.

"Don't worry auntie. I'm not takin' 'em home," he tried

to re-assure her and himself. He was horny as a quartet of shiny, brass baritones.

*Not funny,* blinked the voice behind his mind's eye.

Auntie took his credit card and slid it quickly through the terminal, keeping one eye on the fist fight around the pool table. All the while, she washed glasses, poured draft beer and hit a button on a blender full of Margaritas. Distracted, she slapped the tab on the bar for him to sign and turned away.

'*Now!*' Irish vibed. And in perfect sync, practiced over thousands of years, both devils blinked their vertical eyelids... horizontally. The bartender was forced to turn back to Ole and speak against her will. Auntie's voice boomed out, way too masculine, sounding deep as Barry White's.

"DID YOU READ THE CONTRACT?"

The tab had turned yellow as parchment and was two feet long with a lot of tiny print.

"Y'er a hoot, Auntie," Ole said, as he scribbled his signature on the bottom line.

"*Yes!*" The two demons high-fived each other over their heads. Brilliant sparks snapped out from their fingernail polish like strings of lady-finger firecrackers, 'poppety-pop...snap... pop, pop, pop!'

Everyone in the place stopped drinking, eating or fighting long enough to watch the fingernail fireworks and the two young hookers take Ole by each arm and walk him out the dented metal door of the Sly Mongoose.

Once outside they tightened their grip on Ole's arms

and with a loud, "WHOOMP!" All three rocketed straight up into the night sky like Atlas-Missile-fireworks and exploded with deafening concussions, BOOM! BOOM! BOOM! The street in front of the tavern, usually dark and empty this time of morning, lit up like the Fourth of July. An alley cat with silver eyes dropped a limp mouse she'd had in her teeth and gazed up at all the sparkling, burning glitter falling around her.

## 23  He Knew Where He Was

When Oliver came to, he felt like he'd just dove head first onto some rocks. He was dizzy, disoriented and sweating rivers under his scorched t-shirt. The two cute girls were gone and what was left of his eyebrows smelled like gunpowder. When his vision cleared, he sobered up in a hurry. He knew exactly where he was. It looked just like he'd always pictured it. Up on the side of an erupting volcano instead of spelling out, 'HOLLYWOOD' in big white letters, he saw giant rusty-looking letters spelling out, 'THE GATES OF HELL.'

He was moving along single file, in a line of other humans, thousands of other humans. The line stretched ahead of him along a red-dirt path for at least a half mile. The sulfuric air made it hard to breathe. The heat was unbearable, like Las Vegas in August, at high noon.

*Where 'd the girls go?* He wondered.

He didn't recognize the two soul hookers hiding off to one side of the line. They were back in their normal reptilian bodies looking ugly as sin. They kept one eye on Oliver with smug looks on their burnt faces, they squatted behind some discarded oil barrels. The large bat-like wings on their backs shook with wicked anticipation as they paged through a color travel brochure titled, 'Devilish Barefoot Fun in Antarctica.'

The line was moving fast. The immigration gate into Hell must be a mere formality because the line of humans hustled along in a forced march, almost a run. It was hard to keep up in the oppressive heat. Ole thought about dodging out of line and making a run for it. But, where could he hide? The scorched landscape surrounding him went on forever, a white-hot desert without cactus. In fact, there were open trenches everywhere with flames shooting up out of them, no chance of escape. He kept pace with the rest of the lost souls as best he could.

As Ole approached the entrance to the barb-wire-topped Iron gates, like everyone else, he saw that he was about to be electronically scanned by an ancient-looking bar-code lamp. It read the entire history of each soul and condemned them to eternity with a light beeping sound like the scanner at the grocery store. Ole knew he was in big trouble. He needed a miracle.

"Hit me again!" Oliver desperately shouted. His last-chance card appeared in his mind, in the sharp teeth of a bull dog... *Five of Hearts... sixteen, plus five... twenty-one! A winning hand!* Karma whined like a kicked dog, lifted one hairy hind leg and peed on the casino table. Then he scampered off on all fours to fetch a new deck of cards.

Down at the 'GATES OF HELL,' as soon as Ole was scanned, the bar-code lamp exploded like a half-ton of dynamite! Humans and broken glass flew in all directions, the 'GATES' slammed shut. This hadn't happened in five-hundred years. Not since Martin Luther was turned away from Hell and sent to Purgatory.

Flaming torches shot straight up into the dark sky like emergency boat flares. It looked like a scene from the movie, "Dante's Big, Fat, Titanic Inferno."

Oliver was thrown sideways by the explosion and lay on his back on the scorched sand. He raised himself up on one burnt elbow. There were boulders tumbling down the side of the volcano. The sky tore apart like someone ripping a greasy car rag into small red clouds. An angry scream came erupting out of the volcano's caldera. Ole covered his ears with both hands. The unbearable scream swirled like a siren spinning itself into a monstrous tornado. Sand whirled up off the desert around Oliver and gathered into the tornado's vortex forming a gigantic super-devil made of red dirt and white sand.

The giant stood there with his arms folded like an angry Mister Clean with the body of a red-and-white striped fishing lure. Ole's Dad had one like this in his tackle box; bigger and meaner than all the rest, a red spoon with a white stripe and deadly hooks. Dad called it his 'Dare Devil.'

D. D. Satan / Mister Clean, unfurled his leathery wings wider than a mile. His ugly face rippling with rage, like a pissed off high school principal. He shook his hands up in the air with an over-dramatic, antagonized exaggeration; his fingers were treble-hooks and his voice boomed across the entire expanse of Hell like the roar of a terrible earthquake.

**"WHO BROUGHT THIS GUY IN?"**

The two she-devils ducked down behind the oil barrels, but a tattle-tale laser beam smote down on them from one flank of the volcano. It struck the rocks in front of them like machine gun fire on flint. Sparks flew in every direction. The two soul trappers stood up slowly and raised their lizard-like front legs and black wings in surrender. The big Dare Devil screamed down at them.

**"THIS CONTRACT IS NULL AND VOID!"**

"We seen him sign it, we did!" The Irish demon hollered back. The shorter devil was so shocked all she could do was tremble; shaking her matted tar-black hair from side to side. Thirty-weight, dirty hair oil went flying in all directions.

**"BUT DID HE READ IT?"** The boss-devil was furious.

"Nobody 'eva reads the contract!" Argued the Irish hag. "We've trapped thousands, millions of souls who ne'er read the contract. He signed it, heee did. That's wha' counts! We need tha' bloody soul!" Irish shouted back. Oliver figured only an Irish devil could argue with Satan himself and get away with it.

**"DID YOU CHECK HIS IDENTIFICATION?... NO!"**

"What?" Irish was lost on that one. Shorty shrugged her hunchbacked shoulders, Oliver began to smile.

**"YOU THERE! HUMAN, WITH THE STUPID GRIN ON Y'ER FACE... YOU CAN GO!"**

"What! Wait! Why?" Irish screamed in protest. She wanted that vacation in Antarctica.

**"THIS CONTRACTUAL RECEIPT FOR ETERNAL DAMNATION, SIX BEERS AND THREE RUM DRINKS IS SIGNED... OLIVER G. GOLD!"** Satan turned a deeper shade of fuchsia as he spit-fired the next words.

**"IT WAS SUPPOSED TO BE FOR SOME LOSER CHICK NAMED, DESIREE SCARLIONI. THIS CONTRACT IS VOID. GET THIS OLIVER GUY OUTTA MY SIGHT... NOW!"**

"You stole some woman's wallet?" The short demon bit one of the purple warts on her alligator-sized lizard lip. "This 'Desiree... somebody,' you stole her wallet?"

"I didn't steal it. I found it in the back...I mean...ah...it was lying on the floor at the Sly Mongoose," he lied. "I was gonna call her and tell her I found it, but...I had to think about it for a while. So, when you two couldn't pay for all those drinks... hey, I didn't have that much cash and neither did Desiree's wallet so, I uh... used one of her credit cards. I signed my name without thinking about it. I'd had a bit o' rum ya know. Can I go home now?"

There was another pyrotechnic explosion, "WHOOMP!" Oliver Gold was lying on the curb in front of the Sly Mongoose. His eyes were swollen shut and the last thing he could remember of Hell was the boss daredevil yelling at him.

**"CHANGE Y'ER WAYS OR THERE 'LL BE A TRENCH FULL OF ANGUISH WAITING FOR YOU, OLIVER GOLD!"**

When his vision cleared from the explosion, he saw a black shape hovering over him with two evil eyes bright as dimes. Ole thought it was another devil and started a backward crawl to get away. The thing arched its back with a hissing sound painful as a finger pressed on a hot stove and ran down the street as fast as its little legs could run. Oliver took a deep breath of Lahaina's humid hot air. Even at ninety-something degrees, it felt cool on his dry throat compared to where he'd just been. Somehow, he'd won that hand of karma. The Sly Mongoose lights were off. He looked at his watch.

*You don't have a watch, stupid. You left it out in the cold rain back in Seattle with your wife.*

*She left me, remember?* He thought back at the scolding his forehead was dishing out. *It must be after two in the morning.* Ole shook his head in bewildered relief. He felt in his pockets for Desiree's rhinestone wallet, found it and tossed it in a dumpster. The only car still parked on the street was his beautiful old Cadillac DeVille. It glowed under a street lamp like it was posing for a magazine photo shoot from nineteen-eighty-eight.

*You drive a DeVille? How appropriate brah.*

## 24  Purgatory

It was around two-forty-five or so, in the morning. Oliver stood there on the sidewalk looking at his old car but not seeing it. He'd been to Hell and back; something that only a very few souls had ever done. Martin Luther escaped for sure. Even Jesus was said to have descended into, 'Limbo,' a sort of Beverly Hills neighborhood of Hell where Plato, Socrates, Epicurus, Moses, Abraham, Isaiah, Noah and the other 'unsaved,' patriarchs were under house arrest until the savior gathered them up and took them to his version of Heaven. Unfortunately, there was no mention of their wives or children or friends getting out of limbo with them.

Imagine all the hundreds of millions of people born on earth before Jesus's cousin, Saint John, started the whole concept of 'baptism.' John was famous for being beget by a 'Heavenly miracle,' to his old and barren mother. Oh, and his unusual lifestyle, wandering around in the desert, wearing camel hides and eating locusts and wild honey. He is mentioned in the Quran and was a respected adviser to King Herod, who kept him in jail, but on call, twenty-four-seven, in case Herod needed some practical, kingly advice. Unfortunately, during one of Herod's lavish parties with lots of important Roman dignitaries present and everybody binge drinking themselves out of their skulls, the king promised to grant a wish, *any wish*... to a skinny, cute, sexy and fast dancing girl. She consulted with her conniving mother, who made her wish for John's head on a platter. Herod had to keep his drunken promise. He felt bad about it the next day, but hey it's not easy being a king. Or it might have been just the hangover. Oliver knew this story from childhood, and he always loved Saint John, it was a mean, terrible way for such a good man to meet his last page of life. And all because of the jealousy of a conniving woman.

*Why hadn't he learned a lesson from this story about skinny, fast, sexy dancing girls?*

Anyway, according to his Western religion brain implants, all those millions of people born before John the Baptizer, would never get even a one-day-pass, to visit Heaven. They will remain forever in Purgatory. Talk about bad timing in the re-birth lottery. And ever since baptism became the magic magnetic key card of salvation, there have been millions of cute new born babies who, through no fault of their own, die before being baptized. They too, will never get into Heaven, doomed to everlasting daycare in the cold, crowded basement of limbo where they never learn to talk or get out of diapers.

*Who makes this stuff up,* his forehead wonders?

*It was pretty, Sister Mary Magdalene. She taught him this baloney.* He believed it, hook, line, money and sinker, because she was so pretty and a *teacher;* he trusted her. She did offer a back-up plan for newborn babies. Anyone could baptize a baby in an emergency. So, within days of each of his sibling's birth Oliver had waited until his mom was out of the room and with his Flash Gordon squirt gun, he declared an emergency and squirt-baptized his sister, Judy and his brother, Walter with the sacred words Sister Mary had taught him.

"I baptize thee in the name of the Father and of the Son and of the Holy Spirit." It made him feel like a priest and he was secure in his belief that if either of them did die before an official baptism, he... the good older brother was the one who had saved them from eternal Purgatory.

Even though Ole was a skeptic, he'd baptized his own three daughters right after birth. He didn't use a squirt gun, just water from the tap and a paper cup from the hospital vending machines. He didn't want eternal daycare in limbo for any of his kids.

Later each of his children was 'officially' baptized in whatever church happened to be near where the family lived at the time. His young family moved around a lot from rental to rental. Gretchen was a Catholic, Elsa was a Lutheran and Brita was an Episcopalian. To Oliver, a church is a church, no matter what the sign out on the front lawn says. An official baptism seemed like the, 'Pascal,' safe-bet, thing to do.

Oliver tried to think of others that may have been turned away from Hell. George Washington? Maybe. John F. Kennedy? For sure. Buddy Holly? Yep.

There was a famous Italian writer who walked all through Hell and got out the side door. Dante Alighieri did it in his first book, 'The Inferno.' *His Divine Comedy* proved more divine than funny. Oliver never laughed once when he read the *Inferno,* the *Purgatorio* and the *Paradiso* while serving his mandatory four-year sentence at an all-boys Catholic high school.

So, besides himself, Martin Luther, George Washington, Dante, JFK and Buddy Holly, the only other escapee from Hell he could think of was the beautiful Greek goddess, Persephone. She was carried off to Hell by the king of Hell, Hades. If that wasn't bad enough. She was tricked into being his bride. While touring his underworld castle, she tasted some of the food of Hades, a few pomegranate seeds. Because of this, she was forced to stay most of the year with her husband in Hell. Zeus, the most powerful and lecherous of the Greek gods, did allow her to return to the earth once a year on a few months parole, so he could have is way with her. While she's above ground, she brings Spring and warm weather, the fruiting of grain and most important of all, the flowering of grapes in Zeus's vineyards. Then, it's back to Hell for the winter months; kind of like living in Iowa or in the frozen, darkest level of Dante's Hell.

*That's a mean story brah, but It's not as wicked as new-born babies doomed to eternal daycare.* All the voices in his head agree.

He was still standing there in front of the Sly Mongoose in the early morning darkness. Somehow, he'd escaped from Hell. Things were looking up. His imagination leaped into overdrive. He suddenly thought of a place to hide the body!

## 25  Hidden Beach

Beaches along the north shore of Maui are far and few between. It's a beautiful drive along the shoreline except at three o-clock in the morning when you can't see it. Oliver kept his eyes on the highway as it twisted in his headlight beams like a wet, gray snake with yellow dashes painted down its back. He did know of one lonely beach that was seldom used even by locals. He found the turn. It wasn't even a driveway, just a level spot even with the paved road. Across this abandoned cane field was the hidden beach he was looking for. He'd been there before, under happier stars. This was where Desi and Ole had first kissed. Now, inside his old Cadillac, he shivered, haunted by that ghostly quote from Edgar's raven, *"Never more."* Never more would he kiss those lying lips.

Ole turned off his headlights, but his big car reflected starlight like a white whale, as it lunged through the wet cane field. To add to his woes, the car had only breached a few leaps, when the whale's white-walled tires sunk deep into mud. Ole floored it. The wheels gurgled a scream with that terrible, "we're done" high-pitched whine he remembered from snow drifts back in Iowa. He threw the automatic transmission into reverse. The Cadillac jerked backwards, its four-hundred Detroit horses throwing mud along both sides of the car. The cane field was slosh. He floored the gas pedal again. He sank deeper, the tires continued to wail. He wanted to scream with them.

"Stuck!" Ole threw the word like a curse. "Why didn't I plan for this?" There was no answer coming from the universe. "My first mistake," he grumbled, pounding on the steering wheel with his 'dad' hand.

*Getting involved with her at all was your first mistake.*

That didn't sound like the universe. It sounded more like Karma.

*"New hand,"* called out the dealer. This time Karma sort of resembled Sean Connery with the tuxedo, bow-tie and diamond cuff links. He dealt two cards each to Re-Birth and Death. He skipped Oliver and dealt himself two off the bottom.

*"I saw that,"* protested Oliver.

*"So... do something about it."* Karma 007 taunted.

Ole shrugged. Karma knows he can deal off the bottom of the deck if he wants to. He's the great 'leveler' of humanity. It was like arguing with gravity. Even Death and Re-birth must play by Karma's rules. Karma 007 was leaning in the passenger side window of the Cadillac.

"Take your cards," he insisted and counted out two soiled cards to Oliver. Someone chuckled in the back seat. Ole turned to look, sure enough, Death was still in the back seat. Ole panicked for a moment, then relaxed. If it was his turn to go, so be it. Life on Maui was too expensive and he didn't care to live anywhere else on earth. Death looked... dead. He lay there all sprawled out with his new cards held loosely in his boney fingers and that emotionless poker grin on his eyeless skull.

Ole saw Re-birth-cupid fly past his windshield. She zipped around like a fat Tinkerbell in the early morning starlight. Her bow slung over her tiny shoulder, all her arrows bundled in her quiver. She was frowning at her two cards as she approached Ole's windshield. Never looking up, she flew too low and crashed smack into the big chrome grill of the Cadillac. Ole heard a muffled scream and she dropped into the mud in front of the car.

Oliver and 007 burst into laughter. Even Death sat up and sort of rattled his bones as if he was chuckling. Cupid / Re-birth shook like a fat little dog, splattering wet mud every direction, then flew off toward the ocean.

Ole didn't laugh long, he had a hard task ahead of him and dawn was just a few hours away. He looked in the rear-view mirror. Death was gone. He has a way of coming and going that's hard to understand. Maybe he had some lives to reap before he could finish this hand of Blackjack.

Ole floored the gas pedal again, then shifted quickly and floored it again and again, beating the four-hundred horses without mercy. No use, rocking the car back and forth wasn't getting him any traction. All it was doing was making too much noise. He'd have to carry the body the rest of the way in the dark, through the mud. Ole slammed the gear shift into, 'Park.'

"Stuck! Stuck! Stuck!" He growled, pounding on the steering wheel again like some bad actor in a cheap movie. Oliver had never practiced cussing, so when he really needed to, he wasn't any good at it. He wondered for a moment what this horror movie might be titled? *How about, "Escaped from Hell and Stuck in Paradise,"* suggested you know who, Sarcasm.

He pulled the trunk release and stepped out into the mud. It was warm, oozing over his rubba slippas and up to his ankles. Once he shut the car door, the darkness pressed in on him like black paint. He held on to the door handle until starlight gave him a glimpse of the early morning paradise around him. Ole felt along the side of the car and lifted the rear lid. Reaching under the horrible mess in the trunk, he found his second mistake of the night, a flashlight full of dead batteries.

*Ya know what Oliver? For a retired college teacher, y' er about as dumb as a brick.*

He should have thought to check his flashlight. In the dim light of the open trunk, he stood miserably dejected, like the pale ghost of a modern King Macbeth. *How could people in Hawaii be such liars?* He wondered.

*She was from California remember? That's where the word 'crazy' was minted.*

Oliver reached into the trunk...

## 26  He Almost Whispered Her Name

Ole shut the trunk and the Cadillac latch screwed itself down tight with a soft whirring sound. Newer cars no longer have this feature after the thousands of lawsuits won by plaintiffs with missing fingers.

Darkness troubled him once again. With no moon or flashlight this was going to be more work than he'd planned.

*Just leave the body here,* one lazy voice tempted.

"Gotta get to the beach," Ole grumbled.

So, hoisting the weight of his terrible burden, he set out across the mud toward the silhouette of beach palms dancing beneath the stars. The beauty of the dark morning went completely unnoticed as Oliver trudged through mud one careful step at a time. Hunched over with the weight of his problem, he couldn't see, nor was he in the mood to appreciate hula trees and brilliant stars. He set his course by the sound of the surf. It was beating a dirge. The sad rhythm reminded him of a picture he'd seen long ago of the shores of the river Styx. Ole had been to Hell and back, there was no river Styx. Some ancient Greek just made that up. The catch and release adventure with the two soul hookers had left him with millions of frequent-flier miles on Cosmic Fireworks Airways.

He sloughed along toward that infernal shore. He was ashamed of how stupid he'd been with her. He'd wanted to believe her. He wanted her, the beautiful one, who ~~~ld love him, and introduce his original music to the world. He almost whispered her name, but his teeth were biting down on a bone of determination as he labored along. Another vision came to mind. This time it was a tall-sailing ship running hard, surfing downwind with a 'bone in her teeth,' her bow foaming the sea. The poetic image did nothing to alter his aching guilt.

Eventually, he broke through some shrubs and lurched out onto the sand. Their first kiss that naughty night on this beach came to mind, but this time it brought a bitter taste, salty as the last swallow of a drowning man. That night with Desi was absolutely the wildest, craziest, most bizarre page in the story of His life... until now.

27  Tigers Pacing the Crazy Cage

Uncle Ole set the body down carefully. His hands trembling as he arranged the limp figure into a sitting position with its back resting against a palm tree. He put a pair of sunglasses on its face and a wide Panama hat on its head. If anyone should chance to see it tomorrow, they might think it was just taking a siesta and not disturb it. That was the plan anyway. His thoughts twisted like a DNA Helix on speed or rather too much sweet rum and Coca-Cola. Oliver had never in his life eaten a tablet of 'speed.' But this morning, in the dark, his mind was racing two-hundred worries per second. To make matter's worse; his pulse was trying to pass on a curve.

*You're driving us crazy brah,* complained his forehead.

It felt like three snarling tigers were pacing the small crazy cage of his mind. They were: Anger, Disappointment, and Self-Pity. Three inner-monsters every individual must conquer or be devoured by, at some time in their life. Ole was ashamed that he'd been feeding raw slabs of guilt to all three, ever since that phone call yesterday morning.

The ocean foaming up and down the beach would be stunningly beautiful, except the whole scene was dark and listing dangerously to the west. The shoreline had dropped away by thirty degrees, tipping steeply toward China. To keep the body from sliding across the beach he propped himself up tighter against the palm tree. That took some of the slant out of his view of distant China.

Yes, you must have guessed by now. The body he had carried to the hidden beach, disguised with sunglasses and a Panama hat, was his own. He was hiding the heart-broken, angry, disappointed, self-pitying, semi-intoxicated body of *Oliver Gold.* This was the only plan he could think of: get himself to a remote Maui beach. Then, let the sound of the surf, soothe away this train load of crazy until he became whole again.

So far it wasn't working. The sanity indicator on the back of Oliver's head, just below his Panama hat rim, was blinking on and off in digital red numerals: 6:00 AM, 6:00 AM, 6:00 AM. The Chi-power to his cortex must have blown all its transformers when Godzilla was fighting the high-power lines of reality. There was nobody home. For the first time in his life, even though he was afraid to admit it, he *should* see a psychiatrist.

*Hah! You're stretched so thin you pour water on your cereal. Believe me brah, you can't afford the two, maybe five years of professional shrink help you need.*

The voice in his forehead is such a bore, especially when it tries to balance his checkbook.

But the voice was right again, on a working musician's income and a small pension, he couldn't possibly afford a psychiatrist. Maui is not a cheap place to live. Ole could barely afford his share of the rent. Carrying Oliver to this beach and trying to fix his broken self, by himself, was all he could do. He listened for his breathing... *too shallow and too quick.* His pulse was a snare drum. His fingers shook as he dug them into the sand until he convinced them to be still. Maui touched his hands with her warmth. She's always warm. That's just one of the reasons he loved her.

*Maui's a guy, remember?* Sarcasm scolds him. *He's a demi-god who pulled the Hawaiian Islands out of the sea with his magic fishhook.*

Now the sassy voice is an expert on Hawaiian mythology. Ole knew the legend. He didn't have the strength to argue. This could be the bottom of the last page for Oliver Gold.

"Oh well," his Id whispered into the darkness. He would welcome the adventure of the next life. Oliver hoped he'd earned some merit in this life. Most of his dreams had come true except for finding his Mary Beth.

*Let's survive this brah. We're all counting on you.*

## 28  Dad's Advice

Under the palm tree, his limp body started to list toward the Philippines this time. To keep him from falling flat on the beach, he stretched one of his arms out for support. It was the sore arm, no good. His face hit the sand, he bit his lip and his hat fell off. The sunglasses cut into the side of his nose with enough new pain to rouse him back up into a sitting position. When he wound his legs into a full Lotus flower, his forehead seemed pleased.

*That's right, meditate my son and you will find me, I promise to lead you home.*

Now, one of the voices thinks he's Oliver's dad and cosmic tour guide.

But dad was right most of the time. He was always telling young Oliver, *"It's just as easy to fall in love with a rich girl as a poor girl."* Since moving to Maui, a year ago, he'd been trying to take dad's advice. He'd fallen in love with two rich women. Trouble was they hadn't fallen in love with him. Dad never explained that part of the equation.

## 29  Starlight and Live Bait

The full lotus was keeping him from falling over. His eyes were open, he wasn't moving at all. He didn't feel at all sleepy. In fact, he started to notice... the beauty of the dark, early morning scene in front of him. The constellation Orion and his cast of co-stars were starting to hide behind the dark mountains of Molokai. It would be dawn soon. He tried to calm himself with meditation, but those three big cats: Anger, Disappointment and Self-pity were still shaking him by the brain.

There were so many stars up there... a milkshake of stars so far away, yet so bright they lit up the hidden beach. This light had been traveling for millennia at the speed of itself, but it seemed to slow down... fast, as it settled on the beach like a dusting of fine, pale snow. The snow-light touched Oliver's skin with a cosmic tenderness, almost a sigh, as if it was tired from traveling so far. It lay there resting on his arm. Mary Beth hadn't found him, Tanya and Suki had thrown him away, Desiree was a half-empty box of cornflakes, so this morning, starlight was his only companion. Nothing can make you feel more alone than ancient star light. *Lyka found you and wants to meet you.* He made a wish on a very faint star in one corner of the Big Dipper.

"I wish Lacey loved me, instead of the captain..."
*What? Stop that! Wish for something else, stupid.*
"I wish Lyka was here to take my mind off Lacey," he whispered, "how's that?"

*Bet'ta, but why do you wish on the stars? They're just old balls of Hydrogen fighting with Helium. Why don't you wish on rainbows instead? Iridescent atmospheric colors shine out of rainbows. They are shinning proof of the love triangle between hydrogen, oxygen and sunshine. They curve across the sky holding hands and making out in an I' amour a' trois of color, unashamed, for all to see and be inspired by.*

Staring up at the supposedly, hopeful stars, the retired chemistry teacher did get a kind of catalyst-sensation in his chest. The same kind of excitement he'd felt when he fell in love with a woman. Under the heady influence of this morning's starlight-snow, he'd soon love everybody.

*Why are you so dumb when it comes to women?*

*Well, I'm a guy, so that explains a lot. But I'm starting to get it. Women work hard to impress each other and lure men into relationships. Or they tease men into places where relationships or ships of any kind are not meant to go. They dress themselves up, scent themselves up, and pose themselves in such distracting ways. Women are a lot like bait fish. You can swim all around them and never see the hooks they hide. You can even nibble at them; in small bites they're delicious.* But Ole had learned the hard way if you take the whole bait, you're swallowing some hooks that will make you laugh and cry for a lifetime. Buddha said it better, *"Watch the tracks of your desires for they all lead to sorrow."* His teachings always swim up to the surface of Ole's mind after he takes the bait.

It wasn't just about sex. The root of his problem was believing whatever a pretty woman told him. He had believed in his mother, his first-grade nun, Tanya, Suki and Desiree Scarlioni, the God Mother of the liar mafia. Believing was a fool's game.

## 30  Closer to Dawn

Oliver was beginning to reconnect with himself. He still had a wild look in his eyes, barely breathing one moment and not breathing the next. But how could he give himself CPR (Crazy Person Resuscitation)? He had no idea, other than to hide here on this beach and keep breathing until he recovered.

He knew recovery would start with meditation. But *trying* to meditate never works. You must forget trying. You just breathe for a while without thinking too much until you slip past all the ten-thousand distractions that Lao Tzu warned us about. For Oliver, this method was taking too long. He almost wished for a coconut to just fall on his head and knock him out.

*Nah, bad idea, maybe we all die brah.*

Okay, he didn't wish that. Meditation was the medicine he needed to beat Death in this hand of Blackjack.

## 31 Desi-Zilla

Oliver saw something moving out on the star-lit surface of the ocean. It was just a shadow at first, a vague darkness blocking starlight, and then the huge silhouette took on a monstrous shape. It was Godzilla! He was wading out toward the island of Molokai. The monster's face turned and looked over his shoulder at Ole. The horrible face gender-changed into the lovely crazy face of Desiree Scarlioni. She smiled that darling innocent smile of hers. Who knew Godzilla could look sexy to anyone but another Godzilla? He'd been a Godzilla yesterday so, Desi-Zilla still looked hot to him. She was staring back at him over her horned shoulder, oblivious to the wreckage she'd made of his heart and his dreams. The horrid creature swung her gigantic head and gnashed her dragon teeth. When she was neck deep, she screamed one last long anguished roar and plunged down under the waves.

Watching that monster slink off into the ocean left Oliver breathing a little easier. The soft sound of glass-rod on meditation bowls filled the empty space between his Id and his Egos. Ole sat quietly under that palm tree staring into the dark ocean where Godzilla had disappeared. He was deeply concerned for the poor unsuspecting people over there on Molokai.

## 32  Prayer by Bluetooth

The trade wind touching his sore shoulder felt like a gentle massage. It carried a nocturnal, flower-scented bouquet. He wet his lips and took a long slow sip of the night air: *doe, ray, me, fah, sew, la, tea, dough.* The draft was thick with what a yogi calls, *prana.* It tasted sweet as sacramental wine. Three deep drafts of tropical air-wine got him high as the nearest palm trees. Before long, Ole was humming along with the meditation bowls. He watched a swarm of fireflies behind his closed eyes. They flew around and around inside the vast, empty casino of his mind.

Oliver could use a sacrament tonight, a healing one, not the Extreme Unction kind given on your death bed. He didn't plan to die out here on this beach. His thoughts chased the fireflies. *How was he going to live without Desiree? Without her vending machine of erotic confections? Her home on the golf course?*

"Is there any hope?" he asked the distant stars. It was still dark, too early for rainbows to wish on. He waited. No message vibed down from the stars. Of course not, how could the stars hear him?

*Can God hear us,* he wondered? The obvious fact is that when he said a silent prayer, no one, not even someone standing right next to him could hear it. Only Ole's mind could hear it. So, if God can hear silent prayer, he must have receiving units (supernatural sensors? Mic pickups? Eavesdropping devices?) embedded genetically within our brains. Or maybe, the mind itself is a cosmic, 'blue-tooth' transmitter, that relays our silent prayers to the 'cloud,' where Microsoft passes our prayers onto God for a small monthly subscription fee. The fee would be paid by donations to whatever church you attend. The bigger the donation, the faster the broadband. Silent prayer had always baffled Oliver. He wanted to stop thinking about it. He'd had enough 'baffle' in the past twenty-four hours. His head tipped forward resting on his chest. His thoughts flitted this way and that as he followed the blinking, yellow fog lights of a swarm of lightening bugs inside the casino. They went around and around and around.

## 33  The Haunted House Upcountry

He opened his eyes. He was riding in the passenger seat of a car, a Mercedes from the emblem on the hood. The black leather seat was soft, smelled real and was adjustable in ten directions. He got a happy shock when he saw the driver. He quickly looked in the back seat. Her husband, the captain, wasn't with them.

"Lacey, where we going?"

"Oh... silly, you remember, don't you? We're going to look at that house for sale up in Pukalani. The realtor ..."

"You're buying a house on Maui? Are you rich or something?"

Lacey looked worried as her attention went back to the curvy mountain road ahead of them. Ole stared at her and his heart nearly burst with affection. She and Lyka could be twins, but Lyka was in the Philippines and Lacey was sitting right here next to him. She smelled nice.

*Probably uses deodorant... careful what you be thinking brah. Why you riding in Lacey's car anyway?*

Oliver didn't dare talk back to his brain this time, Lacey would hear. The realtor from Maui Homes was waiting. She looked like a real estate sales person, professional and desperate. She was smiling too much for a normal person, even on Maui where people smile a lot. Oliver used to count the number of smiling people he saw in Seattle on any given day. Sometimes, he'd get to four. One sunny day, he counted seven. The real estate agent opened both halves of a weathered-looking, ornamental driveway gate. Then, as she got back in her Cadillac SUV, she waved a friendly welcome, signaling 'follow me,' and drove up the winding driveway, disappearing in a grove of

Kiawe trees at the top of the hill. Lacey followed.

The front pasture was overgrown with tangled, wild trees. The driveway was rough tarmac, pot-holed and broken. Oliver was subtracting thousands of dollars off any purchase offer that Lacey might make, if she should want his opinion. When they reached the top of the hill, the size of the old house surprised him. It looked like one of those big plantation houses from the cotton states of the South. There were four, faded white-washed Greek columns standing tall along the front portico of the home. The effect was like looking at a scaled down version of the Supreme Court Building in D. C. The columns were kind of pink-looking from years of Maui's red dust blown off the fields. The exterior of the whole place needed re-painting. The dollar signs in Ole's mind-calculator were adding up. Overall, the place had a neglected look about it yet with a stoic charm as if it were so filled with fond memories, it didn't care about its future anymore. Oliver felt the same, so he kept his mouth shut. It was none of his business anyway.

"It looks like a haunted house from some movie," Lacey said, as if she had read Ole's thoughts.

The realtor met them at the impressive front doors.

"Betty Mano, from Maui Homes. Nice to meet you." She smiled too wide and handed Oliver her business card. He handed it to Lacey. Betty unlocked the mansion's wide, dry-looking Koa-wood doors. She waited for them to walk in. The grand hallway did look like a movie set for a haunted house. Dust lay sleeping on every surface. There were piles of furniture along both walls. Ole imagined digging down through years of furniture sedation layers. Outdated stuff rested on top of old furniture that was piled on top of antiques resting on older antiques. All separated by thick layers of gray dust. The house looked more abandoned, than scary. It was a diamond in the dust.

There was a narrow trail winding through the canyon of old furniture. Ole saw bronze statues, mismatched dining room chairs and two grandfather clocks. On the tallest, the hands were stopped at one o'clock. On the shorter one, a grandmother clock perhaps, the hands were stuck at two.

"Oh my," said Betty. "It's a new listing. I should have done a preview inspection, I'm so sorry." Betty went on apologizing and then added, "the owner of this magnificent house has recently moved into a rest home. Her heirs live in New York and want a quick sale. This is great news for the buyer. Everything you see: furniture, appliances, cars in the garage, everything included with a full price offer."

There were two cars in the attached, four-car garage. The center stall had an aqua-green, nineteen-fifty-five, Ford Thunderbird convertible. Its white hard-top was hung from ropes above a work bench covered with dust and tools. Parked alongside the T-bird was a black, maybe one-year old BMW, two-door sedan. The keys were in the ignitions, so Ole started them up. The BMW growled like a panther ready to run. The odometer read fifteen-hundred and nine miles, an almost new car. The T-bird roared to life like a hungry tiger sending a bluish exhaust into the garage. It had thirty-one-thousand miles on it. He revved the engine just to hear it rage, then shut them both down. The third and fourth garage spaces were empty pavement. The value calculator in Ole's head was doing the math. *There must be over ninety-grand parked in this garage plus, there's a lawn tractor, a John Deere riding mower, hand mowers and a workbench with tools hanging on peg board and boxes of gardening stuff.* The dollars were adding up on the plus-side of the ledger.

"All included," Betty repeated as she ran her fingers along the fender of the T-bird. She must figure that Lacey and him were a couple. For Lacey's sake, Ole put on his poker face and shrugged. He hoped it conveyed the message that he wasn't even mildly interested in this kind of junk.

Meeting up with Lacey in the dust bowl of the grand hall they climbed the marble stairway that curved up to the second floor. Betty stayed behind to let them explore on their own.

"I'm falling in love with this house," Lacey whispered to Oliver as they reached the top of the stairs. Each bedroom they peeked into, looked like a poorly organized museum. There were mirrored night-tables with wash basins, antique wardrobe closets, Marilyn Monroe and Elvis posters, hundreds of LP records and a six-foot long mahogany-cabinet Hi-Fi, with an AM/FM radio and a record-changer that looked right out of nineteen-sixty-five. In amongst the antiques were stacks of magazines and faded newspapers dating back to the mid-fifties.

"This woman didn't believe in garage sales, did she?" remarked Oliver.

"Amazing," Lacey sighed, then sneezed again. "It's like she never threw anything away for eighty years. This looks like a closet," she opened a door. It wasn't a closet. A narrow stairway led up to another level above them. On both sides of the stairs were melted nubs of old candles, just lumps of wax resting in the base of each holder.

"Oooo," said Lacey, "a hidden, candle-lit stairway?"

Oliver di...
She was wea...
little butt a v...
legs were tal...
where there's...

*Stop it bra...*
*anything stupi...*

Lacey lifted...
floor of the atti...
helped him up ...
by side raising s...

"How's your a...
here in this dark...

"Okay today,"...
hurting.

second floor. Ole looked under the...
leaks. He was getting into this re...
The faucets ran rusty water f...
nothing. Lacey opened tw...
the master bedroom. ...
rest of the house. A...
would open int...
hundred ye...
open an...
cauli...
Ol...

"I feel like were a couple of kids," she said with a tiny giggle. Her laugh made Ole want to kiss her. But, his fire-wall of friendship with the captain wouldn't allow such a wrong move. They had just enough head room to sit there in the heat while their eyes adjusted to the darkness. Small lines of sunshine slanted through louvers at the far end of the attic. Dust mites powdered around in the sunlight like a swarm of gnats going nowhere. There was a circle of dark stains on the wood floor. In the middle of the circle was an incense burner and a velvet cushion in front of a crystal ball. A pentagram was drawn in white chalk extending its points out in five directions to the circular stain on the floor.

"Let's forget we saw this," Lacey whispered.

"Uh huh, the old lady was a hippie or a bloody witch."

"Don't say bloody," she whispered, as she lifted the trap door and hurried down to the well-lit safety of the

athroom sinks for
al estate thing. No leaks.
r a whole minute, then
o paneled doors and entered
t was brighter and cleaner than the
nother set of doors looked like they
a walk-in closet. Expecting to find a
rs of vintage clothing, Lacey pulled them
turned on the light. She blanched like a boiled
ower. Imagine a dark Filipina turned snow white!
ver followed her into the closet.

Black hair hung from the ceiling... human hair. Long ponytails of it, and figure-eight knots of it, and braids that nearly reached the floor. A note was hair-pinned to each bundle, *"My wonderful hair, nineteen-fifty-one."* *"Nineteen-sixty-one."* *"Nineteen-seventy-one."* *"Nineteen eighty-one."* *"Nineteen-ninety-one."* *"Two-thousand and one."*

"She cut her hair every ten years and saved it? Ehueee." Lacey turned a whiter-shade of Filapina pale.

On the closet's shelves there were one-gallon glass jars, lots of them. At first glance it looked like they were full of Skittles or candy of some kind. But, on closer inspection, the red yellow and orange colors were painted crescents of human fingernails. The jars were labeled, *"My lovelies, nineteen fifty-one."* The next jar, *"Nineteen-sixty-one,"* and so on, six decades of fingernails.

"Eeew..." Lacey cringed again. The glass jars on the next shelf down were all labeled, *"My toe-nail darlings"* and therein were sixty years of the old lady's colorful toe nail clippings.

"I think I'm gonna be sick," said snow-white. Ole took her hand and was about to lead her out of the closet when they noticed all the glass jars on the floor. There were lots of them maybe a dozen gallon-size jars filled with gray dust. They both moved closer to read the neatly printed labels, *"My soft skin, collected by my vacuum cleaner. "Nineteen-fifty-one"*...

"Nooooo!" Lacy screamed. Rooster skin rippled up Ole's arms as well. Pain cock-a-doodle-dooed into his sore shoulder, then knifed its way down his arm to the tips of his monkey fingers.

The real estate agent came bounding up the stairs and rushed into the bedroom. Lacey hadn't fainted, but her knees had given out. She sat in a daze on the bedroom floor. Sweat was running down her face like she'd just been baptized.

Ole held her in his arms, while Betty fanned her with an old 'LIFE' magazine. It had a black and white photo of President JFK on the cover. Lacey raised one pale, ghostly hand and pointed to the closet. Betty went in to look and with a tiny whimpering sound, she slumped to the floor, fainted away.

"Let Betty rest," Lacey whispered. "We need to talk. I love this house. It's amazing. So, what, if the old lady was a little weird?"

"A little weird? How about the devil-worship chapel up in the attic?"

"What do you think we should do?"

"Can you and the captain afford this place?"

Lacey gave him that concerned look again. She didn't answer, so he went on.

"With all these antiques and the cars included, it's a great deal. This is a solid house with real character, plus five acres of bananas and flowering trees. It's on Maui. If you can swing it, you guys should buy it today, right now… before anyone else sees this place."

Betty was moaning, coming around. Oliver helped her sit up.

"Oh, my stars. That's…" she was momentarily at a loss for words. "In my twenty years in the real estate biz… *that,* is the weirdest thing I've ever seen. I am soo, sorry. As I said, it's a new listing. I'm very sorry about all this…"

Lacey interrupted her, "Betty, the old lady… the previous owner…was she… was she dangerous? Was anybody… murdered here?"

Real estate agents are not obligated to tell you such things unless you ask. If you do, they are bound by law to tell the truth.

"No nothing like that, she checked her notes. "It says here, she was a widow, never went out much. It looks like she hoarded her possessions, even the most personal."

"We need some air," Lacey was choking on dust.

"Me too, let's go see the garden," Betty decided.

She led them down the grand staircase and out through the French doors of the kitchen. The formal English garden was a mess of neglect; the weeds out numbering and taller than the flowers. Along the grass pathways were neat, garden signs: *"My Darling Basil," "My Happy Thyme," "My Sweet Periwinkles," "My Lovely Roses."*

The path led to a gate where a tropical jungle took over the rest of the property. Above the iron gate was another carved sign, "My Secret Garden."

"After you," Ole bowed to Lacey.

"No way, you first."

The old gate fit the grand scheme of the place, haunted-looking, with brass-tipped spikes along its top edge. Sure enough, it creaked eerily on its hinges just like in the movies.

"This just gets better and better," Ole whispered. Lacey smiled at him. *She's so darn cute*, his thoughts running with the wolves of his Id.

*Careful brah, don't get yourself in trouble,* vibed his wise ego in the saddle of his forehead.

*That would be some sweet trouble...*

Betty was still feeling woozy, so she sat down on a wrought-Iron bench that matched the secret garden gate.

Ole walked ahead of Lacey following a foot path into the brush. It was late afternoon, plenty of light and warmth, but Lacey seemed to be shivering. They pushed their way through banana trees thick as stage curtains. They passed one sandal lying on the red dirt path. When they rounded a thorn-covered Kiawe tree Oliver came to full stop. Lacey came up behind him and put one hand on his sore shoulder. It didn't hurt. In fact, it felt like an angel's touch, all golden and warm.

"What is it?" She whispered. Her touch thrilled Ole so much he could hardly answer. She was one of those skinny, cute, fast-looking kind of women; 'da kine' as they say in Hawaii.

There in front of them was a sobering sight. Two short granite tombstones stood knee deep in ferns under the shade of the Kiawe. Both headstones were professionally inscribed with lovely script.

*"My wonderful cat Sasha."* On the other, was carved, *"Bongo-Bongo, Son of Sasha."*

Ole took Lacey's cold hand and they stepped past the graves and deeper into the jungle.

*Why are you holding the hand of your best friend's*

*wife?* His forehead wanted to know.

*******

Lacey's terrifying screams lifted Betty right off the iron bench. She wasn't sure if she should run to help Lacey, call 911 or just run. The ground under her feet was vibrating... pounding. Something or someone was running toward her. She had to leap out of the way as Lacey went rushing past with panic twisting her face into knots. Ole was right behind her. He bid a polite nod to Betty as he raced Lacey to her car. The instant he climbed in, she burned get-away rubber onto the old driveway. Betty dropped back down on the bench and stared at the open gate. She was in a flux-quan-drum. There would be no sale today. When she'd caught her breath, curiosity overcame her fear. She stepped through the gate, eased through the bananas and came upon the small grave stones.

"Why that's nothing to get excited about," she murmured to herself and kept moving forward on the path. It was almost sunset, another beautiful Maui evening. She passed the abandoned sandal lying on the path. Betty smiled and hummed a little nonsense tune as she walked on. In a clearing up ahead, she suddenly came upon it. An open grave with a lone shovel stuck in a freshly turned mound of Maui red dirt. Betty couldn't stop her feet from moving closer. A tombstone at the head of the black hole read...

### OLIVER GOLD
BORN   DECEMBER 5, 1948
DIED

## 34  The Question

That by far, was the most detailed dream that had ever delighted and frightened him. Lacey had put her arm on his shoulder, she sat near him in her car and in that spooky hot attic. Ole was proud of his self-control; he was sure he hadn't kissed her or he'd remember. When he thought about the weird end of the dream, he smiled. His own death was certain, it didn't scare him. Everyone's story comes to an end. But it did make him wonder if there was a big old house in his future.

Ole shifted his legs into the opposite full lotus sitting quietly in the dark wee hours of tomorrow. He desperately wanted to be one in spirit, body and mind again. Ole adjusted his hat, folded his hands in a Namaste position over his heart chakra and hoped for a message from the stars or Jesus or Buddha, or even Santa. He'd believe in Big Foot if it would help him get over the shock of losing Desiree and her promises of big money. *A miracle would be appreciated,* he vibed up at the stars.

Instead of a miracle, he heard a curious voice somewhere in his third ear. *What do you suppose will become of Desiree?*

He'd deleted her number from his cracked cell phone, but he did sort of wonder what would happen to Desiree Scarlioni.

## 35  The Legend of One Slippa

The world-class liar-beautician of Oakland made one final visit to Maui. Since Oliver wouldn't answer her calls, she set out looking for another lonely, gullible guy to mess with. She dressed up her pyrotechnic, vending-machine-body in some sexy clothes she'd just purchased at a store called, *Maui Resort Wear*. A new Hawaiian-print blouse and sandals with rhinestone bling-bling all over them made her feel clean and sexy as Lady Macbeth. To this she added an excitingly too-short mini-skirt that made her legs look like she was seven-feet tall. Looking fresh, tropical and innocent as ever, she set out for a Luau at the Hyatt Hotel.

*******

The beating drums had Desi swinging her long legs under her luau table. One of her sparkling new slippers flew off and landed under the feet of tourists at the next table. She didn't even notice. She tossed back her fifth Mai Tai and waved the empty glass of ice at the bare-chested young man who was her server.

"Alooww… wha, hey buoy! That last drink didn't have any booze in it. Make the next one a double or I'll tell your boss to fire you. I paid a hundred bucks for this luuu… wow." She sounded upset, but she was winking one eye and licking her full lips with her tongue.

"Sure 'ting hot wahine, next one gonna rock yo' boat." He flashed perfect white teeth. His tattooed chest was shiny with sweat. His name was Tavika. He was more than a boy and much more than a luau waiter. He walked between two worlds. He knew chants that could recall his ancestors back ten generations to the islands of Tahiti.

The drinks were full strength, he watched the bartender mix them. These tourists were never satisfied. Tavika headed back to the bar with a protection chant on his lips.

"Mahalo ke akua, malama pono a lono kanaka uo'ki make," roughly translated this means, "Thank you god of righteousness for stopping me from killing these crazy people."

Tonight, for some reason, maybe the unseen, but powerful new moon rising; some tourists at his other tables were even worse than the drunken Mai Tai chick. There were grumblers, whiners, spoiled children throwing fits over nothing; there were obnoxious salesmen cursing loudly, and Hollywood types with their noses in the air and no eye contact with a mere waiter. There were the sloppy eaters spilling more food on themselves than they ate. Worst of all were the wasters, piling more food on their plate than they could possibly finish and *then,* heading for the dessert tables to over-fill another plate and waste that one too. It made Tavika cringe, but he could stay connected with his Polynesian heritage by working at the luau. Plus, it was a great way to make a living *in this world.* His friendly smile and natural charm usually earned him a pocketful of twenty-dollar tips.

Desi finished her sixth Mai Tai and wondered why her table was slanting toward the ocean. She was going to complain and have that good-looking waiter find her a more-level table, one closer to the stage, but the drums were beating louder and making her sweat. She kicked off her other slipper and thought about taking off her new blouse.

The hula girls were wearing coconuts, flower leis or just long black hair over their breasts. At least that's what it looked like from way back here in the hundred-dollar seats. She knew the VIPs got to sit at tables up front which cost a 'Very Important' extra fifty-bucks. Those people got a lei made of real orchids and were seated first. She and the rest of the crowd had sweltered in a long line; waiting for the VIPs to get lei'd and sit down. When she was finally welcomed in with a brisk, "aloha" Desi got a pukka-shell lei that looked like it cost ten cents.

The VIPs also got to eat first. But after a long hungry wait, people at Desi's table were now enjoying drinks and dinner. Desi had scooped her way down the buffet table three times so far, trying to eat a hundred-dollars-worth of food. She judged the meal as marginal hospital food at best, but her mouth was too stuffed to complain when Tavika floated by asking if everything was okay?

Desi chewed on her ninth Teriyaki chicken leg and watched the show. The drums were full-strength like the Mai-tais. She was under the spell of the drums and the booze. The kane dancers with muscled brown chests covered in tattoo ink and their short loin cloths were kindling a loin fire under Desi's skirt. Her Teriyaki-sticky fingers came up and started unbuttoning the front of her colorful Hawaiian-print blouse. Her bare legs swung faster under the table; she wanted to dance.

At that very moment, the drummers softened the beat and the master of ceremonies, with the big Hawaiian accent, invited everyone who wanted to dance to come up on stage.

Desi was quite a sight throwing off her blouse and running bare-breasted around the crowded luau tables. Tavika saw her coming, but she didn't see him. He tried to step aside as she shoved past him. He lost his balance and dropped the tray of waster plates he'd been carrying. Uneaten fish and poi flew in all directions, but even that messy distraction didn't take anyone's eyes off Desi's topless dash. She jiggled up the stairs and onto the stage as the audience roared its approval.

A crowd of the show's professional dancers surrounded Desi and hustled her behind the other tourists who wanted to 'Hukilau.' All during the hula everyone tried to get a peek at Desi as she went koholo left and koholo right. When the tourists on stage took a bow, Desi did not. The audience gave her a standing ovation.

Tavika met her as she strolled proudly down the stairs waving her alohas back and forth. He wrapped a bar towel over her shoulders and led her back to her table. She smiled shyly up at him and leaned on his tattoos.

"Bad me..."

"No worry tipsy wahine, happens all 'a time." Which wasn't true, but he was an ancient spirit and a gentleman waiter. More importantly he had promised his ancestors and his God that he would not kill these people.

"Mah... 'loha," she slurred as she plunked down in her chair. Tavika went to find a broom and dustpan.

The drums beat faster, louder, wilder than ever. Fire dancers jumped out from behind boulders on stage and threw flaming torches at each other. Desi felt dizzy as the luau came to a spectacular close. The overhead lights in the palm trees came up, the crowd milled around briefly and then headed for their waiting buses.

Desi didn't bother to tip Tavika, didn't even say goodbye. She staggered down the beach to her rented condo. She was still wrapped in that white bar towel the bare-chested waiter had given her. The warm sand felt great between her toes.

*Bare toes? Where's my pretty new slippers,* she wondered? *Oops! Tha'z a problem.* She was one of those cheap tourists who buy luau clothes at the mall, leave the price tags on, wear them one night to a luau, then take them back the next day for a full refund. She'd never wear hibiscus-flower clothes at her station in the Oakland beauty salon. And those open-toe slippers, no way she could afford to keep those darlings. The lost blouse had cost her forty-one dollars, the rhinestone slippers were one-hundred and twenty.

*Ooo,* she tried to add it up, but her head was spinning when she got to her condo. The dark moon was rolling up over the mountains like a black eight ball, hiding from the sun. She still wanted to dance. She pulled a Dallas Cowboys t-shirt over her head, fluffed out her messy hair and looked in the mirror. She figured she looked as good as those cowboy cheerleaders. So still barefoot, she headed for Lahaina, a three-mile walk.

By the time Desi got into town, the stores were closed and only a couple of bars were still open. Disco music pounded out of Longhi's restaurant, but after that long night-march Desi's feet were bleeding and too sore for climbing stairs or dancing.

She walked past Bubba Gump's restaurant and sat on a low stone wall. On the ocean side was a small rocky beach out of the glare of the town's lights. She climbed over the wall and cooled her feet in the gentle waves until they stopped hurting. She was crying, not sobbing, but broken-hearted over the clothing refund she would never see on her credit card statement.

********

Tavika, the conscientious waiter had tried to find the drunk, topless girl as the tourists left the luau. But she was gone by the time he'd swept up all the broken plates. He didn't care about, 'no tip' or that she didn't even say goodbye. He simply wanted to make sure she got on the right bus. After Tavika helped the staff clean up the luau area, he took a walk through the empty tables, filling a net snorkel bag with the usual treasures' tourists leave behind. All the cell phones, cameras, car keys, room keys and kid's toys he dropped in the lost-and-found box at the Hyatt's front desk. What remained in his bag was what Tavika found under the tables. He called these random slippas, 'tourist souls.' He knew just what to do with them. He hoisted the sack over his shoulder, flipped his skate board up with one foot, hopped on and found his rhythm as he pushed off toward Lahaina town.

Tavika made a graceful skateboard turn onto Wainee Street and rolled past an old white Cadillac that was weaving from one side of the street to the other, going about two miles per hour. If he'd stayed on Front Street, he would have passed the barefooted Desi stumbling and cussing her way into town. He kicked his foot on the pavement, skateboarding along until he came to a well-kept graveyard. Here he slowed down, bowing his head as he passed his mother's tombstone marked simply, *Mother of Tavika.* At this moment, his mortal body began to glow like shave ice under a diamond light in a jewelry store. He was between two worlds now, floating over his skateboard as a Hawaiian 'Slippa'hune' a spirit of the night, carrying his bag of tourist 'slippa-souls.' He cruised down Lahaina's dark streets in long sweeping curves, pulling out one sole at a time. He could feel the weight of karma attached to each sandal as he held it in his hand. Then, just as a paperboy tosses the morning news, he threw one slippa here and one slippa there, and one slippa under a bush and one up on the roof of a church.

Legend has it that Hawaii once had spirit-people called, 'Menehune's.' They were the first people of Hawaii, long before people came in the canoes. It was the Menehune's that built the fish ponds and stone walls found on every Hawaiian island.

The islands now have, 'Slippa'hune's,' like Tavika; spirits who find lost slippers and throw them all over the place. If you've been to Hawaii, you've seen these lost sandals lying around, everywhere.

The meat of the legend goes something like this: If you lose a slippa in Hawaii, a night Slippa'hune will find it, weigh it and throw it somewhere in this world or the next. The Slippa'hune will know when he pulls your lost 'sole' out of his bag, what kind of person you are. If you live with respect and aloha, he'll throw it underhanded, like a softball pitch and it lands in this world where there's a chance you may find it again on your next visit to Hawaii.

If your slippa is heavy with lies, bitterness or other

wicked karma he pitches your slippa overhand, fastball style far into the 'Other World.' Once that happens, you are 'kapu' or taboo and you can never ever return to Hawaii. When the ghost of Tavika skateboarded past Bubba Gump's, he had just one slippa left to throw. He weighed its karma and gave it a fast-pitch out toward a distant world.

********

Desi was still crying over her lost clothing refund when one of her own rhinestone slippas hit her hard, right up the side of her face. She picked it up in shock.

"*No way,*" she groaned; her thoughts sobering a little with the pain. She leaped up which made her so dizzy she fell back down. By the time she crawled up the rocky beach to the low wall, her knees were bleeding as badly as her feet. She pulled herself over the edge, cussing like a sailor. The only thing she saw moving that late at night was some guy way down the street on a skateboard.

## 36 Prana-Chablis

Back on the hidden beach, the Pacific trade wind was the cosmic waiter. It still carried a heady fragrance, light and sweet as fine wine. Oliver took a few more sips then, tipped back the whole carafe of *Prana-Chablis.* He burped long and loud with contentment. Nothing had ever tasted so good as this delicious holy wind. He felt sober, better, calmer. Maui was working her magic.

*We've been over this, dummy. Maui is NOT a her.*

*Don't get so hung up on a pronoun.* Ole smarted back at the smart ass in his mind. He opened another bottle of fresh breeze. *Doe, ray, me, fa, so, la, tea, doe,* he counted as he pulled all that life-giving nitrogen deep into his lungs, held it for another eight counts, *doe, tea, la, so, fa, me, ray, doe.* Then exhaled, pushing carnal-dioxide out with all the Desiree Voodoo. Eventually, his lungs and mind began to fall into sync with the Tibetan meditation bowls still humming on his inner jukebox. He felt a vibration deep within him. It reminded him of the powerful vibration a sailboat sings when close-hauled on the wind.

His exhilaration was suddenly interrupted by a very loud 'CLICK,' as if someone had thrown the master circuit-breaker inside his head. Halogen lights came on, flooding the tennis court of his mind with light. He heard their buzzing, it sounded like a hive of bees.

Ole saw himself standing down there on his end of the clay court blinded by the white glare of the lights. An announcer began tapping his microphone.

"THUD, THUD… SSSKREEEEEEEECH," feedback came squealing out of the loudspeakers of the empty sports stadium in his skull.

"Today's Wimbledon event, the 'Oliver Gold Sanity Challenge' is... about to begin!" The announcer bellowed. There was no cheering from the crowd. There was no crowd. An excellent recording of the national anthem began to play in his ears. He stood up right there on hidden beach, took off his Panama hat and placed it over his heart. When the grand old song was done, he sat back down under the palm tree. Starlight was white-washing the beach. It was beautiful, but Ole couldn't keep his eyes open.

Back on the brilliantly lit tennis court in his mind (brilliant is an overstatement of fact) one of the line referees blew his whistle and nodded in Ole's direction, his serve. Oliver arched his back and with a furious swing, smashed the tight ball of his own guilt over the net of his cortex. There, on the other side of the net, his Ego was ready. With an arrogant smile, Ego whacked the ball back as hard as he could. It came over the net fast and low, hot as barbequed sin off a backyard grill. Spilled coals tumbled all over the court. Smoke blurred Ole's eyes. He missed the return; Love, or 0 /15.

Ego's serve. It came fast and mean, deep into a corner of Ole's self-pity. He swung and sent the ball back over the net. Ego was ready. He let it bounce, then smashed the tennis ball of Ole's pride so hard he nearly passed out. Ole missed the return; Love, 0 /30.

Ole's serve. He aimed this one out along the outside edge of forgiveness. Ego swung a whiff and missed; 15/30.

Ego's serve. This was another screamer, low over the net headed for Ole's backhanded anger. He followed through with great form and managed to return the ball with even more forgiveness. Still mad at Desiree, Ego rushed the net, set an upright racket to block the shot, but the ball of forgiveness shot past Ego's racket like a bullet, bounced inside the far line and stuck in the fence. A tied game; Love / Love, 30/30.

Ole put his next serve right where he aimed, deep into blaming others for his problems. This one came back harder than he expected. He missed the return; Add out, 30 / 45.

Ego smashed a screamer serve aimed right at Ole's feet. He dodged left, swung and with his racket digging clay he lobbed the ball gently over the net remembering Buddha's sutras of compassion, even onto oneself. Ego didn't see that coming and rushed the net but again, he was too late, a miss. Tied game; Love / Love.

Seeing the weakness in his opponent, Ole served the next one with kindness, right into Ego's forehand. It surprised him so much he whiffed another miss. Oliver was now ahead of the game; Add in.

Ego does not like to lose. He served the ball so hard it went out of bounds. The next serve hit the net for a double fault, game over! Ego was lost. So, without him, Oliver finally went out of body.

## 37  Out of Body

**(Completely indescribable)**

## 38  Share of Soul (SoS)

Our soul of course, is not ours alone. Contrary to what we've been told, there is only one soul, the soul of all living things. So, if you hurt or cheat someone or intentionally step on an ant, who are you really harming? Uh huh, yourself. And the great karma dealer is always keeping score on your Share of Soul).

Every living thing owns a share in this marvelous divine soul of living things. After a few blissful, completely indescribable seconds, Oliver's share wasn't ready to join the rest of the Buddhas in Nirvana. There was too much selfish pride still hiding in him. Instead of rising to the pure land of the enlightened, Ole's Share of Soul bounced out on the dark sand like an inflatable beach ball. It rolled along, glowing inside with what appeared to be strings of tiny white Christmas lights. They were bound together in a twisting DNA Helix, blinking on and off. Maybe they were atoms of Hydrogen, but it looked more like swarms of lightening bugs flying in tight formation.

In fact, that's just what Oliver's SoS became, a flying swarm of blinking fireflies. He was seeing out of hundreds of tiny eyes. This made him extremely dizzy until he got his sense of focus back and formed one consciousness again. Ole was a share of the great soul, *and* still a share of himself. He banked the swarm to his left and there, down the beach, under a palm tree was Oliver's body wearing a Panama hat. It looked like he was taking a nap.

### 39  Naked Ghosts on the Beach

Oliver's Share of Soul swarm detected a sweet perfume on the wind. It was a sexy, girlish, disco-dancing kind of perfume. Intrigued, he followed his hundreds of excited sensory antennae. As they / he flew closer to the delicious fragrance he heard women laughing. He quickened the beat of all his hundreds of wasp-sized wings.

Above a rise of sand at the far end of the beach, a soft light glowed up into the darkness. It shimmered there like miniature Aurora Borealis. Ole could detect three, individual spectral patterns shining up into the morning darkness.

*Ghosts! Nothing else gives off such eerie shades of ultraviolet, three of 'em brah!*

How his forehead knows stuff like this he has no clue. Plus, the fact, that Oliver's forehead was still back there under the Panama hat, made this discovery even more eerie. Ole's forehead is trying to explain himself to himself.

*Ego lost the sanity-challenge tennis match, Super Ego is reserving judgment until you mess up again, so it must be your bad boy, Mr. Id, flying you around the beach seeing ghosts. Watch out!*

*Cool,* Ole's Id did a double back flip. *Let's check out the ghosts. You know, maybe Freud should have spent more time inventing Legos, instead of Egos. He'd be rich by now.*

*He's been dead a long time brah,* his forehead countered back.

*Okay, his grandchildren would be rich.*

*Sigh.*

So, Ole's Share of Soul wasn't totally out of body after all. His Id flew toward the ultraviolet spirits glowing beyond that sand dune. His imagination soaring with exciting possibilities.

*Maybe, they're departed Hawaiian warriors who fought and died here? Or the ghosts of tourists who drowned near this beach? Travel magazines claim Maui is the number-one vacation-destination in the world. It may be true in the after world as well.*

*Are you in the after world, brah?*

Ole wasn't sure. Even with Sigmund's lecture, this was the strangest out of body ride Oliver's SoS had ever been on. His Id approached the perfume from downwind like any good hunter would. He didn't want whoever it was, to smell or see him first, so he morphoralized himself into even smaller bugs, the kind without yellow fog lights. He became a swarm of tiny gnats.

*How you make shape shift like this, brah?*

Ole didn't know. He just thought it and it happened, like magic or a miracle or something. Being almost out of body like this was much more fun than being all the way gone. When you're all the way out, you're traveling at the speed of light's imagination (six-hundred and seventy-one-million-miles per hour, really. Look it up.). No one except the Buddha knows what light can imagine going that fast. It's that formless Zen bliss, where thinking isn't required or even possible. Ole had almost been there once or twice while studying meditation back in college.

This morning on this dark beach glowing with ghosts, Ole could probably spy on people and turtles and just about any other living thing; they wouldn't notice him. But ghosts might, if he wasn't careful.

When his hundreds of pairs of tiny gnat eyes coalesced into one wide field of vision, he flew closer for a better look. His gnat swarm almost ran into each other as the ghosts came into focus. There, behind the sand dune, were three naked, ghostly women. That heady perfume was *all* they were wearing. They were laughing in their macabre way and looking up at the stars.

They looked so beautiful to him...us, he meant, kind of familiar, like movie actresses that he should know the names of. Ole remained a swarm of gnats to enjoy the view and listen in. The pale ghost with the blonde hair was talking.

*"What I really want to do… is start another war..."* She lifted herself up on one elbow and gazed wistfully out to sea. *"One with battleships and ferocious storms. I just love a good fight, especially sea battles. You know, with brave warriors dying for ridiculous causes and ships sinking in flames and sword fights and lots of cussing and..."*

*"Where this time?"* The petite, black-haired Japanese ghost interrupted her.

*"I'm thinking North Korea and South Korea again, only a sea-battle this time, none of that demilitarized zone bullshit. It'll be sink or swim, Kim Cheeeee!"* She almost slobbered she was so full of lust for battle. She reminded Ole of his ex-wife Tanya.

"North Korea doesn't have much of a surface navy," said the Japanese nude. "Some patrol boats and a few tanker ships. However, they are remodeling their navy and looking for handsome men with mechanical skill to volunteer." She sounded and looked like Suki the millionaire home owner that put Ole to work for weeks, promised to pay, and still owed him the money.

"Nah... too boring," groused the blonde. "I want a sea battle like the mean old days. Spanish Armada, the English Navy, Lord Nelson, tall ships, only instead of cannons blazing and splinters flying, I want heavy artillery and missiles this time. Flags burning and lots of ruin, chaos and suffering." She caught her breath.

That's Tanya all right. Ole's Id decided.

"Okay, not Korea." Tanya snapped. "How about North Ireland, versus South Ireland? That's always a bloody mess."

The long-legged naked doll with the black forest of hair cascading down her nicely pointed breasts laughed like a wild loon, then spoke up for the first time.

"Ireland doesn't have a navy, north or south. But, they both have dozens of nuclear missiles."

What a liar. That's got to be Desiree. His Id is certain. She looks so hot, even as a spirit.

"Kosovo, Bosnia," Tanya asked?

"Nope," said Suki, scratching herself below the waist.

"Afghanistan?"

"No ocean front," explained Suki.

"Venezuela?"

"Yeah, they have the most powerful navy in the world and everybody there is rich cause they have more oil than Saudi Arabia," Desiree blurted out.

"They aren't fighting currently with any of their

neighbors," added Suki.

"I could piss off Venezuela's neighbors in a heartbeat," threatened Tanya.

"I don't think any of Venezuela's neighbors have navies. How come you know so little about current events?" asked the ghost of Suki.

"They call me 'the Ghoooost of Hissss-tor yeee," Tanya howled. "I don't need current events. I'm the reason humans repeat their mistakes Meeeeeeeeeeeeeee," she woo-wooed with a spooky voice as she waved her arms around in a scary way.

"Ooo, I'm so terrified," Desiree hooted.

All of Oliver's tiny gnat thoraxes contracted in belly laughs. Suki laughed in her cute Japanese way with her hand covering her perfect teeth. When Tanya stopped her wicked cackling, she attacked.

"Nobody, especially you two losers, studies history, so nobody ever learns. Starting wars is fun. It's easy, bloody, senseless, and I'm good at it."

It's Tanya. She brought that same attitude to divorce court, brah.

"I know everything about current events," Desiree lied.

"Of course, you're the 'Gho-ooost of fake boooo-ooking agents,' "Wooo-oooooooooo!" Tanya waved her arms around again.

All his laughing gnat bellies went into spasm. A couple of him were laughing so hard they crashed into each other. Both spun down like dog-fighting bi-planes and crashed with a soundless impact in the sand next to Suki's small bare feet. Nobody noticed except Ole's Id. It didn't hurt too much, but the loss of even tiny lives made him sad.

Looking at world-class liar, naked Desiree, was making him sad as well. He could sense dozens of his tiny hearts breaking, one at a time. That made him angry and so, with the change of emotion, tiny monkey wings began forming on every flying gnat.

Blonde, beautiful Tanya interrupted Ole's transmutation,

*"Duh...so what,"* She snapped? *"I'm History. I'm the one who's famous!"*

*"Uh huh, the one nobody studies or remembers?"* Suki jumped into the fight. *"I'm the 'Ghost of What Might Have Been,' guys want me all the time. A string of guys. They want my slender body and my fat bank account. I can see it in their eyes. But, nobody wins for long with the 'Ghoooooost of Might've Been.' "Wrooo wroooo!"* Suki wasn't as good at it as Tanya. Nobody laughed. Suki looked unhappy.

Sentimental sap that Ole was, he still loved them. *How do you stop loving people you've loved? Should you stop, even if they hurt you,* he wondered?

*Keep lovin' brah. Loving is free. It's compassion at its best. It compliments your spirit.* This sounded like that mysterious third voice in his mind. Ole saw tiny bindi dots of white paint on the foreheads of every gnat of himself.

As he flew above the three nude ghosts admiring them, they quit arguing and lay there gazing up at the stars. All three were looking right through his swarm. That gave him a sexy tingling sensation in his hundreds of tiny insect private places. He got so turned on that all his little wings began to vibrate in unison. This strummed a perfect E minor chord. The Desiree spook sat up and looked around, tossing her beautiful dead hair over her shoulders.

*"Did you hear that?"*

*"What,"* asked Tanya?

*"Music… I hear music."*

*She heard me!* Ole buzzed all his tiny wings as hard as he could.

*"There! I heard it again, coming from somewhere above us. Maybe the stars are humming a tune."*

Desiree looked so beautiful smiling up at him or rather through him like that. He had to get down there, but not as swarm of gnats; he'd be brutally swatted to death. He guided 'himselves' over behind some palm trees and changed form. Ole chose the body of a handsome, twenty-something, magic Menehune man, filled with all the strength and desires of youth.

He needed an Ukulele, so he ran eight miles all the way back to the beach bar at the Sands of Kahana. It took him less than a minute. Ah, but, that minute was a leap back in time as well because when he arrived, it was months ago and Oliver Gold was the happy-hour musician in the restaurant that evening.

It was almost closing time. Oliver was between songs, chatting up a couple of nice-looking Chinese girls. Ole-hune hid in the shadow of some potted palms behind the stage. He didn't need to hide. He was invisible; but he hid anyway just for the fun of it.

The two Asian chicks flirted with Oliver Gold. He'd gotten his romantic hopes up that night, hoping to score with one or both china dolls. This was a year after Tanya divorced him and months before Desiree Scarlioni.

Ole-Menehune watched as one of the Chinese girls wrote her phone number on a napkin and handed it to Oliver, but her hand was wet from the bottle of beer she was holding. She held the napkin out to him.

"Ca'rll us," she said with a wink of one pretty, almond-shaped eye.

The two gals swayed back to their table giggling happily. While Oliver dreamed his Chinese dreams, the young Menehune stole his ukulele from the stage and walked out the back door onto Kahana Beach.

*So that's where your Ukulele went, brah. YOU stole it!*

Oliver Gold, almost-famous musician at the Beach House Bar didn't notice. When the gig was over, later that evening, he dug deep into his gear bag for his old flip phone. Finding it, he unfolded the wet napkin from the Chinese woman and read the message, "call us tonight, ~ 669-blur, smear, smudge-7"

*So, that's what happened, Dang!*

It took the Menehune-Ole another minute to race back to the hidden beach where the three naked ghosts glowed like Plutonium 235. He slowed down from his super run without breaking a sweat. As he walked the beach toward them Ole didn't look anything like the Oliver Gold that Tanya Suki or Desiree would recognize. He strummed the ukulele singing one of his own songs as he neared the three nude ghosties.

*"Dead men tell no tales, boys. Dead men tell no tales, an' you'll never find John Silver's gold, for dead men tell no tales..."*

Desiree, the fake booking-agent-liar, heard him first. *"There it is again, the music. I've heard that song before. Look, that guy with the ukulele."*

He could hear them giggle, which he took for a good
‾‾ so into omens. They leave them
a like bear scat. He walked up to within
n and stopped singing.

"Aloha cute wahines," he offered. The ghosts didn't seem at all embarrassed by their lack of swimsuits. They just lay there on the sand glowing amazing colors and staring at the handsome young Hawaiian man with the ukulele. He could tell they were sizing him up. Desi was the first to speak.

*"Welcome traveler,"* she stood up tall, and offered him a handshake.

"Hey spooky honey, you're in Hawaii now, gimme a hug." They hugged as only spirits can… kind of like two sponges squeezing each other. Clear ectoplasm gushed in all directions. It sounds gross, but it's an amazing turn on. Suki, then Tanya jumped up and added to the juice, sort of a squishy group-sponge-smoothie.

He whispered in their ears as he hugged them tight, "Tanya, Suki, Desi, it's me, Ole Gold in spirit form. I want you to know that I forgive you, all of you. Please forgive me too."

*"Oh Ole, is it really you? Thank you, you darling man,"* said Desiree.

*"You're not moving back in,"* said Suki as she snuggled into his bare shoulder.

*"Go to Hell,"* Tanya snarled and broke out of the hug.

*"Hey guy, y'er kind of over-dressed for this beach party,"* Desiree said in a sensuous, experienced sort of way. She was staring at the bulge behind his ti-leaf malo.

"Yah, I guess I am."

*"Loose the loin cloth and go native music man."*

So, he untied his leaves and they all lay back on the sand. Ole made sure Desi was between him and Tanya. Her no aloha vibe was a poison-ivy, itchy death ray.

"Wanna hear a ghost story?" Ole offered.

They all burst into laughter and agreed.

"I used to wonder what happens to us after we die."

*"Are you dead?"* Tanya asked hopefully.

"I'm not sure. How about you?"

*"I'm dead to you, just a ghost from your memories."*

"They aren't all bad," Ole offered. Tanya didn't reply.

"Are you dead, Desiree?"

*"Tell me a ghost story,"* she whined.

"Okay, it happened long ago on a fishing trip with my dad. We were out in a small wooden boat on some lake in Ontario. The fish weren't biting, but we were having a good time. I remember a fog came across the lake. Soon, it surrounded us in its mysterious cloud. It was one of those spooky, clammy, metaphysical beer moments. I asked my dad, 'What happens after we die, Pop?' He thought about it for a few seconds and replied, 'Well a few days after you're dead there's usually an article in the paper.'" Desi burst into laughter. 'Then,' dad continued, 'about a week later, eight or ten people show up with a pot luck dish'."

Desi went into hysterics, Suki didn't get it, Tanya frowned. *"That's a mean joke,"* she said. *"Death is much more serious than that."*

"You think a pot luck joke is mean? You start wars! That's mean." Ole fought back.

*"You've been spying on us?"*

"Of course, you're on *my* beach."

*"Your beach?"*

"It's where my body is tonight, right over there under those palm trees. So, bam-a-boom, tonight, this is my beach."

*"Even so, my dad was always more serious than that."*

"Just who was your dad, Ms. History?"

*"He was awesome bad, my dad...the famous Old Testament guy who killed Able with a rock, cause Able was better at burning dead animal sacrifices than my dad was."*

*Is this chick for real,* Ole wondered?

*"I think you're lying, trying to make me feel bad for telling a funny ghost story."*

*"You're lying!"* Tanya shrieked and instantly shape-shifted from an attractive, naked, blonde ghost into a mud-ugly alligator snapping its jaws. Her breath was a mix of dead fish and swamp gas.

At that moment, a boat came motoring along just off shore. The Tanya alligator swept her long tail back and forth and stood up on her back legs resembling a small Godzilla. This was not only something very strange to see, it gave Ole-hune a burning rash of chicken skin.

They all gazed out toward the boat. Ole sat up and saw the running lights and deck lanterns of a fishing boat. There was a family aboard pulling in nets and resetting them. They were chanting in Hawaiian, their musical voices skipping across the water like thrown stones. It was a sweet sound. Desi sighed, reached over and held Ole's hand.

Tanya grinned like only an alligator can grin, showing long side bars of sharp teeth.

*"Sea battle!"* she snapped.

Instantly, the ocean began to rise in a furious storm. The wrong-way wind came on fast from the south. It blew the boat onto a reef so hard the next sound they heard was splintering fiberglass. Tanya waved one small, Godzilla front wrist (fore-foot?) and the boat's gas tanks exploded with an ear splitting, "KA-BOOM!" Flames shot out across the water. Some of the fishing family leaped and some were thrown out of the boat by the explosion. Anguished cries for help came rippling across the burning surface of the water.

*"Damn, that was fun,"* Tanya hissed through her clenched alligator teeth.

*"Why do I even hang out with you?"* Desiree shouted.

*"Duh... I'm your only friend and I'm beautiful as a reptile."*

Ole-Menehune ignored them and dove into the ocean becoming a spinner dolphin. He swam toward the burning boat and nudged a teenage boy and girl up to the surface. He let them take hold of his dorsal fin and bounded back to shallow water while they held on in disbelief. Ole didn't stop until every one of the fishing family were wading ashore. Once he was satisfied that all were safe, Ole swam away from the flames and tail-walked in circles, bobbing his head up and down and smiling like only a dolphin can smile.

Suddenly, a glowing pink cloud came floating down from stars like a big ball of cosmic, cotton-candy. It carried a pretty, Filipina woman on its puffy, pink pillow. It was Lacey! She looked like she was in some painting from the Chang Dynasty or the maybe the Old Testament. The cloud painting hovered a foot off the water.

*What is Captain Billy's wife doing in a pink cloud over the ocean?* He wondered.

*Yah brah, could this day get any more confusing?*

"Billy! Can you hear me?" Lacey called out. "Billy, come back to me..." She looked as confused as Dorothy in Oz, trying to get back to Auntie Em. *Captain Billy is a charter boat skipper. Maybe, he's lost out on the waters of Maui? She really loves that guy.* Ole-dolphin thought to himself.

He felt so sorry for her. He could only dream of a woman's love like that, someday.

*Yah, maybe the captain will never make it back...* he toyed with the idea, *and Lacey will need someone to take care of...*

*Stop that! Fo' shame brah. That's just so wrong. What's the matter with you? Vibed his super ego.*

Ole *was* ashamed of his wrong-way desire for Billy's wife. He dove under the waves and tried to swim away. The fishing boat was still burning, so he surfaced far upwind to find some clear water and air. The impossible pink cloud shrine with Lacey in it was patiently waiting when he surfaced. She was encircled by an aura of white stars, like the statue of a saint in a sacred grotto.

He clacked his teeth together and tried to frown. But, the structure of the dolphin mandible is locked in an eternal smile; one of the many things that endears them to humans.

Lacey called out again, looking everywhere, but not seeing the blushing dolphin. "Billy! Billy! ... Promise you'll come home to me!"

Oliver's big bulbous forehead had gone pink with more shame than usual. His left pectoral fin was tiring. It couldn't keep up with his right anymore. Now that all the rescuing was done, he could only swim in slow, counter-clockwise circles. When he tried to swim with the left fin it hurt something awful. Lacey was crying now looking everywhere but still not seeing the injured dolphin or Billy's charter boat.

"I'll wait for you Billy... I'll always be here for you. Come home Billy!"

Ole shook his dolphin size head, and yelled up at her,

"Lacey! I'll help you. I'll search the whole ocean for Billy Bones. I'll find him! I'll bring him back to you!"

Lacey heard something chatter and squeal, but it made no sense to her. After eighty years of dolphin research, humans are still so clueless they can't understand plain dolphin when they hear it.

## 40  REM

The Rapid Eye Movement of re-awakening began with Ole's Share of Soul seeing flecks of light blinking on the inside of his eye lids. Here were tiny solar suns of magenta, red and white, yellow, blue and green. The vast emptiness of space inside his head seemed emptier and deeper than he could ever remember.

*No surprise there,* punched Sarcasm.

Perhaps it was the brightening light of a Maui morning that brought Ole to the threshold of re-awakening. Suddenly with one convulsive spasm he was ejaculated up from the depths of things seen and unseen. He looked around. Hidden beach was a picture postcard of a Hawaiian morning titled, 'Moth Wings of White Air Melt the Snow Drifts of Ancient Light.'

However, when he re-closed his eyes, he was back in his science lab at University of Washington. This wasn't so unusual. Ole often dreamed of his past career as a chemistry teacher. This time however, it was so real he could smell the stinky ink from the marking pen as he finished a chemical formula all over a whiteboard. There were no students around to bother him. The windows were closed, rain and fog making everything outside gray and blurry, a typical day in Seattle. He was kneeling on the floor writing as fast as he could, the last element symbol on the bottom of a third and final whiteboard.

He opened his eyes again and there was the paradise postcard of a soft, gauze-white morning. The beach and the ocean were a moving water-color being brushed onto wet paper. Maybe the post card should be titled, 'Teach in Seattle, But Paint Your Future on Maui.'

Oliver was still sitting under that same palm tree. He took several deep breaths mesmerized by the beauty of the surf. It was a lefty his favorite, but his boards were back at the condo. Molokai island looked like it was stretching one leg off to the west as sunshine warmed its back. Ole's Panama hat had fallen off. His legs had grown roots. He stretched for a while with Molokai. As his body muscles lengthened his share of soul gave itself back to his mind. Ole was himself again. There was no hangover trying to ring his neck. The triple heartache from the women had by-passed him for now. He could remember forgiving them. This filled him up with warm wooly-bully Buddha stuffing. He loved people, he would go on believing in them for that was his nature even if it hurt sometimes. He loved Maui. He loved Jesus and Santa Claus he loved Martin Luther and Princess Diana and Carl Sagan. All this love took him sliding back into REM sleep.

He was running for miles as a young Hawaiian. He saw visions of naked spirits, ex-girlfriends. He saw a crocodile, an exploding boat and Captain Billy's wife floating in pink clouds. His eyes REM-med around and round inside his head as his face went all blush again. But what thrilled him most, was the chemical diagram written on his class room whiteboard with a black-stink marking pen. He had to get to his laptop and set those symbols into a document before he forgot them.

The yoga with Molokai had done its magic. He shook the sand from his clothes, stood tall and raised his open palms in front of his chest 'Pushing Mountains' then, arms over his head he slowly 'Lifted Sky.' When he'd Tai-chi convinced himself that he could move without pulling a muscle, he ran for the car.

Measured breathing and running are a great combination. Oliver felt more alive than he could ever remember. The reset-plan on hidden beach must have worked. There were no pacing tigers of anger or self-pity. There were lots of paw prints of disappointment, but with time he'd get over it.

Ole reached the muddy Cadillac and leaned on the hood panting, listening. No voices in his forehead, so far. He popped open the trunk and dug through the mess until he found the back pack with his laptop computer. While he waited for it to boot up, he plunked down on the comfortable acre of leather that was the Cadillac's front seat. The laptop blinked on with a blue 'low battery' message and shut itself off.

## 41 Electricity

Electricity was just a parlor trick a hundred-and-fifty years ago. If you rubbed a glass rod with a sheep's skin you could produce a few static sparks. No one could catch it or make it do anything useful. Then Edison and Tesla made a slave of electricity and it's been doing our work for us ever since. Oliver's grandmother, Elsie could remember her dad pulling the string of the one-bulb light fixture above the dining room table, in their house in Nebraska. The neighbors came over to watch. It was that big a deal. A glass bulb that could light a whole room all night. One that never needed oil or a new wick. "What 'll they think of next" was an expression Ole had heard all his life. It's one of the reasons he became a chemist.

But he was wasting time reminiscing. He needed electricity right now, and the message on the screen said, 'No way, time to feed me.' He needed something to write on and quick. He dug into the glove box for a pen and paper. Far in the back he found a pen. He dug deeper for some paper and his fingers closed on his old wedding ring.

*All those good married years and Tanya divorced you rather than move to Hawaii with you. Go figure brah.*

He let that bird fly, hoping she was happy back there in the Seattle rain. He kept searching; nothing but the car registration and the insurance card in the glove box. In the side pocket of the driver's door he found a tourist map of Maui. He went to work. The chemical symbols and equations poured out of the science center behind his forehead and onto the map as if by magic. Stuff he'd never imagined before, came inking out of the tip of the Bank of Hawaii complimentary pen.

*You stole that pen brah. Banks only give away pens*

*when you sign a thirty-year mortgage.*

He had no time to bicker over a pen. He checked every sub-diagram for atomic weight balance. He added every notation he could recall. In a wide empty blue-ocean of the map along Maui's northwest coast, he drew a robot. He struggled with the sketch for some time as his drawing ability was about as good as his golf game. Below the broom-stick legs of the barrel-chested robot, he dashed down another unusual chemical formula, one he'd never imagined before.

*What is that?* His forehead wondered.

Oliver was pretty sure it was a new type of Nano-fiber-graphene. From the element symbols he'd lined out this one was a combination of carbon atoms and sodium-anorthosite. He'd look that up later to be sure. He remembered Anorthosite, it was the main element in moon rocks brought back by the astronauts. He knew there were vast quantities of it here on earth as well. Oliver circled the terrible drawing and wrote 'Robo II' in big block letters. Then, he scribbled the copyright symbol and his signature.

*So, now you're designing Nano-built robots? Yesterday, you couldn't remember to buy flashlight batteries.*

## 42  Pulp or Science Fiction?

A night on the beach, the sound of the surf, and some good old-fashioned, new-age meditation had eased him out of chaos and re-booted his ambition. Ole was done with flying-monkey business. He looked forward to a fresh start in the money-business of science and space.

Trade winds had dried the cane field. Ole backed out of the wheel ruts, turned the car around and bounced his way back toward the main road. Coming up over a rise in the field he caught an expansive view of the ocean. It was so amazing to be alive this early in the morning out on the north shore. He turned off the ignition, set the brake and became one with the Hawaiian panorama around him. He knew Maui was Heaven at sunset. Now he realized how much he'd been missing by sleeping in.

Time did it again. It slowed down... fast. Oliver took a deep breath. It was one of those rare, Newton and his apple moments. He paused in awe of himself. He'd never been good at humble. Humility is for sports. 'Yeah, we won the game, thanks to the whole team.' Humble doesn't work in day-to-day making a living. Oliver had to keep publishing as a college prof. He had to push his music to get it on i-tunes. Now, he would gladly set aside his beach-bum retirement, get organized, patent and publish his new discovery and forget trying to find the illusive Mary Beth of his boyhood dreams.

*Uh huh, give up on Mary Beth? We'll see.*

Re-checking the numbers on the map was like reading a science-fiction story by Arthur C. Clark. It was futurism based in fact. Ole was ninety-nine percent confident that a Robo II made from this new Nano-material was do-able science, not pulp fiction. This was no time to be humble.

Ole thought of Arthur C. Clark's, 'Fountains of Paradise' sky elevators. A wild idea of lifting cargo and people up cables into Space with solar energy instead of blasting it into orbit with rocket fuel. His new graphene could be the answer to manufacturing a cable strong enough to make this happen. His robots could build it. Ole's mind was in warp speed. His robots could also build something else Ole had seen in his REM vision. A satellite habitat that would someday encircle the earth like a gigantic doughnut.

A doughnut sounded good, he was starving. He started up the car and headed back to the paved road. The north shore was a Hawaiian picture postcard this morning. It could be titled, 'Even a Fifteen-Hundred-Dollar Cadillac Feels Like a Lamborghini on Maui's North Shore Highway.' Ole smiled. It had been a while since he'd felt this confident. He was back to normal. It sounded boring, but it felt great.

## 43 Lyka

Arriving back at the Sands, He flopped into his office chair opened his desktop computer to a blank document and started translating the hieroglyphics from the tourist map into something other scientists could understand when published. He needed a shower, He needed food, but for the next two hours his mind was on the discovery that had been gifted to him while returning from the stars.

When he'd saved the file, Mary Beth came to mind once again. He opened his email hoping Lyka had sent a message. The online mail delay was shorter this time. When his AOL mail box with the red flag opened, Ole had nine messages from women in China three from Thailand two from Japan and two from the Philippines. He opened the one from Lyka.

Hi Oliver
How are you today? Are you still playing music at the Pioneer Hotel? Sorry about your friend Desiree. But not very sorry:) Ha, ha, ha. I broke up with my bf in New Hampshire. I have a new friend in Texas now. We talk sometimes on the phone. He's rich, I guess. He may come to meet me someday. I hope not. He is not for me. He has a tattoo on his arm of a big red tongue. Ugh! Will you come to Philippines someday to find a wife? I would like to meet you. Anyway, take care
Lyka

Ole hung his head and sighed. Here's a beautiful young Mary Beth, who found his dating profile and likes him. She keeps on writing even though he told her to find someone her own age. He told her straight up that he was involved with his booking agent. She kept writing. Now that she knows that's over, she wants to meet him when he goes wife shopping.

*No can brah. Your passport expired five years ago, you got no money, she too fah away. Ain't gonna happen. Think about Robo II.*

He opened the other message from the Philippines. It was from a young woman named, Edin. There was a glamour-shot photo embedded in the e mail. She looked like a fourteen-year-old movie star.

Dear Oliver,
I found your profile on Asianeuro dating site and I like you a lot. I want to chat with you in private chat room. Just the two of us, but I am poor and do not have money. And I taking care of my mother now. She sick. Can you help us? Can you send $100.00 US soon. Mother needs medicine and food and I want to be your girlfriend from now on. All for you!
Love, Edin

Ole hit the delete button on every dating message that asked for money. Lyka had been writing to him for six months and never asked for a single peso. He wanted to open the rest of the 'fe-mails,' but he needed food and a shower. He hit the shower. He sang one of his songs while he washed his hair three times to get all the sand and burnt gunpowder out of it.

## 44  A Sweeter Phone Call

Oliver didn't wear a watch anymore, but it was time for breakfast. Retirement meant no watch, no job and no boss. Alas, there was also no more suburban home on a golf course, no more Christmas Day dinners with his daughters, no more raking leaves and no more gym membership, no more paychecks.

*No more wife,* Sarcasm reminds him.

*So true, why does the heart treasure it's sorrow with such fierce fidelity?*

Hunger overcame that old heartache. Oliver almost ran toward the smell of eggs and pancakes calling from the Beach House restaurant at the Sands. There were a dozen people eating breakfast. Ole found a seat by the low wall overlooking the swimming pool and hot tub. There were no bikini clad tourist girls frolicking this early in the morning. So, he sat down and within a heartbeat he had a companion seated across the table from him giving him stink eye. She was an ugly, neurotic, old hag named, 'Worry.' She was always annoying, persistent and no fun to be alone with. He ate his pancakes and eggs trying to ignore her endless stream of questions.

*What 'ta' ya gonna do now wing man? No more Desi brah, all pau (finished). Desi's brother is alive? How do you feel about that good news? Let's order more eggs. You have money for all this food? I'm thirsty. What kind of bird is that over there? What are we gonna do now? It's gonna take more money than you've got, to visit Lyka in the Philippines. Is that the smart thing to do? When you gonna patent your new Nano formula? How can you test it without a lab, brah? Why does your left arm hurt so much?*

The waiter at the Beach House restaurant, a fifty-something, polite man named, Chris, was a mainland retiree like Ole. And like Ole, Chris earned just enough money, month by month to stay on Maui. Chris pretended not to notice Ole arguing with someone or something invisible across his table. When Ole was done with his breakfast Chris left a folder with the bill on the table. Ole peeked at the cost... three dollars and twenty-one cents! He called the waiter over.

"Chris, my friend this can't be right... three bucks? I just ate ten-dollars-worth of food." Uncle Ole's never been a cheat. The waiter looked at the mistaken check and then gratefully at Ole.

"That goes to another table. Sorry, be right back." Chris rushed back to the cash register.

The second time around, Oliver slipped one of his credit cards into the little plastic pocket in the folder without even looking at the price. A cooked breakfast and a dash of honesty had settled his nerves back down to an even smoother normal kind of confidence. That old hag, 'Worry' was gone.

"What day of the week is it, Chris?" Ole asked, "and what time of day?"

"Sunday morning, eight o'clock." He walked away with a most likely, worthless credit card.

*Sunday? Wasn't last night a...?* He couldn't remember.

By the time Chris returned, Ole was re-counting the five, one-dollar bills he had in his shorts pocket. He counted again, it added up to four this time. He added it again, it was back to five.

"Come again," said the waiter, leaving the folder with the card and the receipt.

*So, he did have some room left on that credit card. Things were looking up, or deeper in debt.*

He looked at the receipt, eighteen-dollars and seventy-nine cents. He kind a wished he hadn't been so honest. But honesty becomes a habit like any other. Repeated long enough it creates its own annoying, irresistible power.

The "what will you think of, next?" question hung four feet above him like a cartoon balloon unanswered, and certainly not funny. His confident nothing thoughts were going nowhere, but at least he wasn't hungry anymore.

"New hand," demanded Karma. This time he was Bozo the clown. His painted smile was smudged with pancake syrup. It wasn't a funny smile. Ole looked at his two new cards... *a pair of queens. The Queen of Diamonds and the Queen of Hearts.*

*Hold right there, brah,* his forehead orders.

*I know how to play Blackjack.*

Just then Ole's phone started singing in his short's pocket. He hoped it wasn't another dead person.

"Tues-day-ahf-ter-noon Tues-day..." It was a surprise that his cracked-screen cell phone still worked at all. With

a flip of ...
answered ...
defeated.

"Hello?"

That made ...

"WHO IS IT?"

"It's your mor...

"Oh, sorry mon...
heart. "Things have ...

"What's the matte...

"How are you and L...
question. It worked.

"We're fine. Christmas ................ .. up. I have a
few cards to answer from ............. we heard from, *after*
Christmas. Dad won't put w ..., nis toy train. It's still 'woo-
wooing' around the seven-foot tall fire-hazard shedding
its needles in the living room." She took a breath. "I'm
still baking cookies..." she skipped merrily along with
enough left-over holiday cheer to float a reindeer in
eggnog. Ole shut up, leaned back in the restaurant chair
and relaxed to the 'carol of bells' in her voice. Mom could
make Christmas last into February.

"Now, how are *you* dear?"

So, he had to tell her the whole bang-a-boom
deception story of Desiree. He didn't mention his mental
dissipation or the flying monkey stuff. When he'd told her
the worst of it, he paused knowing what she was about to
say.

ot well. Dad and I

. Oh, and bake

e you feel better."

ise."

oven timer, gotta go or these ginger

ill run away like last time. Ha, ha, ho-ho-ho!

good. Santa's watching, love you."

"Bye... he started," but she was gone.

He closed his phone, put his unshaven chin in his left hand, the one that looked like hers, and smiled with genuine happiness. Mom was the only adult he knew, who still believed in Santa Claus.

## 45 Trying to Pray

Now a promise to your mother, is promise chiseled in granite. Ole got in his car hoping there was enough room on his credit card to buy some oatmeal and other baking stuff at the nearest grocery or find a church and say a prayer... whichever came first.

He pointed his muddy car south, driving along the shoreline toward Lahaina. He didn't need a compass to find south, but his morality compass could use some adjusting. He wanted to kill Desiree not pray for her. The only reason he couldn't do it was because when he was a willful brat of a boy, his mom had taught him right from wrong with a wooden spoon liberally applied to his defiant butt. If that didn't correct Ole's bad behavior Dad, the captain of the family, would apply his leather belt to Ole's butt to explain the consequences of wrong decisions and keep things ship shape. Ole never bit anyone or got arrested by the police; probably because of all the butt-spanking he earned as a child. Immediate punishment taught him the painful facts of cause and effect.

As he drove, Ole tried to avoid wrong thoughts. The voices in his head were wonderfully silent. As you enter Lahaina from the north there's a fork in the road that bends off the highway and becomes Front Street. Ole forked onto Front and slowed to twenty-miles per hour, a tempo easier on his nerves. He drove slowly past the 'Jesus Coming Soon' church and looked in the open front doors. There were three people singing up by the altar, facing nothing but empty pews. Oliver had just read in the local paper that the 'Jesus Coming Soon' church was celebrating its fiftieth anniversary. He wondered if they were disappointed that Jesus wasn't back by now. He kept driving toward Lahaina.

He was nearing one of his favorite places, the Buddhist temple on Baby Beach. He considered stopping. The Jodo Mission is a meditative garden of stillness in the shadow of the largest Buddha statue in the western hemisphere. Oliver had been teaching an introduction to Tai chi at this temple for over a year.

*You know that's not what mom had in mind, so keep driving.*

A half mile further on Front street was a beautiful old Methodist church with a gazebo for weddings out on the front lawn. There was one sandal on the lawn and one lying on the sidewalk. It was as peaceful as a Buddhist temple, a little too peaceful for a Sunday morning. There were no cars in the parking lot. It was almost nine-o'clock. He kept driving, turning mauka (toward the mountains) away from the store fronts, then south again until he came to a church with a dozen cars in its parking lot. Ole could see a small crowd inside because the exterior glass doors that lined both side walls were swung wide open. The well-ventilated design convinced him this would be a good place to pray. He didn't bother to read the name of the church on the sign out on the front lawn. As he entered the front doors, a frail Hawaiian auntie smiled and greeted him with a hug and a kiss on the cheek. He sat down in the empty back row, out of the view of the other thirty people in the church. Up front there was a real Christmas tree left over from last week's holidays. There were potted red and white poinsettias all over the place. The little church had a cheery, welcoming vibe.

Up front, left of the Christmas tree, a regulation American flag hung from a tall wooden floor-standard. On the right side of the sanctuary was a piano topped with red poinsettias and next to the piano stood a very large Hawaiian flag standing considerably taller than the American flag. Ole tried to think about the not-so-subtle message that sent, but he came here to pray not debate the Hawaiian Sovereignty issue.

Just as Oliver closed his eyes and tried to pray, a church bell started ringing.

*Wow, you start praying and 'Shazam!' You hear church bells. It's a miracle brah!* The sarcastic voice has no governor on its mouth.

He looked outside at the bell in the church yard. It was hung about chest high in a sturdy rock structure the size and shape of a large stone barbeque grill. An older Hawaiian uncle was pulling on a white clapper rope.

*It's nine-o'clock,* whispered his inner timekeeper.

Three people stood up in the front pew. Ole recognized two of them right away, his friend Captain Billy Bones and his wife Lacey! *The cutest Filipina on the island of Maui.* His thoughts ran away with her into places he shouldn't be thinking about in a church. His face blushed like a red hibiscus.

*You came to pray remember?*

After just two loud tolls of the bell... a big silence made everyone look outside. The Hawaiian uncle stood with a frayed rope end in his hand, while total surprise worried the smile off his handsome face. The bell rope had given way after who could guess, maybe a hundred years of faithful tugging?

One of the younger men ran outside and with his long arm reached far into the center of the bell, found the clapper and rang the bell by hand, four more times. Everyone in the church began to clap and laugh. The spontaneous rescue by the youngster, the laughing, the Christmas tree and Poinsettia's, the hug from the frail auntie at the front door, all these simple joys turned Oliver's apprehension, into Jell-O.

Billy and Lacey faced the people in the pews and started playing their ukuleles. The song they sang went right to Oliver's heart.

*"The Spirit in me greets the Spirit in you*
*Ah-lay-lu-iah... God's in us and were in God, Ah-lay-lu-iah."*

They repeated it again and again while everyone in the church began walking around hugging each other or shaking hands like they were truly happy to see each other. Oliver sang along. 'Namaste' in yoga means exactly this, 'The divine spirit in me greets the divine spirit in you.' Ole wanted to go up front and hug Lacey.

*What?* His conscience kicked him in his cerebral ribs. *Stay right where you are and keep singing Romeo.*

A few older members walked to the back of the church and shook Oliver's hand. This made him relax even more, but, being the kind of guy he is, he noticed that other than Lacey, there were no young women in this church.

*You came here to pray not find a date, brah.*

The song came to an end, so everyone went back to their pews and sat down. Ole sat down and silently began the only prayer he could almost remember.

"Our father who art…" His prayer was interrupted by the minister talking.

"We are drawn to worship by a reality unseen. The One we call God is beyond all human description."

The congregation began to respond in unison. He opened the bulletin the frail auntie had put in his hand and read along with the kanaka (people).

"God is more than we can ever imagine. We sense God's presence as we meditate."

*You sure y'er in a church brah? This sounds like Nembutsu Buddhism.* His disrespectful brain was really starting to annoy him. The minister was still speaking.

"We are amazed by the wonders all around us. We feel God's presence when we sing together."

The congregation responded with, "we are summoned by the One who is just and merciful."

The minister's words splashed on, but Ole could no longer hear them. He was lost in his thoughts of childhood 'believing.' He could see the minister talking, but the words murmured out from the pulpit like a quiet mountain stream bubbling out of a rock. It cascaded down two carpeted stairs and flooded down a red carpet that ran between the rows of pews. The words flowed past Ole and out the front doors to water the lawn with wisdom. He could see a few individual words rush by. There went 'Hope,' followed by 'Compassion' and random prepositional phrases moving too fast to read. A river of words flowed under his pew and made weak eddies of adverbs and nouns around his feet. The minister's words were unending, like a babbling-brook-lullaby that almost put him to sleep. He remembered learning as a child that when you're asleep, the boring sermons go by faster.

He had just nodded off when the singing started again. Captain Billy and Lacey were harmonizing some old protestant tune that sounded familiar. Everyone knew how to sing in Hawaiian. It sounded simply... Heavenly.

Oliver picked up a beige hymnal. It weighed ten pounds, so he put it down. Instead, he hummed along with the melody. The name of the tune was playing hide and seek with him but it rolled along, stirring up his emotions until a tear of joy pushed out of his good eye. It was slipping down his cheek like a kid on one of those backyard water slides. It was a moment the likes of which hadn't happened in a long time. His bad eye stayed dry. It was looking at a couple of hundred years of tombstones resting under plumeria trees in the graveyard next to the church.

Ole searched through the shadowy tops of the trees for winged monkeys. He didn't see any, but they're good at hiding. He looked along the ground, sometimes they run instead of fly. He thought he saw one slip behind a concrete and red brick crypt. Ole shivered and turned his attention back inside the church. His face felt loose like it might fall off if he shook it too hard. His toes were starting to shake.

*Don't turn into anything weird now brah!*
*Breathe deep buddy, get a grip. Find your inner calm like you did last night.*

He shut his eyes and tried to relax. Across the bombed-out moonscape of his mind, he saw a broken door hung in a door frame standing all by itself; its former walls, bombed away. It looked like a black and white scene from a Twilight Zone episode. Neat painted letters across the cracked glass of the door spelled out, 'Department of Inner Calm.' Below that hung a hand-scrawled sign, 'Closed Until Further Notice' 'Keep Out.' Ole opened his eyes and had to look back at the graveyard.

*There's lot of dead people out there. But not Manny. No, he's alive, playing music in California, and hating his sister. Uh-huh, Desiree the big-shot booking agent. The woman you were gonna marry because she promised to make you a rock star.*

That did it; thinking of Desiree made him so angry again. Angry is a bad emotion for Oliver Gold. Monkey wings sprung out of his shoulders. He flew up in the air like a hairy humming-ape and winged his way backwards over the top of the last pew and out the same doors he'd walked in earlier. Ole easily cleared the flowering trees over the graveyard, circled back and landed on the steep ridge of the church's roof. He monkey-balanced there as easily as if he'd done this sort of thing all his life. There was one rubber sandal on the slope of the roof about half way up. It looked like it'd been there for years. Ole could relate to that lost sandal. He felt like a lonely gargoyle placed up here to keep evil spirits out of the church.

*Maybe you're an evil spirit what got thrown out of 'da church brah.*

*Yah sky monkey. Some power sent you up here.*

Oliver acknowledged that there *is* a God power, or at least a power of *good* in his human view of the world. He had looked for goodness in all things. Okay, not everything. Not in the bad stuff like: war, crime, hurricanes, politics and gorgeous, irresistible, lying beauticians from California that could still make a monkey out of him.

He hunched his monkey wings over his head surveying the misty morning. *If God, is really somehere on earth, why did he get such a lonely feeling every time he tried to pray?*

## 46 Flunking Religion

He shook his wings in despair remembering how all the trouble started between him and God. He was in high school, maybe eleventh-grade. It was a long time ago.

*Forty years... brah.*

It was hard to think. His monkey-size head was scrunching his chemist's brain into a small meatball. Anyway, Oliver had flunked religion class. He didn't mean to flunk. He was in religious history class in a Catholic high school for boys in Iowa. He was half-listening one day as most high school students do until the lunch bell rings, or the first-ever Catholic president whom everybody loved, gets shot in the head by a sniper in Texas. Oliver's problem was a whole lot less terrible than JFK's assassination just a few weeks earlier. However, on a personal level, this was even more tragic. The events of that day in religion class would change everything in Oliver's life.

Ole's school desk was up in the front row, right on the fifty-yard line where his teacher stood tall in a black dress or gown or robe. He wasn't sure what the priests called it. It was as plain as the black dress the nuns wore, only their dress was accented by stiff white cardboard. Ole's religion teacher also had some cardboard, a white collar tightly pinching his neck. His teacher had a dissipated-looking pink face with wattles of neck flesh bulging out from that dog collar of cardboard. It was painful to look at.

It was even more painful to listen to him as he rattled

on and on like a towering floor-mounted fan turning his head in slow oscillations from one side of the room to the other. His lecture lessons were focused on the glorious achievements of all fourteen Popes named, Clement. Really, there were fourteen of them plus, three *anti-popes* who also took the name Clement. It surprised monkey-Ole that he remembered anything at all from that boring class.

Up on the church roof, three doves landed near Ole's monkey feet. He smiled down at them, but it must have looked like an evil Elvis snarl. They flew off in a hurry. He wanted to get back into the church and pray like he promised his mom. The sky all around him rumbled with distant thunder, and a light rain began to tap, tap, tap on the roof of the church. He hunched his shoulders, the left one didn't hunch as well as the right. It hurt like H... he didn't want to cuss, especially on top of a church. His big wings came up sort of lopsided, favoring his left, but it was enough to keep his furry, little head dry.

He tried to remember that teacher's name, the one in the religion class. It was something like Father Rasflannahan. Ole wasn't sure. Maybe he made that up. Every day, while Father Floor Fan blew ancient history from side to side, the class went into its usual coma. It wasn't the priest's fault. He seemed a good man. He was just stuck with a tough subject to sell to teenage boys. Oliver felt sorry for him. A typical fifty-minute- torture droned along something like this, "After the long-awaited death of Pope Tyrannosaurus the XIV the most famous cardinals and several lesser birds met in Saint Peter's cozy castle in Rome and elected Bishop Hapsburg the VIII by a slim margin over the front-runner Cardinal Vince Lombardi. The grand news was announced in the traditional way by white smoke rising from the stacks of the very first steam powered vessel, 'Fulcrum's Folly.' It would be a day that would go down in infamy."

It all seemed so irrelevant, a word Ole applied to most of his classes in high school. He wanted more science and literature and a whole lot less theology. So, he spent his time in religion class reading a novel he'd found in the school library.

The book was a three-pounder, almost nine-hundred pages long. It had him completely enthralled. Forty years later, monkey-sitting on a church roof, he could still remember the title, 'Uhuru!' an African word for freedom. The heroine was a pretty, young, white girl, a missionary's daughter dedicated to helping the African people in their struggle for liberty against their heavy-handed Belgian overlords, whom her father just happened to work for as plantation Chaplin and doctor.

There was inter-tribal warfare and rogue bandits to contend with as well as torrential rainfall, floods and deadly drought. All this drama was set on the immense and still unknown (to Oliver) African continent. What a great escape from class; a story exotic, wild and far, far away from high school religion class in Iowa.

The young teenage girl in the story was kind and compassionate toward all, the perfect Christian heroine. Everyone on the plantation and in all the nearby villages loved her. Oliver loved her. She was brave and smart for a sixteen-year old girl. The author had also described her long blonde hair, her slim waist and long legs with considerable voyeuristic detail for a book found in a parochial school library. Bernadette, was her name and she had discovered an unexpected pleasure from the saddle as she rode her horse. She was just beginning to be sexually conscious. This intrigued Oliver completely; a teenage boy in an all-boys high school, knowing nothing at all about teenage girls.

One day, Bernadette was riding her favorite horse. She called him Mister Handsome; he was good in the saddle. Her father had sent her to deliver much needed medicines and other supplies to the chief of a neighboring village. After pushing Mister Handsome hard for a satisfying rough ride, she stopped by a small stream to water the magnificent horse. While he drank his fill, she rested in the sunshine on a grassy slope and day dreamed of the tall dark and muscled son of the village chief. She untied the drawstring on her blouse, opening it to reveal her shoulders. When she leaned her head back to look at the cloudless African sky, a generous amount of her cupcake-size budding cleavage pushed against her white top. The author really knew how to keep a boy turning pages. Ole wanted to lie down next to Bernadette by that quiet stream and get to … ah… know her better.

Bernadette thought she heard something moving downstream. She looked quickly all around, until her innocent blue eyes noticed a pair of white egrets fly out of the tall grasses along the stream by Mr. Handsome.

To young Oliver, Bernadette had become a real person. A girl that was kind, cute, skinny, fast and curious. After admiring her for over eight-hundred pages, she was just the kind of Mary Beth that Ole hoped to meet and invite to the senior prom. He would remember the turn of the next page for the rest of his life.

*"She heard another rustle in the bushes close by. She turned her head, sending her blonde hair flowing softly over her bare shoulders. Suddenly, two very dark natives*

*with sticks of bone piercing their flat noses, leaped out of the grass waving machetes. One grabbed Mister Handsome by the reins the other yanked Bernadette's head back and slit her pretty, white throat with his machete. He cut away her hair with a second slash and left her to bleed out like a goat. The two men jumped on the back of Mister Handsome and rode away across the African grassland. The medicines and hair would mean much money across the river."*

Eight-hundred and fifty-seven pages into a nine-hundred-page book... Ole's first romantic love since Mary Beth; beautiful, kind, sexually curious Bernadette, is... murdered! His Bernadette! Bernadette the Good. Lovely, innocent Bernadette, was lying there dead, her blood flowing into that quiet stream; staining her nubile young breasts and white blouse. Oliver's heart broke. He was furious! He was a seventeen-year old boy in shock. He jumped up on his feet and threw the book down on his school desk with a resounding 'Slam!' Ole could still picture it there, quivering in its death throes; its paperback spine broken.

"Those God-Damn...!" He began shouting, waving his arms around in anger. The grass lands and the galloping horses began to fade away. When the dry, African dust settled, Oliver was standing in eleventh-grade religion class, front row, just inches away from Father Floor Fan. The priest grabbed him by his long hair and walked him out of the class room, down the stairs and into the principal's office.

Young Oliver Gold had never cussed in his entire short life. His parents didn't swear. His grandparents didn't swear. Those 'GD' words just came out of his mouth in a ıeart break.

ən he was allowed back into

first to finish the final exam. It

ə worst kind. Ole filled in as

ɔer about Pope Alexander the

ᴏⅉᴇᴀᴛ, anᴅ aⅡ ᴛʜe pope Clements, even the illegitimates and all the other saints and criminals of church history.

When he took his answer sheet up to the teacher's desk, Father Fan tore it into little pieces without reading it and threw it in a trash can by his desk. He gave Ole double stink-eye, flaming with revenge.

When the school mailed his report card home, Ole was grounded for the entire summer. The only place he could visit was the local library to attend a summer school typing class. He didn't have a car of course, so he walked. Catholic boys who flunk religion don't get a car from their parents, nor do they even get to drive the family car. However, that was the library summer that Oliver found Albert Camus, R. Buckminster Fuller, Joseph Conrad, Franz Kafka and Herman Hesse. All of them bad company for an impressionable, religious flunky. Seeds from the 'Question Tree' had dropped on a fertile young mind. Hesse wrote, "letting go, not holding on, makes us stronger." Oliver was a junior in high school. He would always keep his love for Jesus, but he was ready to let go of religion. Besides, he wasn't good at it. That 'F' on his student report card would document his failure for the rest of his life, maybe for all time.

## 47 Fewer Rules to Break

The next fall, Oliver *really* fell from 'the Church.' That's not exactly what happened. It would be more correct to admit that he didn't fall, he jumped and ran. He was a senior in high school getting good grades and religion class was a lot more interesting. 'Current Events Concerning the Church,' was the official title of the class.

Bob Dylan was on the radio singing, '*The Times They Are a Changing.*' People of all colors were marching in the streets for peace and civil rights. It was during this upheaval that the Pope sent a Vatican Council Decree around the world and suddenly, Sunday Mass was allowed in languages other than Latin. All those beautiful Gregorian chants and mysterious, mumbling Latin prayers lost their mystique when uttered in plain English. Guitars were allowed at mass to appease the hippie generation, and if that wasn't bad enough, the priests wore Madras and Paisley dresses or robes. It was so sudden it was like the circus had come to town on the midnight train.

Rules that had been carved in granite for millennia were changed to give sinners like Oliver another chance. It was, disappointing for some teenagers. There were fewer rules to break.

On November nineteenth, nineteen-sixty-six, a dogma came barking over the Vatican ticker tape: Catholics could now eat meat on Fridays without committing a mortal sin. You see Catholic families were strictly taught by the church that eating any meat on Fridays, even one teeny slice of bacon was a mortal sin, as in MORTAL. Mortal is the most serious kind of sin you can commit, if you dare. For if you die with even one bacon-smelling mortal sin on your soul, you go straight to Hell. Think of Mortal sin as indelible ink that only comes off your soul with the special magic Catholic spot remover called, 'confession.'

Yep, if you confess your Friday meat eating and other crimes to a priest sitting in a small dark closet, you still have a chance to get into Purgatory when you die. However, all those Mortal sins you committed over the years do leave a kind of dull grass-stain on your soul like a football jersey after a rough game. So, even after a lifetime of confession bleach and hundreds of repeated penance prayers, only a few of the freshly dead go straight to Heaven. Now that Oliver thought more about it, the Virgin Mary was another one who of course, made it into Heaven. She was the sweetest and saddest of any mother who ever lived. The apostles, Saint Peter and Paul got in for sure, that would make the Peter, Paul and Mary Trio complete. John, Matthew, Mark and Luke and most of the other apostles. Certainly not Judas, that rat. How about, 'doubting Thomas'?

In Catholic High School, Ole still believed almost everything his priestly teachers taught him, including the many advantages of Heaven over Hell. His local church, Saint John's, was one of the most impressive cathedrals in Des Moines. His mother and father had married there. He was baptized there. Ash Wednesdays were celebrated(?) there. The solid marble columns holding up its vaulted ceilings were four-feet in diameter, absolutely awe inspiring. Everyone, even noisy little children lowered their voice to a whisper in God's house. For of course, only God could afford such a house. The nuns had taught him that God didn't just float around in this vast space. No, he actually... lived in a small round flat piece of bread encased in a three-inch glass window in the exact center of a solid gold cross up on the altar. This elaborate crucifix looked like it must have cost more than his dad's new Pontiac station wagon. That beautiful cross had all these golden spikes sticking out in every direction like a sculpture of a golden sun. Ole's last name was Gold, he used to kneel and admire that chunk of solid gold during all the secret, Latin mumbling during mass. He didn't want to steal it or anything, he just wanted to touch it someday when nobody was looking. It would be like getting to touch God.

His high school teachers went to college for years to learn the truth about religion and pass it on to the under-educated teenage sheep in high school. Ole never liked being compared to sheep. He'd seen sheep in Iowa; fish are smarter.

Anyway, back to confessing. After you wait for an hour in a long, long, line inside the cathedral with the rest of your classmates who never make eye contact with you, it's finally your turn. You enter the delousing closet by parting two heavy velvet curtains. You kneel on a hard, wooden bench with depressions in its black-walnut surface made by decades of sore knees. There is no place to sit, so it's here you must wait for your turn to confess. As painful as this sounds, it was a big improvement over the church's inquisition centuries when you were mercilessly tortured in ways so cruel Ole didn't want to think about them. The church inquisitors kept torturing you with sadistic zeal, until you confessed. Then, if you were still alive you were killed for confessing.

Inside the modern-day closet of inquisition, Oliver would have to wait some more, because there's always another person confessing on the other side of the closet and if you listen really, hard, sometimes you could hear some of the bad stuff the other sinner did.

When it's your turn, the priest slides a small wooden window open with a loud, 'you're next' kind of slam. This echoes through the cathedral so everyone still standing in line can tell just how bad you've been by how long it takes until the window slam's shut again. Oliver used to wonder why it always took Mary Beth Johnson so long to confess her sins. Every week, she was in the closet for a long time. Even though he tried to time his place in the waiting line so he could be in the closet while Mary Beth was confessing, it never happened. However, it did lead his young thoughts into an exciting minefield of more sins to confess.

When the window slams open in your direction, it's your turn. You can't see the priest and he can't see you. But you know, he knows who you are by your voice, because you grew up in his parish and he's met you in the halls at school. So, young Ole would try to disguise his voice and if it had been a slow week, he would make up awful sins just for fun. The priest would listen, mumble in faux shock at the severity of this stranger's transgressions and then sentence him to do penance. Usually this meant repeating a string of prayers that Oliver was forced to memorize in first grade. Nice prayers though, like Our Fathers and Hail Mary's. This makes all the sins go away immediately and removes over ninety-percent of those pesky sin stains that only get polished off by doing time in Purgatory.

So, under the centuries old Friday-no-meat-eating-taboo, it wouldn't matter if Ole ate one bite of a hot dog or a whole pot roast on a Friday; confessing his mistake would give him a clean slate. But only, if he said every single one of the prayers of penance he'd been tasked with. Sometimes, maybe because he'd made up all that bad stuff he didn't do, he'd be sentenced to pray a whole rosary. Every Catholic boy had to carry a rosary in his pants pockets to keep their hands from touching anything else they could reach down there.

But right after the new decree from Vatican Council II, Catholics could eat meat on Friday like everyone else.

Uh oh! The tiger-cub agnostic in Oliver began to pace its Catholic cage. As a senior in high school, Oliver Imagined what could happen in this new-rule scenario: Dad lets him use his car some Friday night to go to the football game. Never happened, but just suppose. So, Ole eats a hotdog with lots of mustard and pickle relish. Then later, after the game on the way to the dark side of the Des Moines Airport parking lot to make out with Mary Beth Johnson, Ole dies in a tragic car wreck. Fortunately, Mary Beth lives to sin again.

Now, his dad is really, sorry he let Oliver borrow his new car. But no worries, he has All State Car Insurance, so he can get a newer car. And dad knew Ole had gone to confession that week, so chances were sixty-forty, Oliver would get into Purgatory.

Dad was right, Ole had confessed all his sins on Thursday, said his prayers of penance and hasn't had a chance to feel up Mary Beth Johnson yet, so even though he ate that hot dog, he's still Mr. Clean. Oliver goes right up to Purgatory. Or is it down? Maybe, side-ways?

Nobody could explain Purgatory, not even Father Floor Fan with his college-education and four years of additional seminary college. All anyone really knows for sure (uh huh), is that Purgatory is kind of like going through TSA at the airport. But, once through those scanners, you still must wait at an airport gate for days, months or years until your good enough to board your flight to Heaven.

So now, young Oliver's soul has left the car wreck. As his SoS flies away, he notices Mary Beth is flirting with the ambulance driver. When Ole arrives in Purgatory, he gets the good news that he's only going to be punished for twenty-five years or so, to burn off the imperfections that would otherwise keep him from Heaven. You see, everyone must be polished to perfection in Purgatory's eternal rock tumbler. Getting into Heaven is harder than getting accepted to Harvard.

In high school, Ole was taught that Purgatory is not a nice air-conditioned library where you visit with other almost good-enough people and celebrate Christmas and birthdays together until your cosmic plane departs for Heaven. No, that kind of Purgatory does not exist. The real [sic] Purgatory airport-holding-pen will be over-crowded and hot, with no place to sleep except on the concrete floors. Over at the vending machine warm bottles of water cost four dollars. Oh, and no one brought a wallet because you know... "you can't take it with you." But there is a hint of optimism in the stinking sulfurous, stale air because everyone knows they aren't going to Hell. This makes for an underlying cheerfulness blended with all the melancholy, sort of like Norwegian music.

Ole imagined there must be an open funnel in the middle of the Purgatory waiting area where you can look down into Hell and see the all the real suffering going on. Everyone in Purgatory can hear the anguished screams of those poor souls being tortured down there all day and all night which makes it difficult to get any sleep. The open funnel down into Hell is also where all the hot, stinking air is coming from.

The confusing part for young Oliver was that a lot of Catholic teenagers just like him probably missed the 'meat-eating' cut-off date. If they died with hot-dog breath on Friday night a week ago, they would be sent straight to Hell... *forever!* Of course, church rules are inflammable or unflappable or infallible, yes, that's the one and thus strictly enforced. There is no plea-bargaining, no public defender, no blaming their problems on society, no bail bond release until a future court date. Those teens just went straight to Hell. They took the two-dollar hot dog gamble of damnation, and *lost*.

Ole, however, who died after the Pope's Decree, got to go to Purgatory. So, he could look down the funnel into Hell and holler at those teenagers suffering unspeakable torture.

"Too bad you guys! You missed your chance at Purgatory by just seven days!"

Oliver decided on that cold November day in Catholic high school to jump off the church crazy train. He excommunicated himself from all such insanity. He would NEVER, allow anyone to mess with his mind like that again. For the rest of his senior year he ate hot dogs whenever he pleased. But sometimes, he still wondered about all that stuff that everyone else still believed in. No matter how well he behaved for the rest of his life, when he died, would God check Father Flanahan's grade book, notice that 'F' and frown?

## 48 The Vengeful Monkey God

Ole eventually quit worrying about hot dogs and damnation or even Purgatory. He hung on to the common-sense teachings of Jesus, but he decided he would take R. Buckminster Fuller's advice and think for himself.

One of his first independent decisions was that further pursuit of trying to understand religion, philosophy, women or golf was for those who seek impossible challenges. Instead, he studied the science of chemistry with its provable predictability, repeating patterns, measurable rates of chemical reactions and fractal mathematics.

It was raining hard now; the church's steep roof was slippery under his monkey feet. The gutters were awash with the downpour. Ole scrunched his wings over his head and watched the rain run rivulets off the tips of his wet feathers. He was supposed to be praying like he promised his mother.

Ole yearned to truly believe in God again. He listened to the familiar song being sung down there in the church. Only when they sang the fourth verse in English instead of Hawaiian did he get it. 'How Great Thou Art' was a song his mom used to sing as she worked in her gardens. In fact, that was his earliest memory of his mother. There among the orchid-like purple, yellow and white Iris. She wore a garden dress of white with tiny black polka dots. His mom had a large brimmed hat with matching white garden gloves with black polka dots. They say songs trigger memories. The congregation was singing every verse of. 'How Great.' It sounded heavenly.

Memories of his mother in her Iris garden must have

released a burst of good Juju because Oliver suddenly found himself sitting in the back pew again. His clothes were damp, but the horrible monkey wings were gone. Maybe he'd nodded off in another feverish sleep. The minister was talking again.

"The people began to gather rocks to stone the woman... but Jesus said..." Oliver tried to tune him out, but every third word kept getting in his ears like gnats or penny-whistle music.

*Human Monkeys killing each other with rocks,* he thought to himself. *The history of so many religions is filled with torture, war and oppression.* One of the chunks of religious flotsam still bumping around in his mind was that whole God created man in his own image thing. It wasn't God created woman in *her* own image. So, God is male gender. How could any religion be so certain of this? Perhaps it had all been made up by a bunch of mouth-breathing cavemen one night while the women were busy scraping the hides off freshly killed animals.

Ole really hoped that God did not create humans in his own image. For if that were true, then God would look like us, one of the hairless, upright walking apes. Only God would have a flowing white beard and a bed sheet over him like on the ceiling of the Sistine Chapel.

*God looks like a hairless monkey? No way, brah!* All the voices in his head refuse to believe this.

Of all the amazing life forms in this world, butterf'' panthers, dolphins; why would God choose to l-hairless monkey? If He really was a monke-would explain a lot. Earth being a pla-monkey business. Cane killed Ab! and humans have been throwing t.

and killing each other with advanced forms of rocks for hundreds of thousands of years. Add copious amounts of fermented juices from fruit and grains that human apes are so fond of, and you have a planet of drunken monkeys forever fighting for domination or to justify their own territorial adaptations of the monkey god.

Ole remembers seeing black and white newsreels from the early nineteen-forties of world leaders toasting peace with champagne, all the while plotting World War II behind each other's backs.

What's worse, all these drunken human monkeys over-populate, litter, exploit and pollute their planet with the same kind of disregard you'd see in any monkey cage at any zoo. Making a mess of things, fighting and misbehaving is a monkey's nature. From the condition of the earth's oceans, rivers and streams and polluted air plus, the daily violence reported on global news channels, Oliver feared that God just might be a monkey after all.

## 49  The Holy Wind

This morning, while Ole was not listening to the pastor's sermon he did notice the clean rich smell of tropical rain. It was carried by trade winds that caressed his face like a mother's touch. He decided right then and there, in the last row of the small Christian church that God was more like the wind than a vengeful, omnipotent monkey.

He'd spent a lot of rainy Seattle evenings racing sailboats on the wind back in Puget Sound. The wind had taught him things he'd never learned in high school religion classes, college or chemistry labs. For instance, the wind can be everywhere at the same time, just like God. It's eternal, like God. Wind occurs on the other planets in our solar system. Our lungs fill with wind and compress the Nitrogen and Oxygen into our blood stream to keep us alive. It feeds and refreshes our heart, mind, skin, eyes and finds its way into every molecule of our body. This is about as personal as a god could get. Oliver sat there in the back of that church with his jaw ajar, a smile on his face and a 'born-again' burst of revelation shining forth from his mind's eye.

*Brah! The 'Holy Spirit' the churches talk about all the time... is the wind.*

His epiphany continued as the congregation started to sing again. When people sing, the deep breathing makes them feel better than they did before. Wind can tease one flying seed at a time off a dandelion. It can fill your sail, toss your hair, turn your windmill, make electricity or push through your saxophone and become something as amazing as music. Wind is unstoppable and devastatingly powerful. Ole had seen the damage hurricanes, tornadoes and typhoons wreak upon people living in their path.

Humans need the 'wind' of breath to form words. This is where people determine if the wind blows fair or foul. Some, like Jesus or Buddha breathe wonderful words of Compassion. Others breathe in the same amazing grace of the wind and shout out hatred. They start wars, injure loved ones and strangers, lie in divorce court, and do evil just for the bloody Hell of it. The hasty breath of human words can kill. Oliver thought of drunken King Herod and poor John the Baptist. Human breath can sue for peace. Words can weave a love song out of plumeria blossoms. Bob Dylan was right. The answer is 'Blowing in the Wind.' It's also the common denominator of all the world's religions, the 'Holy Spirit of Goodness.'

The Hawaiian custom of touching foreheads and sharing each other's 'ha' or breath of life, binds people together in friendship. As for the, 'made in God's own image thing,' the wind, like God, is invisible. So that's a match. When compared with all the paintings sculptures and images of gods with long beards or gods throwing thunder bolts or being whipped, tortured and crucified or meditating upon the nearly unattainable. The invisible, Holy Spirit, though hard to paint on the ceiling of the Sistine Chapel, brought a breath of inspiration to the artist lying on his back, on a wooden scaffolding.

What child has not spent hours imagining animal shapes in clouds formed by the wind? This ever-changing art may be more than the repeating formation sets found in nature and described by the mathematician, Mandelbrot. Perhaps, it's the Holy wind playing with clouds, spinning dust devils on the desert, or twirling autumn leaves into tiny tornadoes.

*You've got all the answers don' cha?*

Ole shook his head with serious uncertainty. What did he know? Yesterday morning he was a Godzilla and a winged monkey. Could he tack upwind with the Holy Spirit and get back on course again?

*You should pray about that brah.*

*Does anybody know how prayer works?* Ole wondered.

*Say one for mom and let's get out 'ta here.*

"Our Father..." *Oh man there it is again God's a father not a mother.* All his life when he needed advice or help Ole went to his mother. Dad was busy making a living for the family. Mom was the wise Buddha with the answers, encouragement and a hug.

Oliver heard the pastor's voice again.

"...and so even though the traffic on the Pali Highway is terrible these days... everyone just be good. Amen."

*Now there's a sermon to remember,* smirked Sarcasm. *Maybe you should 'a listened to the rest of it.*

## 50  Dream Shark

Ole stood up, made the sign of the cross on himself out of grade-school habit and headed out the front doors of the church. The rain had lightened to a very fine mist.

"I tried mom. I really did try" he whispered. Magically, as if in approval, rainbows began to sparkle in the misting rain riding the wind above the graveyard.

Watching rainbows and walking now as a man without monkey wings Ole went around to the back of the church to find a restroom. His friends Captain Billy and Lacey were leaving the church from the open side doors and intercepted him with greetings and Hawaiian-style hugs. He held onto Lacey just a few seconds beyond appropriate, but Billy didn't seem to mind.

"Hey, How'z it, brah? Asked the captain. Lacey smiled and said, "Come over to the hall and have some brunch."

"Okay," he tried to reply in a voice that would hide his tender, wrong-way lust for her.

Lacey looked back at him with genuine concern, as she and Billy walked away and put their ukuleles in the trunk of their Mercedes. Ole found the door marked, 'Kane' then headed for the free brunch inside the church's air-conditioned hall. This magnificent building looked like it must have cost millions of dollars to build. Ole wondered how a church with thirty people on a Sunday could afford to have built such a tremendous reception hall.

*Maybe it was a miracle brah.*

Was his mind joking or serious?

*If you can't trust your mind, who can you trust?*

Ole wondered how he could trust a mind that thinks it's a flying monkey and can't stop believing in pretty women.

The church hall was twice as big as the church. There

was a smorgasbord of hot dishes and desserts waiting. This took Oliver's mind off his mind. Lacey was talking story but either the captain was fading in and out of focus or he was evaporating before Oliver's eyes. He was there one fuzzy moment and gone the next. Ole could still hear Lacey's voice.

"Here's a plate and a fork, help yourself."

"Do they serve this much food every Sunday?" He asked trying to make the small talk last forever.

"Uh huh, it's kind of a weekend potluck club that also prays and does community outreach." Lacey smiled at Oliver. He lowered his eyes to the large tray of Chow Fun noodles. Lacey spoke again. "We like to be reminded of forgiveness, mercy and compassion at least once a week."

Oliver filled his plate, pushing it down the table with his right hand. His left side was still sore.

*Why the lame arm brah? And why can't you find happiness like the captain and Lacey?*

Ole had no good answers for his brain. In fact, he seemed to be slipping into a trance, mesmerized by Lacey's voice. It was an underwater feeling that he couldn't resist, had he wanted to. He hovered over a green carpet of coral reefs almost swimming alongside Lacey and sat down next to her at a round table. He looked at his fork, but hungry as he was, He couldn't seem to touch his food. Lacey took his sore left hand and held it.

"How's your arm?" She said, giving him a look of such concern, it made him tremble. "I'm praying you'll be all better soon. You made it to church today."

She moved her chair closer, leaned over and gave Ole a soft kiss on the cheek. Oliver's face flamed a blush bright as a sunburn. He looked around to see if the captain was watching. Billy was nowhere in the hall. He looked over his shoulders for monkey wings. No wings, but before he could look back at Lacey, he was shocked to see a shark's dorsal fin rise from the center of his back.

Lacey was still smiling at him, the food smelled wonderful, but where his arms or hands used to be there were two pectoral fins. Above him a Barracuda swam past chasing a school of yellow tangs. Ole turned his big head and with a few quick swings of his tail he caught that Barracuda in his teeth. *Now you're a shark? Gimme some air brah.* His mind tries to hang on, but swallowing a live Barracuda is not an easy or pleasant task for the mind of a chemistry teacher. His shark teeth held on, but his brain let go. The spirit world gathered up what was left of him and once again he was out of one body and swimming in another.

## 51 Butterflies

When Oliver came to, he was sitting on the church lawn with his back against a wall outside the Men's room. He was shaken, but no longer swimming like a shark.

*Brah, you need a psychiatrist at any price.*

For the umpteenth time this morning he ignored that wise voice in his forehead. Right in front of him, lying upside down in the grass was one sandal, a leather one this time. Above that lost slippa was a twisting column of Monarch butterflies. Since he was thinking church stuff, he thought of that pillar of salt story. But these butterflies were a pillar of water-color brush-strokes; a moving collage of orange wings in the air. They looked real, but Ole's mind was shaky-unreliable today. He shut his eyes to re-boot his vision. He knew he was sitting on solid ground, not chewing on live Barracuda. He kept his eyes shut. He was hyperventilating. His pulse beating a war-chant in his ears.

When he did open his eyes, the orange butterflies were still there. They were floating around a bush of small white flowers. The calming effect was immediate; as if he'd just been shot by a zoo dart packed with shark tranquilizer. Ole's arm no longer hurt. He took a long yoga breath then exhaled to the count of eight while trying to count butterflies. There were too many of them, all fluttering too fast in slow motion. He crawled across the lawn for a closer look. The Monarchs were landing on milkweed flowers that looked like tiny white and purple crowns. Under the bush was another lone sandal. Of course, this one didn't match the leather one in the short grass.

Oliver knew a bit about botany and biology as well as chemistry. After the caterpillars eat every leaf off the Crown Flower bush, they crawl to nearby trees and buildings and hang upside down like miniature bats. Every third grader knows what comes next. But most people think that inside the chrysalis the caterpillar grows some wings and becomes a butterfly. No, that's too simple for Mother Nature. The caterpillar's body completely dissolves. It turns into white goo. No blueprint of a caterpillar is left over or necessary. Oliver couldn't remember what the goo was called; it was the stuff of ectoplasm. The caterpillar reforms itself with it's million-year morphogenesis experience and becomes a totally new creature. When its internal oven timer starts to buzz, the butterfly breaks out of its green windbreaker of magic and stays upside down until it opens and dries its beautiful new wings for a while. Then, after a few yoga stretches, it realizes what wings can do and bravely let's go, head first into its new life.

To its own amazement it no longer must crawl to work every day. It can fly! It doesn't have to chew tough sappy green-leaf veggies. This new creature drinks, 'born again' flower nectar and travels upon the Spirit wind like a reincarnated, eternal, Share of Soul should. With that fresh-start attitude that all creatures should have on their way to Nirvana.

*Hmmm, you think you're so smart, don't you?*

*Hey this is science fact, it's an observable and an esoteric lesson of amazing beauty that makes more sense than monkeys being tortured by other monkeys in the name of religion.*

Ole felt a prayer rising to his lips, "Oh Holy Spirit Wind of the Good and Divine, please lift Desiree out of her lying madness. Blow her down the streets of Oakland to a psychiatrist's office. Open the door and push her in. Turn her into goo and make her a whole new creature. Make her well, Oh and make her forget my phone number forever and ever, world without end. Amen."

It sounded like a prayer. *Yes, it was a prayer.* He'd done it. He prayed and not for himself, but for Desiree. Ole looked up to see the Monarch butterflies forming a wide arch over him like the entrance to a grotto. Ole knelt there painted into the scene like a saint in a Renaissance masterpiece. The Holy Wind dropped a misty rain of botanical baptism or maybe it was butterfly pee. No matter, this was truly a magic, Maui moment. Promise to mom fulfilled, he tried to think of one more prayer before the spell wore off. "As for me, Oh Holy Spirit, sail me home to the... me... I use to be. Amen."

## 52 The Gardener

An old man came pushing a wheelbarrow around the corner of the church hall. He saw Ole kneeling by the Crown flower bushes. Realizing he'd already interrupted a prayer session, he offered a friendly smile. This sent drops of sweat and-red dirt running down his chin. Oliver broke the silence.

"Hello"

"Butterfly worship?" The gardener asked.

Oliver was too pleased with himself to be embarrassed. Mom would be proud.

"Yeah, they're amazing, right?" Ole answered.

"For sure" the gardener agreed. "They're God's best lesson on how things can change. I saw you in church this morning."

"Yah, I was in the back…" recognition came suddenly. "You're the priest here... and the gardener?"

"Minister, not what some call a priest I'm Kahu at this church. Kahu Tama, ordained gardener." he added, offering a hand to shake.

"I'm Oliver, Oliver Gold." Ole stood and shook the gardener's wet, gloved hand.

"Oliver…? I... ah... I've heard you playing music at the Pioneer Inn. I liked it, especially the penny whistle and the old sailor's concertina."

"Thanks, I write most of the music I play."

"I thought so, it's passionate. I also write music, mostly for Sunday school."

Kahu Tama got a more serious look on his weathered face. "What's the matter my friend?"

"Matter?"

"You're kneeling out here in the rain by some bushes.

What's the matter, son?"

How could he explain becoming a flying monkey and landing on the roof of the church? Or arguing with two, sometimes three voices in his head or his left arm which looked normal, but felt broken? He decided to keep it simple.

"I'm just looking for some answers, father."

"Call me Tama. Maybe I can help."

"Okay Tama. God seems to be playing a clever game of hide and seek with us. Here's God hiding in these butterflies where most people would never think to look for him...or her. Let's start with that. Is God male or female?"

"Figure of traditional speech" said Tama. "Don't get hung out to dry on a pronoun. I hear God in the voices of men and women. I see God in the actions of people. I look for God in all things."

"Tama, you sound like a pantheist."

"I'm a Christian Oliver. This is a Church of Christ. Christ is the answer to your questions."

Ole hesitated, not wanting to sound offensive. "Your Christian God story is so strange, weird even. Why would the creator of the universe force His son to be born down here on this far flung monkey planet to be tortured and nailed on a cross and left to die?" He drew a breath of light rain and added the hard words born from Buckminster, thinking for himself. "I reject a manipulative, punishing, vengeful God like that; no matter how Blaise Pascal bets, no thanks."

Kahu said nothing, so, Ole vented on. "The God I embrace is like the solar-powered wind lifting these butterflies from flower to flower."

"Life isn't just about happy things," Kahu replied.

"I know and I'm not blaming God for all the bad stuff that happens. I just want to send him a text or talk story with him sometimes. But how? How does silent prayer work? Does God have time to listen to me, or to you? Does God even have ears? Or is God just a human invention, an abbreviation of the word Good?"

"I wonder these things myself Ole. Prayer is more than just talking to God from the heart. He may not answer prayer the way you wish. He may not answer at all, but the act of praying is an integral part of what it means to be human. It may not be scientific, but it is historic. For that matter, even prehistoric. Early upright humans buried their dead and built altars. Much later, the Assyrians, Babylonians, Greeks, Romans, even Hawaiians built immense stone temples and heiau's to have a sense of place to pray in. All cultures, world-wide, have aspired to connect with the supernatural by offering prayers. The act of praying has shaped the course of human development, art, architecture, warfare, peace and language. On a personal level it can change you and me."

"Huh?"

"Do you meditate, Oliver?"

"Yes, I do father. Every morning. There are twenty-four hours in a day; my first hour is yoga... most days." He didn't go into the details of this morning's out of body episode on hidden beach.

"When you pray or meditate with gratitude for all that you have, the things you don't have seem to matter less." Kahu Tama said, as he took off his work gloves.

"Yah, but..."

"You marvel at the butterflies and other creatures of the earth, right?

"Uh huh," he nodded and smiled. *Yah, in the pa twenty-four hours, I've been creatures of the earth science fiction: a Godzilla, a flying monkey, lightening bugs, a swarm of gnats, a naked Menehune, a dolphin, a beach ball, and a shark.* Kahu Tama was still talking.

"All that we see around us, is but a small, small fraction of what we discover through microscopes and telescopes..." Tama spoke as softly as the misting rain beading up on his shirt. Ole interrupted him.

"Yes! Tama you said it. When NASA launched the Hubble Telescope into space, oh my stars! That changed my mind about all these earth religions that claim to be the truth. They believe they are soooo right, they'll kill you if you don't agree with them. So many wars and torture taking the name of 'God,' in vain, down through history. These vengeful, self-righteous religions all making bitter enemies with their Jihads and 'pay in advance' indulgences and Purgatory and Zeus throwing thunder bolts and born-again crazies waving their arms around, and Shiva the destroyer and the sad, sad, Wailing Wall, and you know, on and on and on."

"People strive for understanding as best they can..." Tama started, but Ole interrupted him again.

"Allow me to continue, Kahu... "The best we can, is the Hubble Telescope's 'see-for-yourself' gospel. It brings us a new level of truth. One that is measurable, standing on its own merits; no leap of faith necessary. Hubble has shown us photos of so many millions of galaxies, billions of suns that stretch across space in every direction. Hubble Genesis, book one has already packed all of earth's simplistic creation stories and religions into the attic of history like a cardboard box full of old comic books. They'll be treasured by some, for many generations I'm sure, just as I treasure the lessons Jesus and Buddha taught us, but eventually they'll all be as forgotten as the long, gone nightmares of Neanderthals. We will grow up, lose our fear and move on."

"Ole please *try* to accept, as I do, that we understand God as little as a butterfly understands a jet airliner."

"That's what I thought you'd say. You're using your faith for a telescope. One with a rather narrow field of view."

Oliver started walking toward his mud-splattered car. Tama walked with him continuing to explain his version of cosmic things.

"Intelligent Christians today believe that God is still speaking. We don't reject science, we embrace it. We understand that even though we make mistakes, if we strive to be good and pray daily with thankfulness, sometimes we get it right."

"What about Heaven, Hell and Purgatory?"

"These places live in our minds Ole. Hell is not mentioned in the Old Testament. It is mentioned only once in the New Testament. Heaven is spoken of in both books many times. Purgatory is not found in the Bible at all. Each of us has the awesome power to make our lives a living Hell a Purgatory or a Heaven. We are what we think, our thoughts shape our words which shape our actions which shape our lives."

Ole stopped walking. He studied the minister for a long moment.

"No offense intended, but you sound like a Buddhist, Tama."

"None taken. Before he became Buddha, Siddhartha Gautama lived a very austere life. He found his way to compassion and once found, taught it for over fifty years before he died. His teachings are still with us today."

"You make him sound nicer than history says he was." replied Ole. "Siddhartha had been protected from real life, its suffering, old age and dying by his very rich dad. When he realized these things are an essential part of living, he left his dad, abandoned his beautiful new wife and his Infant son, and journeyed out into the world to experience all that painful, suffering junk for himself. He went downhill fast. There is no account that says he ever sent any money home for child support, not one rupee.

"In fact, talk about austere, Kahu Tama, Gau-tama became a homeless guy and lived under a tree on the edge of town. He stayed there for years panhandling, growing his hair and fingernails and meditating on lots of esoteric Zen doodah with some other homeless guys.

"Then one rainy day, he got something that nobody else had ever chanced to get, 'Enlightenment!' It's unclear if he ever took a bath, cut his hair or visited his father, his wife or his now seven-year-old-son. Enlightenment had such an impact on him that he walked away from that old tree and as you mentioned spent the next fifty years teaching compassion for all living things. Most certainly, he was a wonderful influence on the world." Ole took a breath of wind and continued.

"Like Confucius, Siddhartha wasn't taken seriously for a long time. It was over two-hundred years before anyone thought to write down his teachings. Several generations of Buddhas came along, each adding to the dialogue, which became the sacred sutras." Ole paused to breathe again. "All the sutras are wise and peaceful with no mention of torture or crowns of thorns or nailing anybody to a cross."

"You've done your homework," Kahu Tama said. Are you a Buddhist?"

"No, but I am drawn to the meditation and self-realization, Zen part. I still value my childhood love for Jesus. But I'm a retired chemist I look to science for the big answers."

"I believe that the God who created everything we see and don't see, brought Jesus into the world to show all people that the creator loves us," said Tama.

"Yeah, but those Roman monkeys tortured and murdered Him."

"Yes, it's true and people have remembered that moment of guilt and built cathedrals to Christ's memory ever since."

"I thought the whole coming back to life part... I thought *that* was what Christians built a religion on."

"Yes, that's it! The most important part was Christ's resurrection from the dead."

"Uh huh," Ole nodded, but didn't smile.

Did you notice that there is no Jesus nailed to the large cross above the altar in our church?

"Uh huh"

That's how you can tell you are in a protestant church. Only in Catholic churches is Jesus forever nailed to the cross." Tama explained. Ole had never known this; never really thought about it. All this talk of torture was making him feel sad. He'd loved Jesus since he was a child. But Tama was still preaching.

"Jesus gave us the two greatest commandments."

"How about the other ten?"

"Those are important, but those are the old school rules that were necessary for a civil society. They still are. Jesus gave us only two commandments, *'Love God and love your neighbor as you love yourself.'* It's not complicated, yet it's very hard to do, right?"

"Uh huh, especially if your neighbor is your booking agent and she's a lying bitch... Oh! Sorry father."

Kahu Tama didn't seem to mind. They were standing next to Ole's old Cadillac and the misting rain was still not getting them wet. Tama offered another handshake.

"Seek and ye' shall find; you are always welcome here... Oliver."

## 53  Tai Chi Man in Angkor Wat

Lahaina on a Sunday afternoon in late December, is no sleepy village. The sidewalks are worse traffic jams than the street. Ole cruised along Front street at a top speed of one-mile-per-hour in a line of rental cars, but he didn't mind at all; there was plenty to see. Surf schools dot this stretch of waterfront. Ole stopped his Cadillac to allow a line of pretty women carrying surf boards over their heads, to cross in front of his car. This was normal driver etiquette in Lahaina. Plus, it gave him another chance to appreciate the rounded curves of female anatomy. These surfer girls wore rash guards on their torsos, very tight rash guards. Their bare belly buttons and long legs wore tanning oil that glistened in the Hawaiian sunshine like fresh car wax. Ole watched with a sigh as they wiggled their heart-shaped bikini bottoms past his windshield. The optimist inside him imagined one of these precious jewels just might sparkle a wink or a wave at him, but they hurried across the street thinking only of catching waves.

"I love this town," he whispered to himself, feeling momentarily back to normal. Maybe praying had changed him like Kahu said it would. Ole drove along one edge of the banyan forest.

*There's the Pioneer Inn, brah. Remember her room of earthly delights upstairs? How Desi tried to tie you to the bed posts?*

*Hmmmm, there's a memory that doesn't hurt*, he remembered.

Just the thought of his lying booking agent lying naked on her bed, sent his blood rushing to his... monkey wings. They burst out of his shoulders like collision air bags. They were so big they crushed his chest up against the steering wheel, his face mashed flat on the inside of the windshield. He reached over with his good right arm and turned on his car radio.

"Some...where... ova.. da.. rainbow..." a soft voice came to his rescue. The sweet, effortless song from the land of Oz, by Bruddha IZ, untied the mess of knots in Ole's mind and gradually the monkey wings disappeared back into the folds of his imagination. Ole leaned back into the Cadillac's leather and sighed. Prayer wasn't enough. Maybe, he should bake up some oatmeal cookie therapy.

Traffic thinned out. By the time he passed the Bubba Gump's restaurant, he was cruising at almost three-miles-per-hour. Ole felt the warm, holy wind messing with his hair. It was a normal everyday human experience, but Oliver was a spiritual being that treasured every fleeting human experience. A few moments of 'normal' felt great.

He passed the Methodist church, again. The parking lot was full of cars now, The Sunday church people were out on the lawn fellow shipping and *woman*-shipping; everybody drinking coffee and smiling at each other.

*Sorry mom, I'm done with church for today.*

A few blocks north of town he felt a familiar tugging on his mind as he approached the Buddhist temple. He drove in and parked in his usual spot. The large statue of Buddha gazes down on the peaceful park-like grounds. Raked rocks and shade from a large Bodhi tree add to the peacefulness of the Jodo Mission. It's like being in Japan or China. There is no other place like it on the touristy west side of Maui. Every Friday at dawn for over a year now, Oliver had been teaching Qi-gong and Tai-Chi in the shadow of the Buddha. No matter if two people came or twenty, this was his way of giving back some of the kindness he'd received since moving to Hawaii. Volunteering was a life-long habit of his. Back in Seattle it was playing dinner music at rest homes. Oliver still did that some evenings here on Maui. He hoped it made the old folks happy, but underneath all his shiny good intentions, Ole was hoping to meet his next wife. Maybe an Asian Tai chi enthusiast or a cute nurse, caring for the old folks in the rest homes. He missed his ex every day. Tanya had been a very nice person, a beautiful woman and a caring mother until her plot with the evil divorce attorneys to rip his pension and his skin from him, failed.

Ole parked his Cadillac, left the windows down and entered under the Tori gate to the Jodo mission. Thankful for no monkey wings, he folded a couple of dollars into the slot on the large donation box. Buddhists are world-class optimists. The heavy three-foot square steel box bolted to the sidewalk looked big enough to accept a million dollars in small bills and still have room for a bars of gold bullion. The gentle Buddhist monk and his wife at the mission, were supported by donations.

The Buddhist concept of a person shaping his or her own destiny can be found in the teachings of Confucius, Socrates and Jesus as well. It's a personal passage of cause and effect, karma and common sense. Ole was drawn to the humanism of Buddha because he didn't claim to be God. Instead he spoke of compassion right from the start. Buddha was revered as a philosopher like Confucius. Neither of them forced their message on the world at the point of a spear. There is no jealous, 'choose me or die' kind of God in the practice of compassion. That came much later, dressed up in the powerful clothes of 'religion.'

Oliver's favorite spot to practice Tai Chi was a shady spot under the Bodhi tree. However, there was a tall man in flowing white clothes doing Tai Chi in Ole's shady spot this afternoon. The man looked somewhat familiar as he slowly moved from 'pushing clouds' into 'parting the wild pony's mane.' Ole took a seat in the covered gazebo to just watch. He needed a rest. He hadn't slept last night on the hidden beach.

The Tai chi man's relaxed motions flowed gracefully into 'Lifting sky' then, slowly into 'pushing mountains.'

Oliver's vision began to blur as if blinded by white cataracts of snow. This had never happened before, but the day had been so bizarre he remained calm and waited for the storm to pass. It may have been five minutes or more. Time was always confusing, speeding up slowly, slowing down fast and stopping on a dime. He became confused. He thought he heard Lacey's voice calling to him from up in the trees.

The man in white rose up in the air until he was floating three feet above the raked rocks. He moved even slower now into 'archer and bow.' He was encircled in a cloud of mist, or fog, or cotton candy or something. As Ole stared at him, the man turned from 'view the moon' and noticed Ole watching him. Mutual recognition flew across both of their faces like small flocks of rising birds. The man in white was Oliver Gold! He gave himself a knowing smile. It came as a blessing and yet it felt like a warning.

Two days of wings, sharks and Godzilla should have prepared Ole for this. But seeing himself outside himself was a ten-thousand-volt buzz-shock. There he was, his Tai chi self, floating in mid-air in the exact spot where he had practiced his Tai Chi for over a year. Ole could remember a sensation of flying from time to time in that spot while in slow-motion meditation. After such an experience last month, he had written a haiku poem to remember the moment.

*Standing on one breath*
*Parting the wild pony's mane*
*Sweet smell of green hay*

But, seeing himself levitate while sitting in the gazebo gave him a sudden chicken skin rash up and down both wings. He was glowing like a Jack-o-Monkey-Buddha lantern with a look on his face that wasn't enlightenment.

The two of them locked their four eyes for maybe, ten seconds; who knows? No one was counting. Then, Ole turned his eyes away and vise-verse. The Tai chi man morphed down into his fog and became a blue lotus flower floating in a Koi pond that had never been there before. There was a wooden bridge arching gracefully over the pond. On the other side of the bridge was an open garden gate shimmering in a moving archway of Monarch butterflies. This was a path he was meant to follow. Ole crossed the bridge over the blue lotus with a confidence he hadn't had a few minutes ago. He could see past the gate now into the garden beyond. *Is that snow falling on blooming flowers?* He wondered. He heard a viola playing way off somewhere inside the gate. Ole stepped under the fluttering arch of orange butterflies...and into the palatial gardens of the ancient city of Angkor Wat.

*Nothing you do surprises me anymore brah.*

distance. Oliver's feet hurt. He was shivering.

"Why are we meeting like this?" He asked himself.

"You prayed for this, remember? *"As for me Lord, sail me back to the me I used to be. Amen.* I'm here to help," said the Tai chi Oliver.

"Since when did you become my psychiatrist?"

"I'm the only one you can afford, remember? Take it from me, you're messed up brah. I'm trying to reach you from another time and place sort a like a Star Trek episode. Just believe in me. I want to help you."

This reminded Ole of something Ram Dass had said. *"When I am not sure who I am, I serve you. When I know who I am, I am you."*

"Angkor Wat in winter?"

"I've always wanted to see Angkor Wat. What does it matter what time of year? The mind can travel anywhere. Your imagination is the only thing in the universe faster than the speed of light. Like the Moody Blues song, "you could be outside... looking in."

"My feet are freezing. It never snows in Cambodia too close to the equator."

"Quit complaining. We have bigger monkeys to fry."

"I'm listening."

Tai Chi man just stared into Oliver's eyes with a sad look of utter disappointment. Ole wanted to hide away somewhere, but he didn't know his way around Angkor Wat without a map and a snow shovel.

"Are you going to stop being a winged monkey from OZ?" Tai chi asked.

"How do I know? I have no say in the matter. It just happens!"

"Why?"

"Suppose you tell me! You're the one who led me here!" he growled. With those angry words, one monkey wing pushed out from his sore shoulder and Ole fell off his chair from the sudden imbalance.

"Great! Now look what you've done!" He hollered up at himself. He was madder than ever, lying on his face in the impossible cold snow of Angkor Wat. His other monkey wing sprung out of his right shoulder knocking over his chair. He didn't feel the cold any more. He was so mad at himself and at Desiree Scarlioni.

"Maybe anger has something to do with it?" Suggested Tai Chi man.

Oliver stood up on his bow-legged monkey legs and stretched those wings out in a threatening display.

"I want some answers!" He shouted. (Now he's a hopping mad, flying monkey, throwing a tantrum, in a snowstorm, in Angkor Wat.)

"Oh, get over yourself. You're pathetic. What did mom tell you to do?"

"She said to pray… bake and pray. You know mom, she'll forgive anybody for anything and bring them a plate of cookies."

The sweet thoughts of mom and forgiveness made the monkey wings disappear again. He set the chair right side up and sat back down. The man in white across the table was getting harder to see. The snow was swirling in a sudden white out.

"Be patient. It's better to win control over yourself than to rule over whole cities." Tai chi man's voice was heavily muffled by the falling snow.

*Now, you're quoting Proverbs from the Bible to yourself?*

Oliver had read the Old Testament or rather tried to

read it a few times. Proverbs was the only part he wanted to remember. Tai Chi man's voice diminished to a mere whisper.

"Can you forgive Desiree?"

"I tried. I prayed for the Holy Winds of Fate to blow her into a psychiatrist's office."

"Forgive Desiree completely, and I promise I will find you again."

"How brah? I'm as busted up inside today as we were when Tanya divorced us."

The man in white was silent after Ole hit him with that old ice ball. It got so quiet in Angkor Wat he could hear the snowflakes slumping one at a time onto the piled snow on his ears. Tai-chi man spoke.

"We got through that one without becoming a Godzilla. Face it, our life and everyone's life is a dharma drama, brah. Tai chi stood up. "Here's the plan," he said, as he put his arm around Ole's shoulder like a baseball coach. "Go home and get some sleep. Drink plenty of water. Bake some oatmeal cookies, mom's recipe. Meditate. You got all that?"

"Uh huh,"

"You didn't write it down."

"I *am* you, remember. I won't forget.

## 54  Life is But a Dream

Taking his own advice, Ole made it back to his rented room at the Sands of Kahana. He took a quick shower and set a course for his computer desk. He wanted to admire his brilliant equation again and read all those messages from pretty women in far-away countries. When He walked past the super-slumber-conducting-magnet of his bed, his compass went in circles. The desk looked like it was in distant country. He hadn't slept last night while touring Hell, running sixteen miles in the dark at spirit speeds and swimming like a wounded dolphin. The mag-bed welcomed him, holding him firmly as only mother gravity-magnet can. He pushed his pillow under his head thinking of his new Nano-material. He wanted to go through the math again. But his eye doors were rolling down on his brain garage. It was Lyka, not robots that took him by the hand and led him into a dream....

*She walked along the beach with an elegance that made you think she was a visiting princess from Thailand. Lyka held her head high with her long black hair tied in a pony tail. She was bare shoulders, yellow-bikini, adorable. All ninety-five pounds of her. Ole watched her go walking by. Of course, Carlos Jobim came to mind. "Tall and tan and..." she was just like the song. Especially the sad part about how she just went walking by and didn't see Oliver balanced on one hand, muscles tensed, his legs straight up in the air as he showed off for her.*

*It made Ole ache to see Lyka's companion jogging along behind her. He was way-fat, real old, wearing a ten-gallon Texas cowboy hat and trying his best to look athletic. He waggled along behind her like a wheel out of alignment. Lyka paused long enough for him to catch up, then reached out and took his hand. She leaned her lovely body into his flabby white sweaty shoulder with the Mick Jagger tongue tattoo. They strolled along the sand like one of those romantic Hawaiian post cards. This one might be titled, "If This Guy Can… Why You No Can?"*

It was a short unhappy dream. In his final REM moments, he lowered himself down on the sand from his one-arm show-off handstand. Lyka and her fat boyfriend were gone.

*Thought that was your sore arm brah.*

*Yah, what's with that sore arm anyway?*

Ole woke himself up rubbing his left arm mumbling, "no clue brah...no clue."

Ole's pillow was on the bed, he was on the floor.

"What's that terrible smell?" He grumbled.

*It's you Romeo, go take a shower,* one of the voices in his head complained.

"I just took a shower"

*Hana hou shower, brah.* (take another one)

## 55 Gonna Need Money

After his second shower of the day, Ole noticed his bedside alarm clock facing off at him like a hockey goalie, mean and toothless.

"Liar," Ole accused it.

*It might be telling the truth brah, five o' clock? You slept all afternoon?*

"No way." He went to the living room to see if old Sol was on his way to sunset. It was dark in the kitchen, dark outside. It must be five in the morning!

*You slept all day and most of a night?*

This had never happened before, but what was worse, Ole had fallen in love again with a ninety-five-pound Filapina doll on a beach in a dream, and she was with some fat guy.

*Y'er good at dreaming about women brah. When you gonna catch one?* Sarcasm was back in town itching for another fight.

Ole's thoughts were darker than the kitchen this morning. So, he opened the fridge and saw the light. No... not... *'the light'...* just the refrigerator light, showing fresh carrots, boxes of cereal, precious milk, bread, crackers, three kinds of cheese and a slice of watermelon. Trouble was, none of it was his. He hardly paused a beat, eating everything in sight, breaking cardinal rule number one, important to all room-mates: "Do Not Eat Other People's Food."

His room-mates were a happily married couple. They liked him and they liked the money he paid them to live in their second bedroom. It helped pay down their mortgage. *They shared their home with him; they'd understand,* he told himself as he devoured the last of the watermelon. Certainly, Art and Sandy would not want him to perish in the middle of the night in the middle of their kitchen. Imagine *those* headlines.

"Local Man Starves to Death in Deluxe Maui Condo." 'The deceased has been identified as beloved local musician, Oliver Gold. Authorities are investigating. He may have been held prisoner, neglected for months. His room-mates have been arrested pending further investigation.'

There was one leg of celery and half a red onion left in the crisper when Ole finally stopped eating. Of course, guilt set in. He thought of his shirt with the Nike slogan, 'Just Do It.'

*Yah brah, 'just do it.' The next part of Nike's slogan should read, 'you can apologize later.'*

At seven o'clock that morning, he made fresh coffee something he'd never done before. He wasn't a coffee drinker even after living in Seattle where a Starbucks lives on every corner and two more are being built in the middle of every block. His room-mates wandered out of their bedroom when the rich aroma woke up them up. He poured them a cup and offered to take them to breakfast. His room-mates were delighted.

At the resort café, over pancakes and eggs, he confessed to eating all their food and promised he was on his way to the Times grocery store.

"Make a shopping list and I'll be back in an hour."

They did. On his way to the car, he stopped by the front desk and bought a newspaper. He was gonna need more money to get his new Nano-fiber idea into the patent office. So, that meant finding a *real* job. He'd keep his music mistress by night and find a good paying job by day. Ole sat down in a lounge chair in the no-windows or doors front lobby of the Sands and opened the paper to the classifieds.

Front Desk Help Wanted / Kapalua

Front Desk Manager Wanted / Hyatt

Front Desk Manager Wanted / Marriot

Front Desk Help Wanted / Ritz Carlton

There were a lot of these ads. The requirements were all the same. 'Experienced professionals needed. Some college helpful. Must be highly skilled on computers, type seventy-five words per minute, experience necessary with Quick Books and spread sheets. You are friendly enough to welcome and register guests who are arriving late after a no-frills, no sleep, no movie, seven-thousand-mile flight in a hard-cushioned, narrow airline seat. Then, given the wrong rental car, stuck in traffic, stalled by crowds at Costco, stuck in traffic again and just want to vent at you at the front desk. You must be available to work nights, weekends and holidays. Medical coverage is included with a high-co-pay. Employee parking is available for a small monthly fee. Starting pay is ten-dollars per hour.'

*Ten-bucks an hour? No wonder they can't find anyone with all those skills willing to work nights and weekends for dirt wages.*

There weren't many help-wanted ads. He saw twenty ads for 'Housekeeper Wanted.' The pay was better, nineteen-dollars per hour.

*Too much work brah. You don't even make your own bed. Think you could make fifty beds nice and neat, then clean fifty bathrooms? Keep reading.*

That was about it. There was a large block ad at the bottom of the page with four County Jobs open, all in the same department.

WASTE-WATER TREATMENT MANAGERS WANTEDNEEDED IMMEDIATELY, Will train the right person. Monthly salary starts at $5800.00 plus full benefits. HIRING NOW. APPLY IN PERSON.

*That's thirteen-hundred-bucks a week brah*

Somehow, Ole knew that those guys earned that kind of money; fixing and cleaning *those* stinking, gooey pipes and pumps. Just driving past on the highway smelled awful. He left the newspaper in the lobby for someone else to read and headed for his car.

He followed a flagstone path alongside a Koi pond with olive trees and papyrus reeds shading it. His walk curved past a putting green and some barbeque grills. A short cut to his car took him through the Vacation Club Room. The tables in here were piled high with purple orchids. Lani the owner services manager was teaching a group of time-share owners how to make flower lei.

"Hi Lani," he greeted her like always. He'd been living in this building for over a year and knew almost everyone who worked at the resort.

"I need to see you," it was more of an order than an invitation.

"Oh... kay" He said, following her into her office. She'd never said so many words to him. He'd never been in her office. She closed the door and sat down behind her desk.

"Please sit down," she politely commanded.

"We have a job opening here in owner services. She wrote a dollars-per-hour number on a piece of paper and handed it across her desk for him to read. He read it and left it lay.

"Are you interested?"

"What would I be doing?"

"Teaching orchid and ti-leaf lei making and bracelet making with hala leaves. You would help with our social events. I'm open to other guest activities that you may come up with."

"I don't want a full-time job. I just ran away from the 'nine to five' work-release-camp."

"This job comes with holiday and vacation pay plus, sick leave coverage and a 401k."

"I'll think about it Lani, but probably, no. I'm enjoying my retirement."

"The job also provides full medical, dental, and vision coverage and thirty-thousand in life insurance."

*Medical insurance was a luxury he had not been able to afford. He knew he was taking his chances without it, especially at his age. His tongue worried that one loose tooth back and forth in his lower left jaw. It hurt like it was gonna need some expensive work soon. His left shoulder and arm needed an x-ray...hmmm.*

*Ask her if psychiatric care is included.* His forehead has had enough monkey-winging around.

Ole didn't want to ask that question in a job interview. A regular paycheck was what he had just wished for this morning. Here it was right on the desk in front of him. He picked up the pala-pala and read it again. It wasn't what house-keeping paid, but it was a lot better than front desk.

"No nights or weekends?"

"Days, Monday to Friday eight to five."

"Can I teach Tai chi and give ukulele lessons?"

"That would be great! We're looking for new activities. Maybe I can find enough money in the budget to buy a few ukuleles. Would five be enough?"

"When do I start?"

"Take this form to this address, get a drug test, then we'll talk about it."

"Okay Lani, thanks."

*He hadn't smoked grass in thirty some years; a drug test would be no problem.*

*Thirty-seven...*

He'd enjoyed smoking grass. It made playing the guitar a multimedia event. The music had color, and flavor as well as a richer sound. He'd still be rolling joints today, except asthma attacks had nearly killed him in college. So, he'd set his lungs free with daily yoga. Cause and effect; thirty-seven years later, he could still breathe, still pass a drug test and his lungs weren't all gunked up with cannabis tar.

## 56  A Prayer for a Good Wife

Oliver had only worked for Lani one month when his co-worker Joy, passed him a folded note. It wasn't a personal message. It was a one-page prayer.

**Prayer for a Good Wife:**

Oh Lord, please send _____ (write your name here) a good wife. One who will love, honor and trust in him. A wife that will be kind and true to him, and take good care of him all the days of his life.

I _____ (write your name here) promise you, Oh Lord, that I will be kind to her, love, respect and honor her. I will be true to her all the days of my life. May our marriage be long and blessed. Thank you, Jesus. Amen.

_____ (Sign your full name here)

Dated _____ 20__.

Ole read the note in the spirit it was given, and thanked Joy. They had talked about each other's relationships as co-workers tend to do. She'd been married to her high school sweet heart for thirty years and they were still happy with each other. Joy knew Ole wanted to be married again. He folded the note and kept it with him all day. At lunch time, when he had a moment and a pen, he wrote his name on each of those blank lines. Then signed and dated it. That night he read it again before bed. When he woke up in the night to pee, he read it again.

Oliver remembered how Sister Mary Magdalene had taught him in first grade that his heart was like a dirty little cottage in the woods. So, every time he read the Good Wife prayer, Ole cleaned his heart's cottage. He swept out the trash, put flowers on the table, made tea and invited Jesus to come in and bring a new wife for Ole along with him. He made sure to add a third chair at the table and one more teacup.

Ole read that prayer eight or ten times a day. After his trouble with Tanya, Suki and Desiree, he'd wear a lei of garlic cloves around his neck to repel future vamps, users and crazies. But that was playing defense. This prayer was an 'attraction' kind of magic. He'd learned that 'secret' long ago. Think and meditate on what you want out of life and it will be yours. Of course, it wasn't that simple. You had to work for it. Ole the believer, *believed* in this kind of attraction mantra. Every time he prayed the Good Wife prayer, the 'finder' on the Ouija board in his mind swung over each letter of a woman's name spelling out: L... a... c... e... so, he would sweep the finder counter-clockwise and start over. Only then, did it spell out L... y... k... a.

## 57 Advice He Didn't Want

Sunsets in Hawaii are a nightly celebration of another day you somehow managed to afford living in Hawaii. Neighbors gather to watch the star of our galaxy torch the western sky, singe the horizon and make a watercolor mess all over the ocean. This was the high point of Hawaii life for residents and tourists alike.

One evening at the Valley Isle Resort, Ole was visiting with his neighbors. The sunset had been a 5.0 on the less than magnificent scale. It was ten shades of dismal gray with just a few hundred-mile long magnificent sweeps of curling ribbons of pink light streaking out from where the sun had fallen over the edge of the world. The blowing of the conch was over and almost everyone had gone back to their million-dollar condos.

Jack and Sally were still pouring themselves glasses of wine from a bamboo carafe. Ole liked these nights on a beach with friends. Nights without naked ghosts or swarms of gnats. He missed singing with Captain Billy and Lacey this evening. They were a usual part of the sun down congregation. He especially wanted to see Lacey again.

*Dude!*

Ole liked Jack and Sally. They'd spent a lot of nights in rambling conversations while watching the stars come out one at a time. Beach time is a perfect example of Time slowing down fast. Jack and Sally were both stars. They had appeared as extras in over three-hundred movies and TV shows.

"The international Space Station is supposed to be visible tonight," Jack said.

There was a long silence; Sally and Oliver considered this.

"What time?" Ole asked.

"I can't remember," said Jack.

The conversations of senior citizens are always like this. It's challenging.

"9:17" said Sally, "saw it on AOL this morning."

"What time is it now," Ole asked?

"Time for another carafe of wine." Jack got up and walked away.

"Sally, can I ask your opinion about something kind a personal."

"Sure,"

"I'm thinking of flying to the Philippines to meet a lady, maybe even marry her."

"How old is she?"

"She's twenty-six,"

"How old are you?"

"Fifty-five,"

"There's your answer. She just wants to be an American citizen. You'd spend a lot of money to bring her to the USA. She'll clean out your checking account and be gone as soon as she gets her Green Card. Happens all the time. I don' want you to get hurt again." Sally knew about... the others.

The space station came across the dark sky from north to south. It was moving fast and reflecting sunlight brighter than any satellite they had ever seen. In thirty-seconds it was gone.

"She might just be looking for a good husband."

"You think?"

Jack came back with another carafe of California Chablis.

"You missed it," said Sally.

"Missed what?"

"The Space station went by and the astronauts all waved, but you missed it."

"More wine my dear?"

"Of course, darling, thank you.

## 58  Advice from Jens

The next day, Ole called an old sailing buddy in Seattle.

"Hey Jens, it's Oliver Gold. How hard'z it raining up there today?"

"Gold-digger! Hey, it's not raining."

"What? You're lying right?"

"No, I'm not. It's snowing! Ha, ha, ha." His laugh sounded insincere, like he wasn't too happy about it.

"What's with you Gold? Haven't heard from you since you and Tanya split the main sheet."

"Yah well, I'm bad at all that social media face book stuff. You still racing your boat?"

"Sure, 'Slippery Sue' is my concubine on the water you know that."

Jens was one of the meanest attorneys in Ballard. Suing people was how he could afford the fasted J-boat in the Wednesday night regattas. No matter, Ole hadn't called to talk sailboats.

"Jens, you married a Filipina girl, right?"

"I'm on my third one, why?"

"I was trying to remember how that all went down. I'm thinking of flying to the Philippines to meet a lady. Maybe get married again."

"It's a good thing you called me at home, on a Saturday, or I'd have to charge you two-hundred-bucks an hour for marriage counseling. Ha, ha, ha."

His laughter still sounded artificial. Ole never really liked the guy, he was a terrible yacht club commodore, but he was the only person he knew who had married a Filipina. He said nothing.

"Well Gold, I never liked you much. You were a lousy yacht club commodore, but a great sailing competitor. I think you and your crew on 'Amazing Grace' almost beat me across the finish line one night. That would have been 'amazing' all right! Ha, ha, ha, but it never happened did it? Ha, ha, ha..."

"Well, so long Jens, enjoy the snow."

"Oh Gold, don't let my bluster spill y' er wind. I should warn you about Filipinas. The first one I married was nineteen. She was a living doll from Manila. I met her there in a bar. She was oh so very nice to me, until she got to the states and got her Green Card. Then she took all the money we had in our checking account about ten grand and ran off with a waiter from Anthony's Restaurant. Last time I saw her was in divorce court. She made out like the rippin' pirate that she was.

Two years later, I met a twenty-year old from Cebu. Online dating this time. After a year of immigration roadblocks, she got her papers all stamped and came to Seattle on a fiancé visa. We married and we were happy for about three years. Then, just like the first one. she split after withdrawing all our money from our checking account. I made sure we kept less than two-grand in checking after that first little bitch cleaned me out. But the second one also won big in divorce court, which really pissed me off because I'm an attorney, a damn good one."

"Whoa Jens, that's awful." Ole pretended to sympathize. But this sort of thing couldn't have happened to more deserving guy, twice. Oliver was smiling on the Hawaii side of the phone call. Jens plunged on.

"Now this third one, she's a keeper. We met online. She's thirty-six, from northern Luzon. We've been married five years. She takes good care of me and the house. She appreciates the lifestyle I provide for her. She can't cook, but who cares? I've lost weight and she's good in bed. Ha, ha, ha."

"So, chances are one in three, I may find a good one?"

"More like one in ten, Gold. I got lucky… finally. The third times a charm they say, yah?"

"Yeah. Well thanks for the scary stories Jens. I needed to hear the dark side of this idea."

"Sure, Gold. Maybe you'll win this one. Ha, ha, ha."

## 59 Mom's Advice

Oliver read the 'Book of Proverbs' often. It was right up there on his best reads list with 'Everything I need to know I learned in Kindergarten.' If he didn't find the answer in those two books Ole would call his mom. Ole was her 'Runaway Bunny,' from a kid's book he used to read to his own children. Oliver had runaway to Hawaii, but mom knew where to find him.

"Hi mom,"

"Hi dear, how are you? How's your arm?"

He could not remember mentioning his sore arm to her but he answered honestly

"Still hurts, but I think it's getting better. How are you and dad?"

"Dad's pheasant hunting with his buddy, Ted May. You remember Ted?"

"Sure mom. Hey, I want to ask your opinion on something. I'm thinking about going to the Philippines to meet a lady. Maybe, marry her."

"Is this what you really want?"

"I think so...yes."

"I've heard stories about those foreign brides. I'm worried that you may be spending your money just to get your heart broken. Have you prayed about it?"

He told her about the Good Wife prayer. "...ten times a day mom."

"So, what would Jesus do?"

"Come on mom. Jesus never got married."

"We don't know that for certain, do we? There's that whole Mary Magdalene controversy. I saw a documentary about it on Netflix and..."

"Mom I think what I'll do...is fly over there and meet her."

"So why call me?"

"So, you could talk me out of it?"

"Son, if you prayed on it that much, you've made the right decision."

"Thanks Mom. Wish I could be eating pheasant with you tonight."

"It may be mac and cheese if they don't bring home some birds.

"I'm booking a flight to Leyte, mom... Love you, bye."

"Keep praying son, love you, gotta go!" And she was gone.

## 60  A New Place to Live

Art and Sandy were not as excited as Ole about Lyka moving in to their second bedroom at the Sands. They said they were sorry to say it, but, "no." So, Ole began searching the classifieds and craigslist for an apartment. West Maui, San Francisco, and New York City are the most expensive places in the USA to rent an apartment. He figured that a fiancé visa would take a few months, so he put a message out on the 'coconut wireless,' asking friends to let him know if a place became available.

On a hot Sunday morning in February, Ole was in his Caddy heading for surf waves rumored to be kickin' along the west Maui coast. When he passed the Cannery Mall he saw the fluttering flags and banners of what looked like a Barnum and Bailey Circus. He slowed down to read the first banner:

Open House Today / Two-Bedroom Condo $799,000
One-Thousand Down / Easy Monthly Payments

One-thousand down? Since he'd landed a forty-hour a week job he had that much in his savings at Bank of Hawaii. A two-bedroom condo would be great. Especially, if he could bring Lyka to Maui on a fiancé visa. He turned in at the balloon-lined driveway and parked in front of the open-house unit for sale. More red helium balloons were flying from the 'For Sale' sign stuck in the front yard. Fresh sod covered a lawn five feet by two feet under the front windows of the new building.

*You could mow that with a pair of scissors, brah.*

The real estate agent that met him at the door, was an anemic looking man named, 'Rob' something. He spoke kindly and had a genuine smile. Ole felt he could believe whatever Rob said.

*Believing in people is your best problem, remember the beautician?*

Rob showed Ole through the twelve-hundred square foot, professionally furnished, 'staged' model condo.

"This is amazing," Ole said it out loud, then caught himself. He should be playing his cards like any prospective buyer, with vague indifference. He put on his Blackjack face.

"Everyone who sees this great condo says that. This is the last two bedroom we have left. There is a three-bedroom still available in the next building. It has a garage. We sold the rest of the two-bedroom units in the first thirty days."

"Would you take five-hundred thousand for this orphan?" Ole asked.

"Do you have it with you?" Rob must have seen Ole's twenty-year-old Cadillac.

"No,"

"Neither does anyone else. That's why the low-down payment. Appliances included, but not the furniture. Just sign over a check and fill out a standard mortgage application. No credit-check necessary. We finance in house. No hidden fees, everything is clearly typed out on this purchase agreement right here." Rob pointed to the pala-pala papers stacked neatly on the expensive-looking granite kitchen counter. "You could move in to your own home on Maui this afternoon."

"How much would the monthly payment be?"

Rob took up the stack of paper and read, "Thirty-year mortgage...thirty-seven hundred per month...give or take a hundred, plus the maintenance fees. No property taxes the first year." Rob smiled his honest-looking smile. Oliver wanted to be his friend.

"Forty-year mortgage...only nineteen hundred and twenty-six bucks."

"Forty-year mortgage?"

"We make owning a home easier than ever before...here's a pen, sign here, here and here, date it, hand over a thousand bucks, and you've got a home on Maui."

Ole kept his hands in his pockets. "I'll sleep on it. Thanks Rob. Goin' surfin' while the waves are da kine,' 'loha."

*Lyka would like this place, brah.*

"Yah, but forty years is a big commitment." He was talking to himself again.

*So is marriage.*

## 61 Hawaiian Mortgage Devils

There's a hidden room behind a false wall at the Maui Escrow office in Kahului. On the business side, everything seems normal. There are first-time home buyers, real estate agents wearing Tommy Bahama shirts, escrow professionals, pretty secretaries with white cups of coffee, business as usual.

But, if for some reason you chance to rest against the false wall and flatten your ear against its surface, you would hear a hundred years of over-burdened souls weeping in despair. Their anguish began right there on the business side, scrawling their signatures on the bottom lines of never-ending mortgages. Of course, no one ever leaned against that wall or laid an ear upon it. So, on the other side, devilish Gage and his partner in crime, Uncle Mort, went undetected for decades. You see Hell hath many branch offices and Maui Escrow was the Kahului branch of Satan's lucrative Hawaiian-mortgage trap line.

Mort was the branch manager, unseen and deeply embedded in the minds of his employees. They couldn't possibly have suspected that there were devils in their building or their minds. None of the escrow agents had ever leaned on that wall. All they knew was they were making a ton of money locking people into thirty- and forty-year mortgages they couldn't possibly afford, and would never pay off. It was a kick.

Mort was a famous old demon, once beloved by God. Back then, everyone deferred to him as 'Mortozolla the Brave,' wingman of the most-favored angel, 'Gabriel the Good.' This was way back before the 'Big Mis-understanding. You see Mortozolla flew around with a young hotshot named Lucifer. When the charismatic Lucifer challenged the Chairman of the Board for the throne, Morto saw a ground-floor opportunity for advancement with Lucky Luci and lost his rank and reputation as one of the good guys. He was thrown out of Heaven with the rest of the angel trash and left to his own devices. Mort did okay on his own for millennia, but when he met Gage about a hundred years ago, they put their talents together and things got a lot more fun.

One afternoon behind the wall, Mort and Gage were just messing around lighting cave bats on fire and stepping on cockroaches. Flames burned up through cracks in the rocky floor. There was no such thing as air-conditioning on that side of the wall. During business hours long coffin-like file drawers slid in and out of the Hellish cave and in and out of the business side of Maui Escrow. This was normal. The drawers groaned open and shut a dozen times a day as new purchase contracts were signed in indelible ink. Then, they were filed in those long drawers and slid through the wall to the dark side where they were sealed for all time.

On this humdrum afternoon, one of the heaviest over-stuffed drawers slid away with more than the usual groan. Halfway through the wall the drawer fell off its guides and came to an ear-piercing stop. Mort and Gage looked at each other in shock. This had never happened before. They rushed to lift the heavy file drawer back on its runners. Mort rolled it back and forth a few times, then pulled it into his cave with a 'SLAM-BOOM!' However, just a few seconds too late. Oliver Gold heard the drawer screech to a stop as it fell off its rails. Black smoke came curling out of the open drawer; a lot of smoke. It stank something awful, like somebody was singeing the hair off small animals.

Ole had been about to sign a forty-year contract for an over-priced condominium he'd seen in Lahaina a week ago. He set the pen down. The 'closer' blinked his eyes in surprise at the smoke and at the client who had not yet signed on the bottom line. While the closer ran around waving a sheaf of documents to clear the air, Oliver walked cautiously to the wall of file cabinets.

He sniffed along the edge of the file cabinets and felt along the wall with his hands. It was hot to the touch. He thought he heard crying, so he pressed his ear against the wall. His face went white as chalk and he jumped back rubbing his burnt ear. Painful mortgaged voices echoed in his mind, stabbing his emotions like the Roman Senate knifing Julius Caesar.

Oliver headed for the door. The closer ran after him. Once outside, Ole sprinted for his car and sped out of the parking lot onto Pu'unene Street. The 'closer' was still waving the contract in his hand and shouting,

"What about the condo?"

All he got in reply were screeching tires.

From behind the wall Mort and Gage knew what happened. They'd seen it all on devil-vision broadband.

"We gotta find that guy now!" Mort shouted. Gage had already waved open a hole in the cave's ceiling. He shot up like a guided missile. Mort launched right behind him.

Oliver swerved through traffic pushing his twenty-year-old Cadillac faster than ever before. The voices of suffering mortgage holders were still wailing in his ears. It wasn't just the weeping. He felt the crushing weight of their mortgages and angry echoes of entrapment from endless re-financing scams that would keep them in debt forever.

When Ole looked in his rear-view mirror, he saw nothing in the backseat; but there were two things, two very ugly things. Mort and Gage were lounged there enjoying the soft leather and ice-cold air-conditioning. Oliver heard new voices in his head as he sped along the highway.

*Where you going? You want that condo. Turn around. Go back and buy the condo.* Ole shook his head and kept driving.

*Go back and sign the contract.*

Oliver tried not to listen. He turned on the radio. It played for a half a beat and then, green smoke came poofing out of the cassette slot.

*Turn the car around and go sign the contract! You want that condo! Only a thousand dollars down and easy monthly payments.*

Ole stomped hard on the gas pedal and the big Cadillac leaped into passing gear. He was over the speed limit by three-hundred-bucks in potential fines.

*Easy monthly payments? Hah!* This voice in his head sounded like his own struggling for air. *Nineteen-hundred and twenty-six-dollars a month, mortgage, interest plus maintenance fees... plus utilities and taxes! I'd have to either quit buying groceries or get a real job. One that pays more than the Sands of Kahana. What was I thinking?*

Slowing to fifty, he slammed on the brakes, cranked the wheel left and spun a Hawaii-5-0, one-eighty in front of oncoming cars.

*That's more like it.* One of the strange voices approved. *Let's go buy that condo!*

But Oliver didn't go back. He sped off onto a side street and skidded to a stop in front of Carl's Jr. Burgers. He jumped out of his car frantically looking this way and that for somewhere to escape the voices. He took off running and circled the restaurant three times. He stopped and ran in the opposite direction around the restaurant three more times. This seemed to clear his thoughts. He sat on a curb under some palm trees and tried to think. To his dismay, it hurt to think. It hurt because Mort and Gage had slipped into his mind like two brain worms and were poking their pitchforks into anything they could find, related to the words, *suspicious, smoking file drawers, weeping souls, mortgages.*

*What the Hell?* Ole rubbed his forehead. *Ouch that hurts! Where am I?* His mind was all forked up. *Ooo, that hurts!*

He hadn't been drinking yet today, so this headache surprised him.

*Maybe y'er just getting f'ergetful, old man. Y'er age is slowin' ya down.* He wasn't sure where that came from. It didn't sound like one of *his* inner voices. *Why don't you just kill y'er self and get it over with?* The voice whispered seductively, sounding dead serious.

"What?" Ole shouted! He jumped up off the curb. He'd never do such a thing; never considered such a thing. He shook his head like he was trying to shake water out of his ears. Mort and Gage were tossed side to side, but kept sticking their pitchforks this way and that just for the Hell of it. When the shaking stopped, they slipped out of Oliver's ears and roosted in a palm tree over his head, to keep an eye on him. Oliver sat back down, crying like a baby.

"That was fun," Mort snickered.

"You blew it big shot," scoffed Gage. "You used to be awesome at this stuff."

"Shut y'er muggly-ug! So what, he neva' sign the mortgage? I almost got his pathetic little soul with that 'why not kill y'er self-stuff'."

"You're pathetic, Mort. Really losing it. You bump up against a simple musician with a few shreds of, 'free-will' left, and you cave in. Who are you, and what the devil have you done with my bad-ass partner?"

The scolding by his junior associate made Mort so red-hot mad he accidentally lit the top of the palm tree on fire. Neither demon moved; they were used to flames flaring up around them. In the intense heat however, small coconuts in the top of the tree, began to explode, popping like corn. That drew Oliver's attention and he looked up just as a flaming coconut fell straight down, hitting him right between his eyes, a bindi bulls-eye.

"Nice shot," Gage had to admit, despite his anger.

"Let's go. This guy is wiped," Mort snorted, and like two sparks snapping out of a campfire, they were gone.

********

Later, driving back into Lahaina and rubbing the mysterious bruise on his burnt forehead, Oliver saw colorful circus flags along the side of the road leading to a 'Condo For-Sale' banner. He slowed down to read the next sign:

Open House Today / Two-Bedroom Condo $799,000
One-Thousand Down / Easy Monthly Payments

He had that much in his savings account at Bank of Hawaii. Ole flipped on his right turn signal intending to check it out. But just as he was about to turn in the driveway, his cassette player started working again.

"Lucky-ee come Maui-ee, lucky-ee girl and boy, rainbows, bea-ches... Maui no'ka 'oi..." It was a tape of his own songs in fact, one of his favorites. He whistled along with the happy tune trying to remember something important. He had to admit he was getting older and more forgetful every day. He drove right past all the banners and flags. His right turn signal blinked all the way through town.

## 62  A Ticket to the Philippines

Lani was already at her desk when Ole got to work a little earlier than usual. She looked like she was in a good mood, so he sat down and waited until she was done with whatever busy thing she was doing on her computer. She looked at him.

"What?"

"Lani, I'm going to the Philippines for ten days."

He didn't ask for time off. He just told her he was going. He expected her to say something like, "No. You just got this job," or "Why?" or maybe an argument or a fist fight. He really didn't know what to expect.

"When?" She asked.

"In two weeks."

"The leave request forms are in that cabinet over there. Look in the file marked Employee Forms. Fill one out with the exact dates you'll be away and I'll sign it."

That night he sent Lyka an email telling her the good news. He'd decided that if they married, and it only lasted two years; he would have helped one more person legally enter America to have a better life. Besides, he only had ninety-one dollars in his checking account. Not much to steal there. But he did have enough room on a credit card, to buy a flight to the Philippines. He would pay off the credit card with the money he hadn't put down on an over-priced condo.

The resort job had him all plugged in again, eight to five, medical Insurance, a 401k, a dentist appointment and a steady paycheck. Lani had purchased five ukuleles for his classes. The short notice decision to fly to the Philippines was a bit of a risk, but his core confidence was back. He wanted to meet Lacey's sister even if it meant losing his job.

Oliver's 'Id,' the one that wants to live on the wild side of life and hides in the dark basement of his mind (according to Freud), was naughty dreaming in over-drive. Ten days! He was finally going to meet a woman cute as Lacey who isn't married to his best friend.

*Would you just forget Lacey brah?*

*Just thinkin' tha'z all.*

The Philippines is eight-thousand-miles from Hawaii plus, you lose a day on the calendar. So, he wasn't sure how many time zones that was or when Lyka would read his email. He went online and read her profile again at Asianeuro.com. It made him feel close to her.

Some people can handle loneliness better than others. Oliver missed everybody he'd ever loved. Living in Hawaii was wonderful, but it would be a true paradise, if he had someone to love and take care of. Unfortunately, Desiree came to mind... again. He bundled all he could remember of her into three giant suitcases in his mind, and set them on an imaginary train station. When the Cerebellum Express departed the station, he got on the train and left the luggage on the platform. From now on, he was catching the train or rather the plane, to Lyka.

Back in his bedroom, Ole began to re-write his Nano-material equations into a more concise equation. The kind he could publish without giving away the formula he intended to patent. His stomach rumbled, but food could wait; worrying about how it might work out with Lyka could wait. He had chemistry homework. It felt great to be thinking again. When his ambition got fired up like this, he was unstoppable.

"You've got mail!" the AOL voice shouted out like a ring master in a circus. He wasn't as unstoppable as he thought. He saved his work and opened Lyka's message.
Oh Oliver!
I am so excited to meet you in person. I want to show you my family and my town and be with you in person! I see you will land in Tacloban airport at 1:00 pm on February sixteen. I will be there when you arrive! I'm sorry to ask, but it costs a lot to travel back to my town. Could you send some money for the van driver? Sorry it is more than I have, and it is far, three hours from my town of Palompon. I have never been that far away from home. I wonder, have you been to the Philippines before? Are you meeting other women here in Philippines? Sorry to ask, but are you?
Your friend, Lyka

There was another photo of her enclosed in the email. Lyka was a lovely, younger version of Lacey.

*Brah, there you go again. Stop it.*

Lyka had Lacey's great smile and long black hair. The picture of Jesus pointing at his heart wasn't in the background this time. Instead, was a bare concrete-block wall with sloppy mortar and re-bar sticking out in the corners. But he wasn't flying ten hours to meet a wall. Lyka was wearing a yellow tank top and tight white jeans. She looked like she was nineteen.

*This nev'a gonna work brah. One look at you, old guy and she gonna run for the hills. Why don't you do what you told her to do? Find someone your own age.*

His forehead knew the answer to that. He'd clearly stated in his online personal profile the age-range of the person he was seeking; forty, to sixty years old. Matchme.com had only attracted three in that age group, all from California. All with homes, cars, money, grandchildren, addiction recovery problems. and several, angry ex-husbands. The other two-thousand, seven-hundred hits all came from Asianeuro.com. These were all eighteen, to twenty-four-years old. Lyka was the oldest Asian woman that had ever written to him and she looked like Lacey.

*WHAT! Brah, you seriously need to forget the captain's wife!*

Details about transferring money by Western Union were at the bottom of the email. This was the first time Lyka had asked for money. The amount she requested was three-thousand Philippine pesos. (seventy-US dollars)

The next day he sent her a hundred. Western Union accepted credit cards. He could do this. Why worry about credit card debt or money? Nine-tenths of everything a person worries about, never happens: Failing an exam, losing your wallet, missing your flight, dying. Oops! That one happens, ten-tenths of the time. Death eventually wins at Blackjack. Worrying about it was a waste of time. Especially if you planned to live to one-hundred and fourteen. It's living that takes courage. He'd tasted success in his life from time to time. Maybe this adventure with Lyka would lead to that Walt Disney fantasy that everyone dreams of, *"they lived happily ever after."*

*Good luck wi' that, stupid. What are the odds Lyka won't skip out on you? You never beat, 'Slippery Sue' to the finish line. Aren't you glad you called Jens so he could rub it all over you, from a year ago? You're such a loser.*

*Who needs you?* He thought back at his sarcastic brain. Professor Gold needed to focus. He went back to chemistry, a discipline he trusted; one that wouldn't scold him.

## 63  It's More Fun in the 'Pila-ppines!'

The pretty flight attendants on Philippine Airlines handed out warm wash cloths, hot meals and offered Ole enough pillows and blankets to make a rather comfortable nest in his larger than normal, economy class seat. He passed on the free drinks, so, after sleeping for six of the nine hours on the jet, he walked sober and refreshed off the plane and found himself in a long que at the immigration blockade in Manila. There were only two windows open but the line was moving fast. Not as fast as the line into Hell; he didn't have to run this time. When it was his turn at the window, the fourteen-year-old immigration officer in a starched white shirt and blue police costume, asked only two questions:

"How long will you be staying in the Pila-ppines, sir?"
"Ten days"
"How much money are you bringing into the country?"
"Eleven-hundred, US"
"Welcome to the Pila-ppines!"

He must have got the answers right because he had fresh ink in his passport. The next hurtle was a higher one. Customs guards holding machine guns stood in tight clusters on either side and behind a row of conveyor belts lined with carry-ons. The hand luggage was slowly being searched by x-ray machines that looked forty-years out of date. Oliver emptied his pockets of everything except for his cash, his passport and just for fun, a package of foil-wrapped gum and a bunch of coins. The kind of dangerous stuff that sets off alarms in the USA. He walked through the scanner... green light. A fifteen-year-old customs officer waved him on without welcoming him to the 'Pila-ppines.' Ole guessed right, either the x-ray machines were too old, or not working at all. *Why bother with the machines? This detail of well-armed, trigger-nervous kids in blue uniforms should be enough to keep away smugglers and terrorists.*

He was now officially in a foreign country, and what's the first thing anyone wants to do when entering another country? Find a place to pee. Fortunately, the designers of airports know this. There were ample Men's restrooms in the Manila airport. Oliver knew exactly how to find them. He looked for a long line of anxious looking women and headed their direction. Right next to the door with all the women lined up, clear into the lobby, he found the door for men, with no line. Architects of airports train stations theaters sports stadiums schools and other public places may be good at big building design, but they have a lot to learn about women.

*Hah! Look who's talking,* Sarcasm jibes.

Oliver found a currency exchange and turned his eleven-hundred into fifty-two thousand pesos. He felt rich for the first time since retiring from teaching at University of Washington and moving to Maui. He quickly stuffed the thick wad of bills in his shorts and walked a mile to the street level of the airport. He got a little lost because instead of down, street level and taxis were on the third floor above him.

"Inter-Continental Hotel," he tossed himself and his carry-on into the back seat of a worn-out looking taxi. He probably should have asked how much first. Nah, he felt too rich for that.

"Okay Joe, where's home?"

"My name's Oliver, what's yours?"

"My kids call me dad. You can call me June."

"Okay, June. How many kids?"

"Eight with this wife, two more before her, all grown up now."

"Big family, brah"

"Yah Joe, I got a restless rocket."

Oliver made no reply, so June rattled on.

"Inter-Continental is a nice place Joe. Want me... take you downtown...hit the girlie-bars?"

Ole thought about it. It didn't take long. "No thanks."

"Sure? Those bar girls find out you stay at the Inter-Continental, zoom-bang-a-boom, a whole car-load of 'em wanna go home wi' you. Nice-girls. Like American Joe Rocket."

"Just take me to the Inter-Continental, June. I'm here to meet just one special lady, that's all."

"Okay Joe, almost there."

He shut up and drove for another half hour. Ole knew he wasn't taking him on a tourist 'jack up the fare' loop. The Inter-Continental was in the center of Manila, a half hour or more from the airport. He'd looked it up on Google maps.

They were on a street built for five traffic lanes in each direction. Ole counted seven, not five lines of trucks and buses moving the same direction as his cab. Helmeted dare-devils raced their motorcycles through these lanes of solid mass like quantum atoms appearing to be in two places at once. They would zip around cars, then brake just before they hit the wall of trucks ahead of them. Seizing the first gap that opened, they disappeared through the impossible narrow canyons between the semi-trucks, somehow making it all the way through before the crevasse closed to smash them. Ole got out his camera and started shooting from the backseat of the cab.

He was amazed to see three to five people on a Honda one-fifty. Some motorcycles were driven by ten-year old kids, boys and girls; some looked too young to drive a bicycle. There were motorcycles carrying whole families with three or four kids squeezed in between book-end parents. There were parents carrying babies in shoulder bags. Every one of them, except the babies were holding onto plastic bags full of stuff. Everyone had a plastic bag of stuff. He tried to see what they were carrying; everything was moving too fast. There were dozens of bicycles and pedestrians weaving through traffic as well.

Ole took a picture of a guy and his girl on a motorcycle. Behind the girl, tied on the back, was a live pig. A pig with scared, bulging eyes. June saw Ole shooting pictures of the pig.

"Welcome to the Pila-ppines," he said with a friendly laugh.

Traffic had slowed to about five-miles-per-hour, when an old man on foot ran alongside the cab and pounded on Ole's window.

"Ciga-wettes! Grum! Candry!" He hawked trying to keep up with the moving cab. He had only one tooth which stuck out at an odd angle from his lower jaw and made it hard for him to yell clearly. He wore a wooden box tied to his waist with all his wares in neat rows. Ole didn't want to buy anything, but he wanted to give the old guy a hundred pesos as a reward for his ambition and courage. It looked like a dangerous way to make a living. He tried to open his window but it wouldn't go down. Maybe it was glued shut. The old man ran in front of Ole's cab and pounded on the windows of another taxi. Suddenly, there were four or five of these pedestrian traveling salesmen. All running, weaving bravely through the traffic chaos. One was a boy about ten-years-old, One, was a young woman carrying a baby in a shoulder bag. The others were far ahead, running between moving buses. Apparently, it was a family run, candy, gum and cigarette franchise.

As they got closer to downtown, the traffic got even slower and thicker with more people walking and running through the seven lanes of vehicles. Ole saw a woman pushing a baby carriage making better time through the jam, than the gaily decorated Jeepneys. A Jeepney is built to hold maybe ten people, side by side, on two long benches in the back. Every Jeepney on the street looked like it had over twenty people squished inside. The back doors were open. Ole looked closer there were no back doors.

On the nearest, overloaded Jeepney, two teenagers were standing on the rear bumper hanging on to open windows. Up on the roof, four pre-school-age children bounced like popcorn; laughing like they were on a ride in a theme park. When traffic stopped again, a woman carrying a twenty-pound bag of rice ran up to the back of the Jeepney. The teenage boys helped pushed her in with the crowd inside. She held on to her bag of rice which was still hanging out the back opening. One of the teens hanging there, put his foot under the bag to help her hold up the weight. She smiled out at him. He laughed.

Oliver had seen some of the world in his thirty-year chemistry career. He'd ridden crowded trains in Japan, Hong Kong, Singapore and all over Europe, but nowhere did people seem so carefree and happy about being smushed together. Lyka had written in an email, "*It's more fun in the Pila-ppines.*" He was starting to get it.

When traffic started moving again, June blew his horn over and over and jabbed his cab in a threatening way toward the right-hand lane. Eventually, this intrusion worked and he was driving next to a sidewalk. It was so full of people, it looked carpeted, thick as hair on a winged monkey. Their faces were a blur. The cab turned into an elaborate gate in a high concrete wall.

"Inter-Continental Hotel, Joe."

"How much you need, June?"

"I need millions, but tonight for you, only one-thousand."

It sounded like highway robbery, but Ole did the math. June was asking for less than twenty bucks, US. A half hour cab fare on Maui would be eighty to a hundred. He gave the cabbie with eight kids, two-thousand pesos.

"Thanks Oliver. June got his name right for the first time. "How about those girlie-bars tonight?"

"No, it's been a long day."

"Then, you should at least try the department stores across the street. You'll have fun."

"Maybe, thanks June."

## 64 Department Store Girls in Manila

From the ninth floor, Ole had a view of the city. It wasn't a pretty sight. Downtown Manila was gray as any other city, but gloomier than most. It's tall, square and rectangular buildings held no architectural interest. It's crowded streets and sidewalks were littered with people and the plastic-litter of people. Looking down onto the grounds of his hotel he saw a tropical paradise of coconut trees and neat lawns. There were four tennis courts with no players and a large swimming pool with no one in it. It was as beautiful as any resort in Hawaii. The hotel property covered an entire city block of downtown real estate. Its lush tropical gardens protected from the locals by a castle-like wall with one defensible gate and no windows.

After a shower and change of clothes, Ole was a little hungry. He decided to go out on the town. Mostly, he was curious about the department store across the street. He found his way out of the hotel lobby, past all the buses idling their stinking smoke into the evening's already polluted air. *Too thick for tennis that's for sure.* Ole thought, as he passed through the gate of the walled city. He stood on a corner with one-hundred and fifty other people waiting for the cross-walk light to change. A wild herd of autos, buses and motorcycles rushed past. Most of the bikes were two-stroke, spewing worse clouds of blue exhaust than the buses. Ole held his breath. He looked around. Everyone was staring at him. Men, women, kids, even dogs. He was the only Caucasian on the sidewalk, a foot taller than everyone else. His inner warning system kicked in. He took his hands out of his pockets and put them into fists held casually at his waist. He moved his feet into a basic karate stance and bent his knees slightly. He held his back straight and kept his eyes moving. Self-defense starts with an alert stance. He taught this stuff back in Lahaina at the Buddhist Temple.

The light changed, the paranoid feeling went away. He walked to the front doors of the department store. There, an armed sixteen-year-old, uniformed guard opened the door for him and bowed. Immediately inside the door, were two of the prettiest Filipinas he had ever seen. They bowed and welcomed him in with a sway of their arms and lovely smiles. He wanted to stop and chat them up a bit, maybe ask directions to the food court or something, but there were four-hundred people behind him, so rather than be crushed to death, he kept moving. The store took up the first five floors of the boxy building it was in. Ole smelled food and followed his nose. There was a McDonald's, a Kentucky Fried Chicken and a whole lot of Chinese and Filipino restaurants. He found his bowl of chop suey and some green tea and sat alone at a table for one. He watched the flood of people go shopping by.

*How can a person feel so alone when surrounded by so many people?* He was fine alone on a beach with no one around, but this was a terrible loneliness. He didn't want to feel this way, it just came upon him like a rush of vertigo. He wasn't a dizzy victim of circumstance. He'd put himself in this moment intentionally, on his way to meet Lyka. Oliver closed his eyes and stopped time on a dime. He smiled at that old cliché, when he considered inflation and the 'Pila'pine' currency exchange, it would be more like stopping time, on a five-hundred-peso bill.

The five-hundred note was Ole's favorite. Its color is a faded yellow, with a large green parrot on one side and the smiling faces of Mr. And Mrs. Aquino on the other. They are both wearing glasses and they look so happy to be living in the 'Pila-ppines.' They made Ole smile.

US currency was boring in the extreme, with its solemn, green-faced dead presidents. Lyka had told him, *"It's gonna be more fun in the Pila-ppines."* Even the money was more fun. He pictured young Lyka in his mind, a blooming flower growing out of a rough concrete wall. He deeply inhaled the green scent of the tea.

*Be the tea brah. Be the tea.*

By the time he'd finished his chop suey he was over his loneliness. He didn't need any clothes, but decided to look around. Men's clothing was on the fourth floor. He took the very tired-looking escalators up and walked into the Tommy Bahama store on his left. There must have been shirts and clothes in the store, but all he saw were the beautiful young women staring at him. They were the cutest store clerks he'd ever seen in all his world travels. Each one dressed professionally in store-policy strictness. Their short, pleated skirts and white blouses were offset by brightly colored scarves loosely tied around their necks. This gave them a rather dangerous, sexy look. Or he might have imagined that. Two of them came over to offer their smiles and assistance.

"What size sir?" One of them asked.

He looked at her and her helper. They looked alike. Maybe twenty-one-year-old identical, Filipina twins.

"Large please." Then, remembering he was in Asia where clothes size always ran a little smaller than the tags, he changed his answer, "Extra-large." Both young women started giggling leading him toward the back of the store. Ole would have followed them over a cliff they were so darn cute.

"Here you are sir, extra-large." They giggled in stereo, one on either side of him.

He looked at the prices. He ran the currency conversion and realized these Tommy Bahama shirts were twenty-two dollars. Back in Hawaii, they would each cost over a hundred. He chose two. The twins led him to the changing room, slid a curtain across and stood like palace guards outside the curtain. Ole entered, slid the yellow curtain closed and took off his shirt. Standing there like that, his chest hairs could feel their feminine heat on the other side of that thin cloth. It felt a little too exciting. His manifest male, wild man wanted to invite them into the dressing room. It was big enough for three. He stayed on task, trying to think only of Lyka. The shirts fit perfect. His next surprise was at the cash register. A lovely fifteen-year-old dressed the same way, with a blue scarf around her neck, pushed the buttons on a retail computer. This seemed to take longer than it should. Maybe she was a trainee. Ole was the only customer in the store, so he patiently admired her as she pressed buttons and checked the codes on the shirts to make sure she got it right before pushing more buttons. When he'd paid for the shirts. The computer girl handed them off to a darling seventeen-year-old clone who folded each one carefully. She handed the shirts to the eighteen-year-old girl standing next to her who unfolded the shirts and re-folded them doing a much better job of it. When she was satisfied that the folds were perfect, she handed them off to another doll who carefully put them one at a time in a plastic bag. Every one of these women stood straight and professional, smiling up at Ole the whole time. He reached for the bag of shirts, but it was handed off to another slim twenty-year-old who placed it carefully in a bag with the Tommy Bahama logo on it. She offered the bag to him with two hands like the Japanese do, but instead of bowing, she looked up at him and smiled.

Ole didn't care much for shopping. He was a guy. Wandering around in stores all day looking at things to buy seemed so ridiculous. But after this experience, he shopped for another two hours enjoying the attention of pretty department store girls.

*What 'd June the cabbie say, brah? Tell the girls you are staying at the Inter-Continental, you'll have a car load of 'em wanna come to your room."*

Oliver figured this was his 'Id' yearning for trouble. Fortunately, his Ego (the guy holding the reins) kept him on the straight and narrow. He'd come all this way to meet a nice normal woman. One that his Super Ego would approve of. A woman who he'd gotten to know by e mail, who looked like a younger Lacey.

*Oh, my stars, brah!*

He shook his head to scramble the picture in his mind of the young Lacey. He didn't give any Inter-Continental invitations to the department store clerks, but he did buy two more shirts and four pairs of shorts just to watch this scene play out again and again.

## 65  Meeting Lyka on Leyte Island

The instant the inter-island's tires hit the runway, the pilot threw the engines into reverse. He knew how short this strip of World War II concrete was. He slowed the jet down enough to turn the front wheels before they dropped into the ocean less than a half-mile from touch down. The jet swung around and forward-blasted its way to the Leyte airport terminal. Workers rolled out an old-fashioned stairway by hand, and fastened it to door with bungee cords. As Ole climbed down the stairs he waved to the dozens of happy faces waiting behind a chain link fence. They waved back. Oliver didn't see Lyka along the fence.

The airport in Tacloban is about the size of a three-bay car garage. It's made of concrete block with high ceilings and has all the inviting ambiance and same color paint as an empty, public swimming pool. Only this pool was packed with hundreds of sweating, t-shirted men and women all smiling laughing and have a grand old time. Oliver stood by the wooden tables at the open-air, luggage retrieval bay. Everyone waiting for the slow-moving, Ford farm tractor pulling a wagon load of suitcases including his, to the tables. His carry-on, no longer fit in the passenger overhead after all that shopping in Manila.

The suitcases were thrown off the wagon onto the waiting tables just as carelessly as everywhere else in the world. These two guys threw with such disrespect, Ole figured they must be drop-outs from 'Baggage Handling College.' Incredibly, they got hired anyway. Ole was glad he had hand-carried his ukulele.

He suddenly heard roosters crowing so loud they hurt his ears with their angry, screaming, 'DOODLE-DOO-YOU' expletives! Looking across the luggage tables, he saw tail feathers sticking out of cardboard boxes being set down very gently by the baggage college dropouts. *'Welcome to the Pila-pinnes,'* his mind reminded him.

Carrying his ukulele case on his shoulder and pulling his carry-on behind him, he made it through the closest chain-link gate. Taxi drivers rushed him trying to pull away his carry-on and lead him to their waiting vans. He was shaking his head 'no,' in their language when he spotted Lyka waving.

*Oh, my stars, brah. She too good for you. Look how young and pretty she is. An' you old...*

"Shut up brain," he whispered under his breath. He walked out another gate in the perimeter fence to where Lyka and her mother waited by a newish-looking Toyota window van. Ole knew mom would be there. He was ready for this moment. He opened his carry-on and brought out the two orchid leis he'd made. He placed one over the head of Lyka's mom and gave her a hug. Then he tenderly placed a longer lei of purple orchids over Lyka, kissed her on the cheek and gave her hug. Both smiled like they'd just graduated from high school.

Lyka introduced Ole to Edgar, the van driver and off they went. They were the only passengers in the nine-passenger van. Lyka's mom sat up front with Edgar, Lyka put Ole next to her in the back seat and held his hand. It kind of surprised him. He took this for a good omen.

"Lyka, this is kind of embarrassing, but I have to pee so bad."

She hollered some Visaya commands at Edgar and he started looking from side to side for a place to stop the van. Ole was about to burst. As soon as the driver pulled up in front of a small family store, Ole was out the door and Lyka right behind him. She spoke pleadingly to an old woman inside the store and got permission for Ole to go around back. Lyka led the way. She pointed to a shed attached to the back of the store like a metal parasite. It was a mess of dented, dangerously-sharp, corrugated sheets of tin. It could have been space junk that crashed there and nobody had bothered to clear it away. On the back side, there was a waist-high privacy door made of warped plywood. Ole swung it open and relieved himself into a porcelain-rimmed hole in the ground. No toilet seat, no toilet, just a hole in the ground. Lyka stood right next to him on the other side of the half-door.

She told him later, that she was afraid someone might kidnap him away from her. He had no idea such things could happen in the Philippines. He wondered if anyone he knew would pay ransom money to get him back. Not his ex-wife, Tanya that's for sure. His daughters? Not gonna happen, they were just starting their working careers. They had nothing to pawn. His parents? Yes, surely dad would second mortgage their house to get him back. Or would he? *Mom would pawn her wedding ring to get me back,* he assured himself. He didn't want to keep thinking about it. He got back in the van, closer to Lyka.

They'd only traveled a kilometer or two when Edgar stopped the van at a Tacloban beach that's still on history's map of famous places. He wanted to show his 'American Joe,' the seven bronze statues wading to shore in water up to their knees. The monumental figures, twice as tall as the average American Joe, were a tribute to General Mac Arthur's return to the Philippines during

World War II. Oliver's dad was a World War II veteran and had been stationed on Samar island; the one Ole could see right across the bay from Tacloban. Dad told Ole that this famous, invasion photograph was a bit misleading. Dad and his navy air-corps buddies had been swimming at this very secure beach for a month before the army press corps staged this dramatic photo-op for General Mac Arthur.

Lyka and Ole did more touching than talking during the rest of the three-hour ride to her town. As Edgar drove, she played with the curly blonde hair on his arms, she rubbed her leg on his. She even put her arm around him. Something his wife hadn't done in the last five years of their marriage. He could tell she was just as attracted to him as he was to her.

Edgar sped along the narrow, two-lane, concrete road built by the US Army Corps of Engineers over seventy years ago. It looked brand new; not a pot-hole or a crack in it anywhere. The most annoying thing about the drive was Edgar blowing his horn all the time. The constant blaring and beep-beeping was driving Ole nuts. After a whole hour of this, Ole began to notice that this was normal driving etiquette in the Philippines. Every vehicle blew its horn all the time. These narrow concrete roads are not just paved rivers of motorized cargo and human transport. They are the drying beds for rice on long blue plastic tarps. They are sidewalks for pedestrians, parking lots for broken-down vehicles, workshops for repairing motorcycles, welding re-bar, sawing coconut lumber and playgrounds for children of all ages on bicycles. Oliver saw more real-life, abject poverty in the first hour of this ride, than he'd ever thought possible.

Here in the Philippines, it looked like the poor built

themselves affordable housing out of bamboo and dented sheets of tin. The shoulders of the concrete roadway on both sides were what Lyka called 'squatter land.' It was free, first come first squat. It looked like all the good spots had been settled generations ago. These people had no running water, no electricity, no furniture, no glass windows or screens, no lanai, no doors. Ole didn't want to think about the porcelain pipe in the ground.

It was impossible to count with any accuracy, but he guesstimated more than ten-thousand people were squatting along the banks of this fifty-mile stretch of concrete river between two towns. All the vans, motorcycles, trucks and buses blew their horns not to be annoying, but as a friendly warning.

"Daplin," (pronounced, Dah-plain) said Lyka.

"When you hear a horn beep, you holler, 'Da-plin!' Which means, 'Eva' body run... get off the road!"

It's the driver's way of saying, "Excuse me, but I'm driving through your front yard and I'm not slowing down." By hitting his horn, Edgar was just being polite.

## 66  Whispering Beach Resort

When they arrived in Palompon, Lyka instructed the
driver to take Ole to what she assured him was the nicest
hotel in town. It was a quaint looking, five cabin, ocean-
front resort called, 'Whispering Beach.' It sounded
romantic.

The nice old auntie who owned the place took a
deposit of a thousand and gave Ole the key to his room
and two scratchy, but clean faded bath towels. Lyka
insisted on carrying the towels. Her mom stayed in
Edgar's air-conditioned van.

When Ole opened the cabin door he got the Deja-Vue-
Bama-BOOM-flashback of his life. This was the same
dismal motel room as his dream. The one where he
thought he was waking up in prison. This was the room
where he'd seen Lacey sleeping on the bed, naked. He
leaned against the rough door frame. His knees were
about to give out. He couldn't believe how in real life, it
could look the same as his dream. There was the same
antique refrigerator the same weathered-looking desk
and plastic pink chair, the same rope strung from two iron
nails hammered into the bare concrete wall.

The jalousie window slats in the windows were
covered with dust. Ole rolled his carry-on to the foot of
the bed. The same bed... *Lacey had been sleeping on that
bed...he'd thought she was dead. His head was bandaged
and his purple swollen arm... the one that still hurts.*
Oliver's mind went diving down that too-familiar pain
dive. His knees were shaking, his vision went all blurry. A
rooster crowed outside the front door and then another
screeched a challenge, then another. A dog started
barking like mad. *Whispering Beach Resort?*

*Are you still dreaming brah?*

Oliver would have passed out at that very moment, except Lyka suddenly had her arms around his neck, standing on her tip toes and kissing him right on his lips. He put his arms around her for support. The kiss was wonderful, but he felt kind of dirty kissing Lyka while thinking about her naked sister. It was their first real kiss. It was deliciously sexy, but conflicted. He wanted to try doing it over, thinking about Lyka this time. She pulled away. Lyka had felt his reluctance. Deeply hurt, she led him back to the van.

"I want you to meet the rest of my family."

## 67  Lyka's family

Edgar delivered them to the overgrown dead end of a paved street. Ole tipped the driver with a five-hundred-peso parrot. He thought about the fifty-thousand he had in his shorts pocket. He double-checked to make sure it was still there after all that snuggling in the van. *Yep, all there. Lyka is no pick pocket.* Then, he was ashamed he'd ever thought such a thing.

Lyka's mom was leading the way down a narrow unpaved driveway. Lyka took Ole's hand and they followed at their own pace. A wide-open expanse of low Jungle spread away to their left. The distant green hills looked inviting. Leyte was more lush and greener than Maui. *Lots of rain, yah?*

Ole was more interested in the way Lyka caressed his hand as they walked. To their right there were two big homes that looked like they could be featured in Sunset Magazine. These were expensive-looking homes with gates closed and chained. *She said she was poor. She sure lives in a rich neighborhood.* His thoughts were even more conflicted. *He didn't really know her, did he?* The next house was partially hidden behind a high, unpainted cinder-block wall. The ugly walls were lined with strands of barb wire. If that wasn't forbidding enough there were broken shards of glass sticking up out of the dry cement on the top of the wall. *Please God, not this house.*

*Thought you didn't know how to pray, brah?*

Ole stopped at a crumbling gap in the gray wall and looked in. The place was a dump. There were ugly piles of trash everywhere. Abused looking dogs in small cages smelled Ole looking at them and started barking. Busted motorcycles, beer bottles, crushed water bottles, plastic bags of every color and random bricks and boards littered the bare dirt yard. The house in the center of all this junk looked like a jail with steel bars on the windows and a tin roof. Ole said nothing, Lyka's mom was walking past this one.

The grass driveway became a paved, narrow sidewalk that led them between closely built homes. On the left were shacks covered with sheets of corrugated metal. Towering above and behind them was another modern home with two new motorcycles in the front yard. On his right, Ole stopped at a house with a small store window in what should have been the front wall of its living room. The large window was covered with hog-wire fencing. On the inside of all that wire, shiny packages of candy and snacks were hung on display. There was a small wooden counter jutting out from a square hole in the fence about waist high. A woman's face looked out the hole and stared at the 'Joe' walking past her home.

Ole waded through a half-dozen small children playing happily between the fancy homes and the dismal shacks. He was enjoying their wide-eyed stares so much that he almost smacked his head on a wooden awning swung out over the sidewalk. It was exactly forehead height for an American Joe. He ducked just in time.

*Thanks, brah,* whispered his bindi eye.

*You owe me one,* Oliver thought back at his forehead.

Lyka and her mom entered the next bamboo gate on the right. Their front yard was paved with many nicely potted plants. Excited children rushed out the front door of a clean, well-cared for, one-story concrete home. One at a time, each child took Ole's hand and placed it against his or her little forehead. Lyka whispered in his ear that this was a gesture of respect paid to older people. He looked around at her siblings and parents. He was the oldest person there.

The handsome children were making a whole lot of family-sized noise. Oliver liked them right away. Lyka's dad stood in his front doorway and watched all this commotion with great interest. He offered Ole a handshake and invited him in. Artemio was wearing no shirt. He looked strong and fit with just a slight sag to his shoulders showing the wear and tear of years of hard work. He was about Ole's age, fifty-something. Oliver looked over at Lacey still outside with her sister's kids. She looked like a teenager.

*It's Lyka! Forget Lacey, will you? Man, y'er dumb.*

*I saved you from a nasty bash back there on the sidewalk, so ease off.* Ole pushed back.

Ole and Lyka's dad sat down together on the bamboo chairs in the living room and talked about stuff: the house, the motorcycles parked out front, his job.

"Artemio?" Oliver paused, collecting his thoughts. This was the moment. "What do you think about an old guy like me, marrying your daughter?"

"I'd be very happy for my daughter." He shook Ole's hand.

## 68  Chicken and Put-Put

Ole enjoyed hanging out with the family the rest of the afternoon. When he got a chance, he took Lyka aside and asked her if she'd like to have dinner with him tonight at a little restaurant he'd seen from Edgar's van. It would be their first 'date.' She agreed. Soon after, Lyka excused herself from the family. She led Ole back to the main road. It was just a short walk to the restaurant maybe a half mile, but Lyka waved down a passing 'put-put.' A sixty-year-old man circled his bicycle around and paused for them to climb aboard. They sat on a small padded bench above an extended rear axle and a third bicycle wheel. There was a fiberglass roof over their heads. It was a pedal-powered rickshaw of sorts. The old man started pumping his skinny legs. Lyka took Ole's hand and said nothing. She was still confused by his mixed reaction to their first kiss. The ride was too quiet.

The restaurant was air-conditioned and clean. They had just sat down at a table when Lyka's dad and mom walked in followed by all six of her brothers and sisters and some of the kids. Oliver waved them over. Waiters slid tables together until there was a chair for everyone. Ole ordered lots of chicken and rice. He was shocked by the bill when the impromptu feast was done. He converted the peso's in his mind; dinner for eight adults and two kids: nine-dollars and fifty-one cents, US.

They all said goodnight. Put-puts headed away in various directions. Lyka put Ole in a put-put, sat next to him and spoke to the driver, a boy this time. A boy who looked eight-years-old. He started pedaling. After a mile or so, he tired and stopped in the middle of the main highway through town. A Coca-Cola semi-trailer truck with its headlights off, blew its horn and passed. The little boy climbed on the back of the put-put and stood in a metal basket probably meant for groceries or other cargo. An older boy who Ole hadn't noticed jogging along behind, climbed on the bike seat and started pedaling.

Their late arrival at 'Whispering Beach' woke up the dogs and roosters. Lyka paid the boys for the one-mile ride.

"How much did you give them?" Ole asked.

"Five pesos,"

"What? That's like eleven cents, US"

"Is that too much?"

Ole shook his head. Apparently even pennies were worth more here in the 'Pila-pinnes' than back home. He wondered if Lyka would go home to her parent's or stay the night? The boys were waiting too. He gave them each a twenty-peso note about fifty-cents each. They looked shocked out of their comfort zone; like they were gonna cry or something. The boys hesitated, looking back at Lyka. She sent them away. *Lyka is staying!* He smiled and took her by her lovely hand and led her into their love nest with the prison-cell furnishings. No matter about the décor, Ole was turbo-charged with excitement to have this night with Lyka. He'd deal with the ghost of... what's her name... later.

## 69  Nights in Stained Rayon

As soon as Ole closed the door, Lyka had her arms around
his shoulders. He ignored the pain shooting down his left
arm. At five-foot-five, she was taller than most Filipinas.
She found his lips and pressed hard, kissing him with a
hunger that quickly overcame his earlier hesitation. It felt
so good to be kissed like that. It was as if she wanted to
own him. He quit analyzing and let her take the lead. She
tasted like slow roasted chicken, finger-licking good. He
licked her lips, Lyka moaned and squeezed him tighter.
She pulled him over to the bed and throwing back the
covers fell on top of him. It didn't hurt. She couldn't weigh
more than ninety-pounds. She rolled him over on top of
her. Ole kissed down her neck and pushed his face into
her hair. She smelled more like pan-fried chicken. He
opened his eyes and looked at the bed sheets. They
smelled freshly washed with a heady perfume of fabric
softener, but this wasn't a night in white satin. They were
rayon sheets with dark stains from years of love and lust.
*Welcome to the Pila-pinnes, brah.*
Ole decided to take the lead. He pulled her off the bed.
It was easy as pulling up a skinny tent peg. He hugged her
gently and stood her next to the edge of the bed. She
wobbled there with a worried look on her face like maybe
she'd done something wrong.
"Go take a shower."
"Come with me."
Lyka pulled her yellow tank top over her shoulders. Her
long black hair caught and she shook it loose. Her pink bra
covered her larger than cupcake-size boobs. She
unsnapped it and dropped the bra on the bed. Ole's

counting his lucky stars. Next, she slid each skinny leg out of her white jeans and they fell to the floor. They sort of bunched up around her ankles like a white cloud. She looked like that famous painting of the naked woman standing in a sea shell. He couldn't remember the name of the artist. He couldn't think at all. A vision of Asian beauty, divinely clad only in pink panties, stood there before him.

*Botticelli, the Birth of Venus,* his forehead has a thing for naked fine art.

"Okay I'll race you to the shower," Ole teased. Lyka laughed and ran.

*Look, look, look," said Dick. See Jane run. Run Jane, run. Funny naked Jane. Fun, fun, fun.*

"Shut up brain," Ole whispered with a sigh. He stripped quickly and met Jane for some fun in the badly painted cement shower room. The water was warm, then cold from the same dysfunctional, wall-mounted heater he remembered from his dream.

*Welcome to the Pila-ppines!*

Lyka tore open a foil wrapped package of... 'Smooth as Silk' shampoo and gave Ole a rub down. Which led to a rub up and down... his back. He returned the favor. Her back was a tan hour-glass. Her butt was a Valentine.

Oliver tried not to think about Lacey. But he couldn't help it. She was all he could think about. The two sisters looked so much alike it was easy to pretend it was Lacey.

*That's just twisted, brah.*

Lyka was fun, fun, fun in bed. He stopped thinking and tried to please her as best he could. But, he couldn't shake the feeling that Lacey would be better at this and a whole lot more fun. His forehead stayed quiet the whole time. Maybe it was off hiding somewhere behind his mind's eye chanting mantras or something. He'd just thought that when the voice slapped up him up the side of his conscience.

*Why can't you just love the one you're with, brah. You deserve all the da' karma what gonna smack you.*

## 70  Motel Room of Doubts

It took Ole a long time to get enough of beautiful Lyka. She took great pleasure in the American Joe rocket ride. Then she slipped into a love coma and slept through the entire concert of crowing roosters and barking dogs. Ole looked at his phone. There was no signal in this remote edge on the pie-plate of the world, but it still gave him the local time. Three AM. The barnyard noise was annoying, but nothing compared to what his forehead was scolding him with.

*So wrong brah, to make love to one woman while t'inking 'bout someone else's woman.*

His dream of naked Lacey in this lousy motel room would not go away. He'd been injured with stitches in his head and a broken arm. Did she do it?

*Maybe, the captain broke y'er arm. Either way you deserve it brah.*

No Lacey had spoken to him kindly. "Oh darling, come back to bed. I'll put another ice-pack on your shoulder." Her voice haunted him, but it wasn't a scary haunted feeling. For some unholy reason it felt wonderful. Now, what should he do about Lyka? Did he love her? Did he deserve her?

*Ah... that would be, No, on both counts. Man, y'er dumb.*

## 71 Dive Party

The next day, all six of Lyka's brothers and sisters, plus everyone else in town went to Palompon's waterfront park. If there were a heat-index scale in the Philippines it would have been flashing: "STOP WHATEVER YOU'RE DOING AND GO SWIMMING!"

The park, right in front of city hall, has concrete steps that lead from a green lawn down into the ocean. The steps and the water were crowded with families. Naked children were leaping, diving, splashing and hollering just like kids do back in the USA, only with bathing suits on. It was very foreign to be surrounded by naked kids age one-month, to around twelve-years-old. They swam with wild abandon.

Some of the older teenage boys still thought they were twelve; grounds for indecent exposure in America leading to their arrest and imprisonment. The teen girls were much more modest. All the teenage girls wore t-shirts with water-soaked bras under them. Nobody wore a bikini. Even one-piece swimsuits were out of the question. All the women wore bras under their t-shirts plus, blue jeans or shorts while swimming.

Ole wasn't used to being someplace where he didn't understand anything people were saying. His Philippine Visaya vocabulary was limited to, 'Salamat' (thank you), 'Oo' (yes), 'Dili' (no), 'Daplin' (get off the road) and Lyka had taught him, 'gwapa totoy' (nice boobs). So, because he couldn't say much, he did a lot of soaked bra, totoy watching. He knew gestures and smiles or shaking heads can get a lot across, plus he knew the language of diving, splashing and laughing. He was having a great time in the

'Pila-ppines.'

The ocean was maybe, one degree cooler than the air temperature. Ole guessed ninety degrees. The bravest of the brave, both teens and little kids, dove off a wall about six feet high into deep warm water. Ole was among the brave. It seemed to impress Lyka who didn't swim. He was a bit disappointed by this. Lyka would look good in Hawaii, in a bikini. She sat on the concrete steps with only her feet in the ocean playing with some of the littlest children.

She told him early on, that she was afraid of the water. When she was eleven years old, a typhoon hit her village and a flash flood knocked down the stilts that held up her family's bamboo house. They were all swept into the raging flood. Only by grabbing hold of coconut trees were they able to survive until the water receded enough to wade back to where their home used to be.

Ole wondered how a relationship between a surfer and a woman who won't go in the ocean could possibly work. Lyka looked over at him and waved. Her smile was pretty, as Lacey's. It might work.

## 72  Oops!

Next day, same heat-index. Palompon's waterfront was even more crowded. Ole waited for a naked ten-year-old boy to dive off the high wall. Lyka was saying something to him, but he wasn't listening. He was in a hurry to get in the ocean. Oliver hadn't really noticed that the ten-year-old dove long, further from the base of the wall. Ole had seen him surface and waited until the boy swam out of the way back toward the concrete steps.

Ole's dive was more straight down. He liked the cooler water down deep. BAD OOPs! The tide had gone out! Ole was diving into three feet of water. He could see the bottom too clearly... solid rock made in the Philippines. There was no time for his life to flash before his eyes or wish Lyka good-bye. No time to plead to God for a miracle. None of that. In those last micro-seconds before his left arm and head hit terra-firma-veritas, all he had time to think was, *it's been a great life and now it's over.*

He hit hard but came up to the surface immediately. Blood was running down his face mixed with salt water. When he got a full breath of air he didn't cry out with pain. It was more of a very stunned, stupid feeling. He was so surprised that the tide had gone out, and that he wasn't dead. In fact, nothing hurt. Ole sat there on the rocks with his bare torso above the surface and turned his bloody head from side to side, *no broken neck?* He worked his elbows and then his knees. *I'm not dead or paralyzed? How come?*

Lyka was screaming for help. She wasn't getting in the three-foot-deep ocean to save him, but she got the attention of two nearby swimmers. These teenage boys with swim suits on, rushed to either side of him and helped Ole wade over to the steps and climb them one at a time. He was bleeding from the top of his head, but it still didn't hurt.

*You're alive? How come your neck ain't broke?*

He was in no mood for his forehead's questions. He sure didn't know the answers. Lyka had an arm around his waist and was wiping the blood off his face with a towel. The impact had peeled back a lot of his scalp. His hands were still wet, but he managed to slide that patch of scalp over his skull to where it used to be. Lyka nearly passed out. To her credit, she stayed upright and helped the boys walk Ole to city hall, just across the lawn.

Fortunately, there was a sign above a door that said, 'Emergency Medical Room.' The door was locked. It was a religious holiday of some kind.

Oliver peeked in the ER window. What he saw in there scared him worse than his bleeding head. The room was full of empty computer boxes. They were laying all over in random piles, some on shelves some on the floor. There was no patient table, no sink with running water, no bandages, no first-aid kit hanging on the wall. The ER was a storage closet. What were his options now? *I'm gonna need medical attention soon and there's always infection... I could be dead in week. What about Father Floor Fan's grade book?*

*Wanna pray now, brah?*

A man Lyka didn't know, assessed Ole's situation quickly and offered to drive them to the hospital. Oliver wasn't sure what surprised him more. That there was a hospital in this little town or that he could still say words,

"Salamat," he managed to get across. It looked to Ole, like the helpful stranger had a brand-new car, a small four door white car. Ole had soaked a couple of beach towels with bright red blood so far and was still a mess. The owner of the car pulled a large sheet of plastic out from somewhere covered his new back seat with it and helped Oliver in. It was short drive, a few minutes through the streets of town and then up a driveway to a faded two-story building that looked like an abandoned warehouse.

*You're screwed, brah.*

Even though there were no cars or bicycles in the parking lot of the hospital the place wasn't as abandoned as it first looked. A dozen patients were sitting on the floor in the main hall way. A three-foot-high statue of the Blessed Virgin Mary stood on a wooden table in the center of the lobby. There were votive candles, some burning, some spent on the table by her bare, plaster feet. On the floor there were flowers in cans of water and several bibles and prayer books stacked neatly to one side. Words came to Oliver's lips that he hadn't said in over forty years.

"Holy Mary, mother of God, pray for us sinners now and at the hour of our death. Amen."

Lyka left him leaning against a badly painted, green wall. She started a panicked conversation with a woman behind a desk who was dressed like a nurse, but more likely, was an office clerk. Ole looked at the injuries of the people waiting ahead of him. One old man had an arm in a sling. It looked like he'd stopped the bleeding from the severed fingers missing from that hand. The sling was a t-shirt soaked with his blood. Another old man had crutches next to his chair he was sound asleep his mouth hung open showing no teeth. All the rest were distressed looking women with crying or feverish children on their laps. Most of these mothers and grandmothers were sitting on the cement floor. There were not enough chairs.

Oliver looked out at the afternoon sky. In another three hours the day would be done. There wasn't time for a doctor to see all these people today. Ole would have to come back tomorrow.

*You are so screwed brah. Remember karma?*

He couldn't remember his last hand of Blackjack. He didn't want to think about it. Death was probably on a red-eye flight to Leyte. He'd be looking for Oliver this week. Karma had dealt him his last hand. Without a miracle, he was pretty sure, he wouldn't live to see tomorrow. Lyka came over and took his hand.

"The Doctor will see you next."

"I don't want white man privilege, look at all these injured and sick people waiting for the doctor."

"It's not white-man privilege. It's money privilege." She explained. "These people don't have any money. They've probably been here for days hoping a doctor or nurse will eventually get around to seeing them. You're an American, a tourist with money. We're going to the operating room. She led him down the hall. He was still walking on his own. All his life he'd heard stories of stupid or drunk teenagers diving into the shallow end of the pool or hitting bottom in a lake and spending the rest of their lives unable to move or even swallow. It could have been him today.

*Miracles really happen?* Wonders the bewildered chemist in his head.

Two older women dressed in hospital uniforms met him at the door. Rather the door *way*. There was no door you could open or close. There was no glass in the windows. Sun beams, heat and flies came and went as they pleased. Ole was laid on an operating table that had a stained green sheet on it. It was padded, so comfortable enough. There was a Pine-Sol stink to it. One of the nurses turned on a surgery lamp over his head. It looked like it was left over from World War II. There were three light bulbs, two of them still worked, blinding his eyes. Things were looking up. The nurses set about cleaning his torn scalp. They rubbed away at his head with wet cloths and cold water from a plastic dog dish. Ole didn't care if it was dog dish by night and a surgery dish by day. He was glad to get some medical help right away.

"Ooo, this looks nasty," said one nurses as she pulled his scalp flap from side to side like a piece of thin-crust pizza dough. *Aren't nurses supposed to say nice, soothing things? Like, "just a little scrape, nothing to worry about here.".*

None of this cleaning and prepping caused him any pain. However, his left arm was sore. Sore, accelerated to, 'yikes!' every time he tried to bend or lift it. By the time the nurses finished their prep work, a bunch of Lyka's sisters were standing around the operating table. It looked like he was surrounded by five angels. They all looked like Lacey. Lourdes held his left hand. It was a sweet gesture, but his fingers hurt so bad he had to ask her to let go. One of the Lacey angels wouldn't let go of his right hand.

*Lyka brah, Lyka... for God's sake, it's Lyka!*
Doctor Francis...somebody, came in with blood on his

shirt sleeves and looked at Oliver's head. For the next two hours that good doctor shaved the front of Ole's head and sewed a lot of careful stitches to hold down the post card size loose flap of skin onto the rest of his scalp.

The doctor said it matched up pretty good with the surrounding skin and that he should be good as new before long and cheery professional stuff like that. So, this was a real doctor. Ole had felt the black thread being tugged tight with every stitch, but no pain. The nurses helped him sit up on the edge of the table.

"Salamat, Doctor Francis. Besides my life, how much do I owe you?"

"Two-thousand peso's, you can pay the clerk. I don't like to handle paper money. It's covered in germs."

*His shirt and sleeves, hands and pants are spotted with old and fresh blood stains; and money is covered with germs?* Ole let that slide. The doctor was asking for about thirty-eight dollars for two hours of surgery. In the USA this would have required two doctors, an anesthesiologist, a dozen x-rays, several operation room staff, IV's, surgical supplies, and in-hospital room rates for three days to hold Ole for, 'observation.' It would cost fifteen to twenty-thousand US Dollars.

Oliver handed the clerk all the cash he had in his wallet, fourteen Philippine green parrots (one-hundred and forty US dollars). She looked up from her desk with adoration at Oliver as if he were a saint or something.

"Help some of these people waiting in the hallway, and hey Doc before you go, I think my arm might be broken. I should get an x-ray. Maybe one x-ray of my head would be a good idea too."

Doc Francis touched Ole's arm from his wrist to his shoulder and pushed on every splotch of black and blue.

Ole held back his screams to impress Lyka with his manly courage. She saw the pain doing its evil cha-cha-cha across his face. She started to cry, finally letting her fright and concern wash down her pretty cheeks. Ole put his arm that wasn't broken around her shoulder.

"The nearest x-ray machine is in Ormoc City, about forty miles from here," said Doc Francis.

"You mean in this whole town of Palompon, what... maybe thirty-thousand people, there's not one x-ray machine?" Ole could not believe it.

"As you can see, we are seriously ill-equipped and under-staffed."

Lyka thanked the doctor and said something to her sister. Lourdes sent a text with her cell phone and ten minutes later they were on the way to Ormoc in a hired, air-conditioned van. Most of her family came along, all Lyka's grown siblings and their kids. He thought it was for his moral support. Lyka explained later that some of them had never been to Ormoc City and none of them had ever been in an air-conditioned car before.

The thirteen-year-old-looking nurse that took the x-ray of Ole's arm assured him it was not broken. She showed him the x-ray film which was his to keep. Sure enough, you could see solid white bones all connecting where they should. She gave him a sling for free and sympathized with him about the gauze wrapped around his head. The cost for the x-ray was four dollars, US.

For the next eight days, Ole slowly recovered in his dismal cell at the Whispering Beach Prison and Rooster Ranch Resort by the Sea. His arm changed colors every day, going from black and blue to yellow to purplish magenta. Lyka arranged for a massage therapist (an older woman with no front teeth) to give Ole a long massage, hot packs and sympathy every afternoon. When he asked Lyka for a younger, prettier therapist, Lyka poked him in his sore shoulder.

The day of his return flight to Maui he and Lyka took a walk together. She'd been so nice to him, so good in bed and so kind helping him recover. She cleaned his head wound and wrapped clean gauze on it every day. She was amazing, but Oliver knew it wouldn't work out between him and Lyka. *How do you say to someone, 'I can't marry you because I'm in love with your sister, who's married to a buddy of mine?'* So, he kept his mouth shut and let her do most of the good-bye-ing. He had a lot to think about.

## 73  Tacloban to Manila to Honolulu

The flight to Manila was a quick jump off the short Leyte runway and a one-hour hop to Manila. During the layover, he typed one last text to Lyka. He thanked her for everything, but made it clear he wasn't coming back. She deserved a man closer to her own age. He wished her well, hoped she would find that good man and have a wonderful life. Oliver re-read it three times not wanting to send it. Tears were forming in his good eye. He hit 'send' anyway.

The flight back to Maui was the longest, loneliest flight he'd ever endured. He had a window seat, so he could watch the clouds go by at five-hundred miles per hour. He turned his back on the old man next to him so nobody would see him cry.

*Who you cryin' ova' brah? Lyka or Lacey?*

It was Lyka who nursed him back to health with a look of love in her eyes. How he wished those eyes had belonged to Lacey.

*You deserve to die brah. Even if you live through this, Captain Billy is gonna kill you some day.*

## 74  Maui's Lonely Airport

Riding down the escalator at OGG Maui airport was always a lonely moment for Oliver. He could see the families down below welcoming home loved ones with leis and hugs. No one would be meeting him at the bottom of these slow-moving stairs.

The bandages were still wrapped around his head, but the stitches had been removed. He wore a baseball cap that said, 'It's More Fun in the Philippines!' to hide the shaved spot above his forehead. His arm felt a little better. It was his heart that was broken. Saying goodbye to Lyka felt so wrong. Being in love with Lacey felt much worse, hopelessly worse.

He was chewing on this wad of self-pity when he saw Lacey at the bottom of the escalator, waving! Oliver looked behind him to see who she might be waving to. Her husband wasn't there. Ole looked back down at Lacey and gave her a small wave with his good arm. As soon as he stepped onto the ground floor, she had him in her arms hugging him tight.

"Lacey what...?"

"How was your flight love? How about your arm... still sore?"

"Not too bad. What are..."

"We're gonna get you another x-ray, right now." She took him by his good arm and led him to the parking lot. Oliver had no idea why Lacey was meeting him at the airport. He was thrilled to feel her gripping his good arm. *She came all this way to the airport to pick me up? She likes me more than I thought.* He decided to shut his mouth and let this play out as it will.

Lacey popped open the trunk of her Mercedes. She carefully placed his carry-on and ukulele on top of her golf clubs, then opened the passenger-side door for him. She looked so much like Lyka He felt like he was still in the Philippines, except no one has a Mercedes and the parking lot wasn't littered with plastic bags, and crowing roosters. Lacey looked so cute in a white top and black short-shorts. He wanted to lean over and kiss her on the lips.

*Don't do it brah, bad idea. Remember, the captain's your best friend? Don't 'just do it' and think you can apologize later.*

Of course, he wouldn't do it. He knew his boundaries, but he loved her with the kind of love he'd felt for Sister Mary Magdalene and for Mary Beth Johnson. *Maybe, I could just reach over and touch her on her beautiful knee.*

*Stop it.*

Lacey was busy buckling herself in the driver's seat and she kept talking. "I was so upset that our flight from Manila was over-booked. I wanted to sit by you. When you were bumped until the next day, I had to sit next to this fat slob of a guy who snored for ten hours. I got here yesterday at noon, on time, our original flight. How was yours?" She asked again.

"It was Okay. I sat next to a nice old Hawaiian man who left me alone, so I could cry for a while. I was so sad to leave Lyka. I told her I won't be seeing her anymore."

"Who's Lyka?"

"Lyka... your sister, Lyka."

"I don't have a sister named, Lyka."

Oliver looked at Lacey with a monkey face of utter confusion.

"I've been writing emails to Lyka for months, so I finally flew to the Philippines to meet her." He took a quick breath and sputtered on, "Don't mess with me like that," Ole said, with a nervous laugh.

"I'm not messing with you. I don't have a sister named... Lyka."

Ole let that settle into his mind like freshly poured concrete.

*Who did you sleep with, brah?*

"I slept with your sister, Lyka at the Whispering Beach Resort. She took care of me after my dive into the rocks. Hey, how did you know about my arm?"

"Oh, my stars and little fishes, that was *me*! I sleep with you. I cleaned your stitches and re-wrapped your head wound every day. Don't you remember? That was *ME!* You hit your head hard, got thirty-four stitches. Your arm's still swollen. I'm taking you to the ER for another x-ray right now."

The cement slurry of impossible facts was starting to harden. Ole looked in the back seat to see if the captain was hiding back there with a gun.

"Does your husband know about us?"

Lacey looked like she was about to burst into tears; her grip on the wheel made her light brown knuckles go white.

"You're my husband, Billy. We've been married for seven years. You're wearing the wedding ring I gave you...don't you remember me?"

Now, Lacey really was crying, sobbing with her eyes shut while she drove. He looked down at the sling on his left arm. When he peeled back the cloth he saw a solid gold ring glinting reality back at him from the fourth finger of his purple left hand.

Lacey parked in front of the emergency room doors at Maui Memorial. He got out on his own and went around to open her door. She unbuckled and leaned into him, still crying hard. He put his good arm around her and held her close to his chest. His thoughts were doing 'parkour-leaps,' jumping from every other word that she'd just said and back again. *Billy? I'm Captain Billy? Married for seven years? To Lacey, the woman of my illicit dreams?* He was so happy he nearly peed his shorts. Instead, he held her up and walked her into the ER, Billy smiling, Lacey crying.

The ER staff took one look at them and set Lacey down in a wheelchair thinking she was the one injured. Lacey got a smile out of that. They sat in the air-conditioned, freshly cleaned waiting room on upholstered chairs, talking in small whispers for about an hour. Finally, an x-ray tech took a few pictures of Ole's arm and head. When a doctor had a chance to look at the film, he came in with the good and the bad.

"Your head wound is healing nicely. No fractures of the cranium. That scar is all over the place. Did you sew it up yourself?"

"Of course not, it was a doctor in the Philippines. It took two hours and cost thirty-eight dollars."

The doctor didn't seem to hear him, or didn't want to hear him. "Your arm's broken in two places," He announced.

Ole showed him the x-ray from the Philippines. "They told me it wasn't broken. They gave me that sling to ease the pain."

"I guess we have better x-ray machines here on Maui. Ours are only twenty-seven years old. See these splinters sticking out here and here. That's what's causing the pain.

We call them bone-fractures. Here's another sling, keep ice on it until the swelling goes down."

"No cast?"

"No, it'll take time. but you'll heal up just fine. Bone grows thicker than normal after this kind of injury. Your bone will be stronger than before. I'll write out a prescription for pain and another for physical therapy. You're going to need five or six months of serious P. T. You can pay the clerk on your way out. Good day." The nameless doctor with the spotless white sleeves left the room.

"Four-hundred and ninety-seven dollars and fifty-two cents!" Billy read the invoice lying on the clerk's desk. He didn't touch it not even with his good hand. "For an hour wait, and three snapshots from a twenty-seven-year old x-ray machine? No, way!"

Lacey took the bill and handed over a medical insurance card and fifteen-dollars cash for a co-pay.

"Whoa!" Ole exclaimed. "It's more fun in the Pila-pinnes."

Lacey laughed the sweetest little laugh. Rainbows filled the ER with her smile. His heart laughed over the rainbows with her as her words cured the concrete of this new reality. He was her husband. He'd seen his name on the medical invoice, William B. Bones, Captain.

"Where to now, Missus Bones?"

"I'm taking you home, Mr. Bone Fractures."

"Hit me!" Oliver exclaimed. And suddenly, the casino of his mind lit up with a supernatural brilliance. Karma was Jesus this time. Jesus with the flaming heart pierced by swords. He looked calm as a Buddha, with a look of love in his eyes. Jesus pointed to his heart with one hand and offered a new Blackjack card with the other...*the Ace of Hearts. A symbol of love. Billy added it to his other two cards... Twenty-one.* "Thank you, Jesus!"

"Hit you... thank you Jesus, what?" Lacey's face looked worried.

"Just talking to an old friend. No, don't hit me." He smiled and shut up again. She put her arms around him and kissed him right on the lips. It tasted like fresh rain and green tea, grandma's cookies, and thirty-one flavors of ice cream.

## 75  Home, No Way, Home

The ride in Lacey's Mercedes was a happy blur to Captain Billy. It was ten minutes before he noticed she was driving the wrong direction. They were heading up the side of the volcano on the Haleakala highway.

"Lahaina is back that-away, Lacey."

"We live up in Pukalani, Billy. Don't you remember?"

"Sorry, feels like I've got a vog bank hiding my memories. Are we rich or something? How could we possibly buy a house? I was forty-eight-thousand in debt to my divorce attorney. I must be dreaming again."

*That must be it, brah. You're still asleep on the flight from Manila.*

"This could never be," he whispered. "You an' me... married for years. No way, it's too wonderful!" *Why can't I remember?*

"It's true, my captain. Just lean back and rest. We'll be there soon. This is no dream of yours. It's mine too. I love you my husband. This is *our* dream."

Billy sat quietly and watched the green fields of sugar cane blur past. It was another ten minutes of elevation gain before Lacey turned off the main road into a formal looking estate entrance with two rusty looking gates. She drove up a winding, badly paved driveway. It looked familiar.

"This place? I remember this driveway from a dream." He sat up straight to see out the windows better. There's a big old haunted house up there in the trees."

"It's our house Billy. You've been working on it for months. The painters have finished the exterior. It's so beautiful, now. Don't you remember? You've been puttering around in the garage with your cars and replanting the garden."

"What about the secret garden back in the woods?" He cringed, thinking about the open grave marked with his tombstone.

"That old irrigation ditch? We filled it in. You designed our new collection system. Rain runs off the roof and down into an underground cistern. There's plenty of water now for the house and the gardens."

"Where'd we get all this money? I was in debt; your parents are poor. Lyka had a job in a bookstore, but she couldn't afford anything like this."

"I don't have a sister named, Lyka. That was me you were sleeping with. We work hard, Billy. We both have jobs. Do you remember yours?"

"Sure, I work at the Sands of Kahana guiding garden tours, teaching lei making, Tai chi and ukulele."

"And what else?"

"I play music at the PI two nights a week, the 'Ole Gold happy-hour gig.' I write my own songs, and play the concertina and the penny whistle."

"The *'Captain Billy Bones'* happy hour gig," she corrected him. "The longest running singer-songwriter show on Maui; six and a half years. Your music has caught on, Billy Bones. World-wide sales on i-tunes got you out of debt and paid for this car in just five of those years."

"No way..."

"Stop with the no way," she raised her voice. "It's all true."

The old house came into view. It looked like the grand plantation house that belonged to Forest Gump's mother. Wearing its new coat of paint, it glowed like the White House in D. C.

"Is it enough to buy a home like this...on five acres...on Maui."

"We... came into some money...I'll...tell you… later."

Lacey parked under the formal portico of the grand old house and turned off the engine.

"Welcome home!"

Billy sat there in the front seat, stunned by the 'miracle' that was blessing him. He thought of his original retirement dream when he first arrived on Maui. He wished he knew just one cute Asian woman who owned her own home on the island, drove a Mercedes convertible (this one had an electric sunroof, close enough) and owned a liquor store. Booze wasn't high on his list anymore, so forget that part. *The cute woman is Lacey... Captain Billy's wife. That's me, I'm the captain. Lacey's my wife. This is our car, our home.* He was getting dizzy, about to pass out from happiness and arm pain. Instead, he got out of the car and lifted the trunk lid to retrieve his luggage.

"Leave it. I'm giving you a hot bath and you're going to bed...with me."

*Jesus deals a good hand of Blackjack, brah.*

## 76 Mom's Hair Brush

The very next morning, Lacey was up and singing softly as she dressed for work. Billy lay in bed listening, admiring his wife and his wedding ring.

"I talked to your supervisor at the Sands of Kahana." Lacey stopped singing and explained, "Lani knows you're injured. I told her you won't be coming in this week. She's good with that." Lacey sat on the edge of their canopy bed brushing her long black hair.

"Let me do that," Billy offered. He wanted to be close to her. He took the brush and began to run it down her thick hair... then stopped.

"This looks like my mother's hair brush. She's had it since I was a kid... what's it doing here?"

"Sit down love." Lacey patted the bed next to her. Like an obedient puppy, he sat on the edge of the unmade bed.

"You really don't remember, do you?" She paused. Billy didn't answer. His thoughts were on the hair brush and the sad premonition appearing in his mind.

"Your mom passed away last February. It was a brain aneurism, very sudden. You flew back to Iowa for the funeral. Don't you remember?" Lacey was tenderly massaging his sore, left hand, his mom's hand.

A collage of ice-cold images pasted themselves on the white board of his mind. A cloudless sky above him, blue and cold as eternity, crowds of people dressed in black overcoats, ice-crystal air that hurt his lungs when he breathed. The crunch of crusty snow under people's black dress shoes, a long line of white limousines and dozens of cars parked along a snow-covered hillside. The distant sun that gave no warmth, but reflected off the snow with white lasers that burned his eyes. He could see puffs of steam hanging off the tips of people's noses. Most of the noses he recognized. His brothers and sisters and his daughter, Elsa was there. She was holding onto his arm while they all waited under the navy-blue awning over the grave.

His dad was hunched over with grief and the chill of the moment. When the casket was lowered into the carpet lined hole, dad stood straight and blew the conch shell loud and strong, challenging cold death and the winter sky. Billy could still hear that conch shell moan, a sound from the Pacific islands, mixed with the honking of wild Canadian geese. They rose off an open patch of water on a pond near his mother's grave. A block away a snow and mud-covered back-hoe tractor looked like it was trying to hide behind some leafless trees.

Of course, he remembered, more than he wanted to. He sighed and put his 'dad' arm around Lacey. The other arm hurt worse than ever. Pain begets pain. He wanted to cry again, but he'd cried that day and many days after. He moved the hair brush softly through Lacey's black hair.

"Mom left us some money?"

"Don't you remember?"

"No... I don't remember that. Enough to buy this house?"

Lacey nodded her head. "We bought this place the day Betty Mano showed it to us, almost a full price offer. The antique furniture, sculptures, pots, pans and cars in the garage, all included."

"Then I wasn't dreaming, I was here with you...up in the spooky attic?

"All cleaned out now. No more devil-worship chapel."

"How 'bout the jars full of dust and clipped nails?"

"All gone. Kahu Tama drove up from Lahaina and went room to room shaking holy water from a Ti leaf and shouting lots of prayers in Hawaiian; he even climbed up to the attic. The home is ours and blessed Billy, thanks to your mom. There was money left over to start in on the renovations and we have helped my family buy a nicer house in the Philippines."

Billy hugged her tighter. "Mom would like that." He got very thoughtful… "Lacey, I didn't know she had any money. Maybe a few stocks and bonds, but not this kind of money."

"When her will was read, the mystery came clear. Back in the nineteen-twenties, the roaring twenties, your mom's father bought a farm down in Florida on speculation. He never even saw it; he just bought it. A whole section, six-hundred and forty acres, fifty miles from Miami, not a single house on it. The years passed. He tried to sell it for a profit, but nobody was buying anything in the thirties. When the Depression got worse, grandpa could no longer pay the property taxes. So, rather than loose title to the state of Florida, he entered into a written agreement with a friend, who was an attorney in Perry, Iowa. The attorney promised to pay the annual property taxes from then on, for half-ownership of the land. They recorded the shared-deed with the local Florida tax assessor's office.

Time burned up the decades like firewood and in the nineteen-sixties the federal government decided to build a freeway through that swampy land. The title search showed the owners both deceased by then, so the children of both families were notified. They agreed to sell. Your mom never told anybody but your dad. They invested their share in the stock market. It grew for forty-five years. It was a quite a wonderful shock to your brothers and sisters, too. You don't remember any of this?"

"I remember the funeral and the snow and the geese and Elsa being there... and the wake at my sister's house. I was drinking, dancing and laughing with my siblings one moment, then stepping outside into the snow and leaning on the frozen wall of the house, crying my heart out. Then back inside for another drink and more dancing. Mom would have loved her wake."

"I have to get to work. Are you going to be okay?"

"Sure, I'm fine... ah...where do you work?"

"The same store I opened on Front Street two years ago..."

"You own a liquor store?"

"No! Why would I want to open a liquor store? It's my retail clothing shop, t-shirts, Hawaiian nick-knacks, you know the place. You helped me get it up and running."

"It's your store? You own a store on Maui, on Front Street?"

"I have to go love. If you need me, call me. Your phone is on its charger, right over there. I made you some oatmeal, it's on the stove. There's food in the pantry and in the fridge. Take your pain pill and ice your arm if it gets too sore, promise?"

With this, she kissed him, hugged him gently and went down the marble stairway.

"I promise," he said to the empty bedroom.

The trade wind was blowing the curtains away from the open windows. Ole walked over to one of them and watched Lacey drive away in her Mercedes. *What would mom say about all this,* he wondered? Then it came to him. She'd say,

"Merry Christmas, Billy!"

He knew what else she would say, so he knelt next to the open window. The seductive mistress of Maui island had stolen him away from Tanya and his life and friends in Seattle for this moment. His heart was rejoicing with gratitude for the years he'd been given here on Maui, even if he couldn't remember them this morning. He shouldn't be surprised that his childhood dreams had come true; they were his from the start. He'd studied, become a scientist, a teacher. He'd retired on a shoestring budget in Hawaii, wrote and recorded music, and he'd found his Mary Beth.

*Miracles happen? Even to a skeptical, agnostic? What powers this,* he wondered? *If it wasn't god-believing, what was it? Can the human monkey-mind dream what it needs, and then create what it dreams?*

Oliver thought of mankind's ideas over the eons. People needed fire, then a drum, then a boat; first it was a log, then a canoe, then sailing rigs. People domesticated animals to do the work, then machines, Then computers. Humans invented music, theater, the periodic table, hydraulics, the industrial revolution, electricity, steamships, flying machines, the cure for polio, television, spaceships to the moon, cell phones, the internet, light emitting diodes, Nylon, Dacron, Mylar, Carbon Nano-fiber materials...

He could hear his dad's voice, "what will they think of, next?"

Oliver knelt in thankfulness for his grandpa's swamp purchase and his parent's wise investing. Then he lost it, broken with sweet tears, as he thought of his dearest friend, his mother.

"Hit me," Billy whispered. He waited...nothing happened. Nothing at all. He half expected to see Mark Twain dealing a new hand in the casino of his mind. But, no new Blackjack card appeared. The trade wind, blowing in the open bedroom window, kissed him softly right between his eyes. It left a bindi dot of affection on his forehead. A kiss soft as his mother's.

When he was a child, his mom would kiss him like that after reading him a bed time story about robots or pirates. Then tuck a few extra blankets around him to keep him warm on Iowa's winter nights.

There was a scent of her perfume on the wind this morning, white ginger, mom's favorite. The ginger wind blew in from the north and out the south facing windows. It sent the curtains flying like spinnakers on a sloop. He prayed gratitude to Jesus. He bowed to the sunrise, he chanted to Buddha, he would send a thank you card to Santa at the North Pole if he could. Anything, to show his appreciation for this sweet turn of events.

"Prayer changes the person praying," Kahu Tama had said.

The Universe (or Multiverse) is a mysterious creation. Maybe it's just one of God's dreams, composed of Nano-fiber string theory and grateful protection chants to His ancestors.

The crush of elation and sorrow he felt at this moment was overpowering. He could feel the transmogrification as emotions flooded his mind, his feet, his Share of Soul, with Pentecostal fire. The Holy Spirit had taken off its sandals at the door of his little heart-cabin in the woods, sat down at the table with the fresh flowers and radiated amazing grace in all directions. His aura was glowing bright as Ram Dass. Tea was brewing in the kettle. Captain Billy had never in his life felt so alive! He just might just jump up and start speaking in tongues.

*Uh huh... where's your new Blackjack card brah?*

He was too busy pouring tea for his Holy Guest to worry about cosmic Blackjack. It was like his karma had caught up with his life, at least up to now. Billy would have to make more mistakes or do something right, before he would reap any further punishment or merit from his karma. It was a magic Maui moment of such satisfaction, that his ego slipped out of body... and blew away on the white-ginger wind... through the window and out across the celestial sea.

## 77 Love Tools and Spilled Paint

When Captain Billy returned within himself, or awoke or whatever you may call it, he was sitting behind the wheel of his nineteen-eighty-eight Coupe DeVille. He panicked. All that cosmic astral travel on the wind meant nothing, signified nothing, compared to the fear that paralyzed him now. *How did he get in the car, wearing only a t-shirt and the boxer briefs he'd slept in last night? How did his Cadillac get in Lacey's garage?*

Parked next to him was the fifty-five aqua-marine, Thunderbird and next to it, was the almost new, BMW sedan.

*Lacey kept your old Caddy for you? She stored it in the garage. That's true love brah. Has it ever been in a garage?*

He couldn't remember walking down the stairs or getting behind the wheel of his old car. The last thing he could recall was gratefully inviting Jesus, Buddha and the Holy Wind into his heart.

*When did you learn to astral sleep walk, brah?*

Perhaps his mind's eye did the walking for him.

*No matter, be here now.*

*Hah, that he remembers, it was the title of one of the books written by Ram Dass. He'd read it in high school. It helped him jump off the circus wagon of religion.* Billy stretched one leg out on the vast white leather of the front seat, recalling stuff as best he could. This car for instance... all the worry, trauma and great sex this fine old Cadillac had seen him through.

*Good thing cars can't talk story brah, or Lacey would throw you and this car, out on the street.*

Out of curiosity, he reached into the glove box. Under some tourist maps he found what he was looking for, his old wedding ring. It was lighter than he remembered. Maybe, because it was no longer burdened with heartache over Tanya. Lacey had found him online, believed in him and married him. He looked at the new ring of gold on his left hand, 'mom's' hand. He sighed with tremendous loss and an equal balance of great Joy. He knew he should take the Buddha's advice and walk the middle path of life, less crying, less laughing, a path of great wisdom.

*No, brah. That ain't living! You want the whole roller coaster!* The captain scrunched his eyes. His wild Id was piloting his soul plane again. Billy could imagine his Ego strapping on his parachute while his Super-Ego shook his head from side to side in disdain.

*Have you learned nothing?* Asked that mysterious third voice in his forehead. It sounded kind of like the Tai-chi guy.

The moment passed. His new wedding ring radiated with trust and faith. Lacey was the beautiful woman he had believed in for seven years. The captain held his old ring up in his 'dad' hand comparing it to the one Lacey gave him. The old gold looked tarnished and lifeless. Without a moment's hesitation, he threw that round chunk of pain into a trash can over by the lawn mowers. *An ounce of gold is worth a lot of money brah.*

*Take it as a symbolic gesture. Someday I'll dig it out of there and pawn it.* He re-assured his forehead.

One of the tourist maps had fallen onto the floor of the car. As he picked it up to return it to the glove box, he saw that it was covered in math and chemical formulas. There was a sketch of a something up in one corner.

*What?* Chicken-skin panic rising again, he tore through the glove box to find the Cadillac's registration. He couldn't read it; his eyes were still waking up. He got out of the Caddy and under the fluorescent lights above his work bench, he read,

```
Hawaii State Department of Taxation
Motor Vehicle Registration
Legal Owner: Oliver G. Gold
Year and make: 1988 Cadillac
Model: DeVille Gross Vehicle
Weight: blah blah blah...
```

The registration fell from his trembling fingers. Synapses were doing jumping jacks in his brain. He studied the chemical formula on the tourist map. In the upper left-hand corner, out on the ocean, above the north coast of Maui, was a bad drawing with the name, *Robo II.* Below that a signature, *@ Oliver Gold*

He laid his brilliant, but still unproven formula on the work bench next to the car registration and with a lost-monkey look on his face, he began touching jars of nails and paint cans, wrenches and screwdrivers to see if any of it was real. He saw a hammer hanging on a peg board above the nails. He thought of smashing it down on his thumb to see if he was dreaming.

*Don't do it brah. You're a musician; you need your thumbs.*

He turned around, he was staring eyeballs to headlights with the Ford convertible. He closed his eyes. His third eye assured him the car was still there. When he opened his eyes, he was sitting behind the wheel of the T-bird with the engine running. He felt woozy.

*******

That's how Lacey found him, asleep in the driver's seat of the Thunderbird. The engine was running, muffler rumbling, idling a steady cloud of blue, pre-environmentally-correct exhaust. The smoke would have killed him in ten minutes, but for the fact that Lacey had left the fourth garage door open that morning when she'd left for work.

"BILLY!... BILLY!... WHAT ARE YOU DOING?" she screamed!

He moved his head a little, but he didn't answer. Lacey ran to him and shook him by his shoulders. She woke up the pain in his left arm.

"Ye-ouch!" His eyes bulged in surprise.

"What are you trying to do, KILL yourself?"

She looked into his eyes with a devotion he hadn't seen since he lost Snorty. Lacey had beautiful, brown eyes. She turned off the key in the ignition and pulled him out of the car. She was shaking all over, frantic, talking a hundred-miles-a-minute. She wrapped her arms around his waist, hugging him with all her skinny mighty, might. That hug woke up the tool box in his shorts.

"Answer me! YOU WANNA DIE? What's wrong Billy? How many pain pills did you take? This is all my fault. I should have stayed with you today. Talk to me!"

He was still groggy. She went to open all the rest of the garage doors. The fresh air started clearing the unholy carbon monoxide from his lungs.

"Say SOMETHING!" She shouted. He wasn't

responding.

"That's it. I'm calling 911." She dug in her purse looking for her phone.

"You're home early," he muttered.

"What were you doing in that car with the engine running?"

"I just fell asleep, I guess. I wasn't trying to end it all..." he tried to reassure himself as well as her. He wasn't quite convinced. Neither was she.

"How many pain pills did your swallow?"

"Haven't taken one since yesterday, honest."

"I'm taking you back to the doctor."

"No, I'm okay. I was just messing around with the cars and fell asleep that's all."

*Is that how it happened brah? How about sailing out the window on the Holy Wind like Ram Dass?*

Lacey raised up on her toes and kissed him with a passion that made his brain shut up. The kiss was... well... indescribably delicious. No one had ever kissed him like that. He got his full confidence back. His all-purpose screwdriver was growing longer, ready to get to work. *Lacey loves you brah. She's your wife. Her arms are tight around you. You're the captain. She's yours. Be here now! Wow! wow! What a little Filipina doll she is!*

Lacey kept kissing him like she was so glad he was still alive or maybe, it was her version of sex-crazed, CPR to keep him alive. He felt his ego slipping away like live steam from a moonshiner's still. He was about to evaporate out of body for another trip into the cosmos. She opened her tender lips in such an inviting way she took him to France instead. French kissing has a way of relieving stress that's one-hundred-thousand times faster than meditation.

He lifted her up onto his work bench, she tore off his t-shirt. Her skinny, tan legs wrapped his waist like a bench-vice. She grabbed his screwdriver with both hands. He pushed some paint cans and papers off the workbench. The cans hit the floor like a payload of small bombs. Left-over house paint spread evenly across the garage floor. Sherwin Williams, off-white, exterior satin finish, guaranteed one-coat application, soaked through, and destroyed the paper car registration.

The tourist map with the formula for Nano-fiber Anorthosite floated down like a leaf and landed under the T-bird, escaping the river of house paint.

Had the captain looked down at the mess on the floor, he would have laughed out loud. But he was too busy kissing the lipstick off the pretty lips of his wife. Lacey had switched on his drill press and he was ready to start pressing something. Her long black hair came tumbling down around his face. He wouldn't need safety goggles for this project. She leaned back and growled like a belt sander about to grind away all his rough edges. He pulled her close to his hairy chest and with his sand paper chin, he kissed slowly down her long sexy neck. She moaned, tightening her leg vice.

His hot fingers measured her larger than cupcake sized breasts. Lacey's fingernails scratched his back like ten frantic wood files. They were buzzing like two skill saws about to rip into each other. He found one of her mini-marshmallow nipples and twisted his lips round and round on the tip like a compression socket wrench turning for home. She cried out hotly in his ear,

"Welcome to the Pila-pp... PING!... PING!... PING!"

## 78  The Me, I Used to Be

"Well, good morning everyone. This is your captain speaking. I have turned on the cabin lights as we make our approach to Honolulu International Airport."

Looking around, Oliver awoke with a groaning gut-ache the likes of which he'd never known. He thought he'd just won Gold at the Olympic event called, 'Sex with the wife of your dreams.' But instead, he was crumpled in his economy class seat like a crushed aluminum can. He tried to deny the passenger jet around him, but the cabin lights were too bright. His butt was too sore, his throat, too dry. He tried to swallow, no way. He dug into the airline seat pocket in front of him for his water bottle; it was empty.

"Aloha everyone. This is Captain Vicentillo again. The weather in Honolulu is a balmy eighty-one degrees this morning. We are thirty minutes ahead of schedule, so we'll be landing at... eleven-fifty AM, Hawaii time. Set your watches and enjoy your stay in these beautiful islands. Please raise your curtain shades and return your seats to their full, upright position. Thank you for flying with Philippine Airlines. We hope you'll fly with us again... flight attendants, prepare for landing."

Oliver sobbed out loud. He slumped down into himself. He could see Diamond head out his plexiglass window. It usually made him excited to see Waikiki beach and that landmark crater. Today, it looked like a giant grave where all his foolish dreams and wrong-way love for the captain's wife should be buried. He leaned his head against the window and cried. Waking up from his happy dream with Lacey hurt worse than that cold winter day of his mother's funeral.

*Whoa! If that was all a dream, then mom's still alive!*

The moment the pilot announced that cell phones and electronic devices could blah, blah, blah. He quick-dialed his parents. Mom answered.

"Merry Christmas in February! You've reached Pat and Floyd at the lake. We're either out building a snowman or shoveling him off the driveway. Leave your number and we'll call you as soon as we get these frozen mittens off our hands. Ho, Ho, Ho... bye."

Ole left a message for her to call him back, ASAP. He followed the single-file line of arriving passengers rushing through the airport until the line slowed to a shuffle at US immigration. After those x-ray machines, there was a longer wait at US Customs. No one asked him how much money he was bringing into the country. No one said, "Welcome to the USA!"

He headed for the nearest Men's room. When he had finished the longest pee of his life, he took off his baseball cap and looked in the mirror. His head was still bandaged. Not much blood had seeped through on the long flight. His purple arm hurt almost as bad as his heart. That poor old beater was missing on five cylinders, yet seemed to be racing two-hundred beats per miss.

*"You're messed up brah,"* There was Tai-chi man, staring back at him from the Men's room mirror. Ole shook his head to make the vision go away, but the Tai-chi guy was still there, still staring. He looked older and sadder than before. Oliver took a closer look. There was a lot of gray in his hair that he'd never noticed before. He surveyed his face. Lines of age were making new roads across his forehead, he looked ten years older than before the flight to the Philippines. *Was that a jet plane or a time machine,* he wondered? Ole whispered a prayer. No, he

wasn't praying to the guy in the mirror, he was praying to… God? He tried to Blue-tooth his prayer silently… *as for me, oh Lord, oh Holy Spirit wind, sail me back to the me, I used to be. Amen.* Then, remembering that he'd made no broadband donations to any church recently, he said it again, this time, out loud:

"As for me, Oh Lord, Oh Divine Holy Spirit Wind, sail me back to the me, I used to be. Amen." The other men in the washroom moved further away from his sink and made like they weren't listening. Ole washed his hands out of habit, never wanting to become a leper, and headed for the nearest airport bar.

## 79 The Impermanence of All Things

He didn't drink the rum and Coca-Cola that he paid nine dollars for. The first sip tasted like mold, so he just let it sit there stinking up the air over his table. He was so over the pleasures of self-inflicted alcohol poisoning. He knew if he drank it down, it wouldn't make him feel better. In fact, it would make him feel worse, if that was even possible. He left the bar and somehow found the inter-island flight gate.

The half hour hop to Maui was another adventure that used to thrill him with joy. Today's flight was thirty minutes of Twilight Zone. Nobody on the small jet had a face. Everyone looked like a mannequin. They had foreheads, ears and noses, but no eyes and no mouth. They wore colorful Hawaiian print clothes. They were animated, turning their faceless heads from side to side, sneezing, scratching their ears. He couldn't wait to get off that plane.

The instant the seat-belt light went off, he grabbed his carry-on and made it almost to the exit door before the mannequins in first-class, stood up and blocked his escape. They moved in slow-motion, reaching into the overhead luggage bins like faceless zombies searching for brains.

Descending the escalator to the Maui baggage area gave him that same old sadness. Down there on street level, people stepped off the moving stairway into the arms of their loved ones. Like always, there would be no one waiting for Oliver Gold.

*It was just another of your psycho-dreams, brah. You really need a mental tune-up.*

*Yah, ask the shrink for a brain scan. Yours is defective.*

"Look who's talking," he shot back at his mind. That shut the voices up for a while.

He looked for Lacey at the bottom of the escalator. But of course, she wasn't there. She was married to Captain Billy Bones. Oliver sighed. He was happy for them. They were his friends.

He'd burned all his bridges with Lyka. Maybe that was the wrong thing to do. She was so nice to him. Now, here he was, back on romantic Maui all alone. His carry-on stumbled along behind him like a blind dog. All the cheerful buzz of the airport was making him nauseous. He wished his mom would call. Ole stumbled along with the happy crowd of aloha-shirt mannequins. A tear dripped out of his bad eye. He let it roll. Heading for the parking lot, he heard the roar before he felt it. The wind sounded like a thousand passenger jets all taking off at the same time. A tremendous storm was ripping across the island. Rain slammed against the passing taxis. Passengers ran for their cars.

*How could things get any worse,* he wondered. *Was this another omen? If it was, what could it mean?* He suddenly had a mini-epiphany as he stood there watching the storm. *The word, 'omen' is four-fifths of the word, 'women.'* He looked around to see if there were any more gorgeous omens nearby. Someone cute, fast and skinny that he could believe in, and fall in love with. Someone who would smash his heart like a water balloon when she was done messing with him.

*Don't look for trouble, brah. Remember the impermanence of all things, even of heart break. Find the Joy hiding in the moments you are given.* Oliver shook his head. Wise sutras like that one, bring very little comfort, after your finest water-balloon dreams are dashed on the rocks, lei'd and lied to, then sent out of body.

He stood on the sidewalk, lost in his personal storm of disappointment, trying to remember where he'd anchored his Cadillac. For a small island airport, OGG Maui has a parking lot the size of San Francisco Bay. He stood there in the power-wash rain like the Fool card from the Tarot deck. There was a glazed look in his eyes, no rain coat over his shoulders, totally unaware that he was about to step off the mountain, into traffic.

A shiny wet car drove up and honked. Ole stepped back and focused on his surroundings. The car looked like a Mercedes. It braked to a stop in the passenger pick-up zone, blocking his way, maybe, saving his life. To his amazement, Lacey hopped out smiling like a Philippine teenager. She jumped for joy and rushed down wind and rain, right into his wet arms. Before he could catch his breath, she placed an orchid lei carefully over his bandaged head and arranged it on his shoulders. She kissed him full on the lips with a determined, welcoming smack.

"Lacey, what...?"

"How was your flight, love? How 'bout your arm... still sore?"

"Not too bad. What are..."

"We're gonna get you another x-ray, right now." She took him by his good arm and opened the passenger-side door. She put her other arm around his waist tight as a wood clamp. He wanted to stay glued to her forever, but the rain was soaking them both. He got in, and shook water like a soaked puppy, as Lacey dashed to the driver's side, jumped in, buckled up and drove off into the storm.

## 80 Angry Clouds

X-rays were shot through his head and arm. Then there was a one-hour wait in the ER, before a doctor with no blood on his sleeves, showed them the results on a computer. The doc said the head injury showed evidence of a cranium separation, but it had already healed, somewhat. 'Somewhat' did not sound like an official medical term. *Is he guessing? Is this even a real doctor?* The man with clean sleeves said the stitch marks in the forehead were crude. There'd be a mean looking scar.

*Nope, not a real doctor.*

The arm was fractured in two places, bone splinters, painful, but would heal quickly. The man with no blood on his hands wrote out a prescription for pain meds. Then, without another word, he left, total time... two minutes max.

At the ER payment desk, the clerk read his name out loud as she handed him the invoice, 'William B. Bones, Captain.' The amount owed was nearly five-hundred dollars. Lacey had medical insurance. Billy couldn't stop looking at his typed name and the shiny gold wedding band on his swollen left hand. His mom's hand. He turned to Lacey.

"Mom died." It wasn't a question.

"Yes, love. She passed away last year. What do you remember?"

Those memories were too clear. The cold crunch of the snow under his shoes, the wild geese, dad blowing the conch. "I remember," was all he could manage to say.

They drove into the maelstrom of weather. The onset of the approaching hurricane tried to push the Mercedes back toward the hospital. Lacey drove with determination, heading south on highway thirty.

"Where are we going, Mrs. Bones?"

"I'm taking you home, Mr. Bone Fractures."

"But Pukalani town is up-country, on the side of the volcano... that-a-way." He pointed back over his shoulder.

"Why would I go to Pukalani?"

"Our house, the one we bought. Big house, five acres?

"You hit the rocks pretty hard my husband. We live in Lahaina. We bought a condo there four years ago. You don't remember?"

"Sorry... no... how could we afford to buy a condo? I was forty-some-thousand in debt. This is Maui, where everything costs a trillion dollars. Did we win a lottery?"

"We work Billy. I still have my job. You work at the Sands of Kahana. We paid off your divorce debt last year. You bought this car for me with money made from international music sales on i-tunes. The 'Captain Billy Bones' gig at the Pioneer Inn is the longest running singer / songwriter show on Maui, six years now..."

"I always wanted my music to be heard around the world. I never dreamed I'd make that kind of money."

*You thought you were booked in Las Vegas.*

*Yah, remember those big money dreams? Ole's* 'bad memories' chip seems to be working just fine.

"You're not that famous yet, but we save our money, invest in stocks and we bought our condo in a foreclosure auction. We paid cash. No mortgage. Don't you remember this?"

"Wish I could..." He got depressed thinking of all he'd done in seven years that he couldn't recall. *All because of one stupid dive into shallow water. Water that had been deep the day before. Dang!* Then, another dream surfaced. "Do you own a clothing store on Front Street?"

"No, but my boss *did* open another store on Front. I work there two days a week and three days at the Cannery mall. You have a lot of catching up to do, love."

He shut up and watched the fierce rain that was trying to break the windshield wipers. It was mid-afternoon, but the day was dark already. A dark day of weather, yet he was charged like a cyclotron of nucleonic, speed-of-light joy!

*They owned a home on Maui! No more sharing a bedroom in someone else's condo.* He looked at her, then at his wedding band. He closed his eyes and tried to say a prayer of thanks. He was thankful, very thankful... but prayer? That was still a struggle for a skeptical chemistry teacher.

Angry clouds swept in from the sea like a fleet of Viking Berserkers. They were already waging destruction upon the defenseless beauty of Maui. Trees leaned over like drunkards; many, already blown down, branches blocking some parts of the highway.

Traffic quit moving just before they reached the tunnel on the Pali. The tail lights of all the parked cars blurred in odd psychedelic waves with every swipe of the windshield wipers. It felt like another dream, but it was a wonderful dream. This was a hurricane-Zen, 'be here now' wind shaking the car, kind of life-like dream.

The Mercedes was too heavy to be blown away in this breeze. Lacey reached over and took his hand in hers. He leaned in for a kiss. She tried to meet him midway, but her seat belt wouldn't allow it. She unbuckled and kissed him with a hungry desperation. Time stood still, balanced like a yogi on one hand, it slowed down... fast. That magic kiss made the hurricane disappear along with the rest of the world. *I want to believe this is real,* he nervously thought to himself.

*Y'er an expert at believing, brah. How would you know what's real?*

He thought of a test. With his lips and heart still believing in the magic, he reached over and pressed his passenger-side window button. Water blew in with a vengeance, soaking them as if they'd ducked under a breaking wave with a surf board. That broke the kiss, but not the magic; he was still in the car with Lacey.

"Close the window!" She shouted. "What're you doing!"

He let the wind and rain slap him in the face another few seconds and then closed the window. He didn't wake up in some other body. He wasn't gambling with Death in his mind's riverboat casino. There was no Mark Twain, or Hyena or James Bond, just Lacey and him, sitting in a line of parked car on the highway. Lacey wiped the rain off Billy's face with one hand and her own eyes with the other. It looked like she was crying.

"I had to see if I would wake up from this delicious dream."

"This is real Billy... don't do that again, we'll drown."

Soon they were laughing again... happy as two birds out of the rain. The night looked dark and mean, but rainbows filled the inside of their car with the bright colors of Walt Disney animation. Billy felt more at home with this woman than with anyone he'd ever dated or married. He almost called her Mary Beth, but caught himself just in time and kept his mouth shut. The cars ahead of them were moving again, crawling into the only tunnel on Maui. When Lacey was in the deep dark, half-way through, she leaned on her steering wheel with both hands. The commanding, made in Germany horn, filled the tunnel with awesome echoes.

"I dreamed we bought a big house up-country. It looked like the White House in Washington, D. C. It was so real. How'd that get in my head?"

"We visited the White House, three years ago, on our vacation back east. Maybe you were just remembering that tour."

"In my dream, mom left us some money. That's how we bought the place... did she?"

"No, she had some investments, stocks and bonds mostly. She willed everything she owned, to your dad."

"How is dad?"

"You should call him, you just got back from the Pila-pinnes, he'd like to hear from you, I'm sure."

"I called him from the airport in 'Lu'lu, just got mom's answering machine. The house up-country was a mansion on five acres, there were two cars in the garage... sorry... I've got Vog in my brain so thick it's hard think or even breathe."

He stopped talking. His chest was suddenly tight. Asthma is a monster, one of Death's nasty little helpers. He did some slow breathing. His lifetime of yoga discipline kicked in; trying to keep him alive. They were both quiet. Lacey, battling the wind, Billy making his airways relax. He watched the wind kicking the surf along the shoreline. It looked like messy ten-footers. There were hurricane-chasers out there shredding it.

The ꞁ
Lahaina, ꞁ
miles-per-hꞁ
shaking their ꞁ
language, wild ꜱ
limbs blew throug꞉
the 'Open House' foꞁ
helium balloons had aꞁ
low-down, forty-year-mꜱ
on past. Three blocks furthꜱ
highway, then another turn ꜱ
neighborhood streets and into ꞁ
complex. He counted three, mayꞁ ꜱ two-
story, modern design, and nicely laꞁ ꜱ hibiscus
bushes bent over, trying to hide from ꞁ ꜱd. There
were tall palm trees doing the shimy-shꞁꞁy coco-nut
dance in a circle around the swimming pool. It looked like
one of them had decided to take a dive. Its palm head
stuck in the shallow end of the pool. Or maybe, he just
imagined that.

"Welcome home!" Lacey announced with sigh.

The place did look familiar. However, he couldn't
remember which condo entry was theirs. The wind still
blew like it had something to prove, maybe it was
showing off. Getting out of the car could be dangerous.

"Let's make a run for it, we'll get your carry-on later."
She opened her door and caught it before it tore off its
hinges. He did the same and ran after her. It reminded
him of grade school, chasing Mary Beth. He couldn't have
been happier. Lacey was skinny, cute and fast.

Up one flight of stairs, he caught her and held her tight
with his good arm around her shoulders. A short delay,

...he unlocked the front
...t reminded him of standing
...nts during his charter years. He
...a ship's wheel, sure of himself in this
...moment passed, they were inside. He forced
...or shut behind them. They were in the snug harbor
of their own home. It looked kind of familiar. Lacey
turned on a lamp by the couch. Somehow, the power was
still on. Now, it looked even more familiar.

She kicked off her sandals and leaned in for another
kiss. He grabbed her by her wet, brown shoulders and
pulled her close. *Lacey was his wife!* It was kiss of deep
appreciation. They didn't tear into each other like skill
saws. This kiss was all tenderness. They both held that
kiss with no intention of ever letting go. Gravity settled
them gently down on the couch. There, they curled up
like teenagers necking at the dark end of the Des Moines
airport parking lot. The wind shook their condo building.
Billy's pent-up passion shook Lacey's body mind and soul.
Their wet clothes went flying around the room like soggy
paper airplanes. Mr. Wild 'Id' had his way with Lacey. But
this was a sweeter kind of mad lust; powerful in its
demands, yet chrome-plated with affection. This was
joyful, married sex, warmed with Hawaiian-style 'malama
pono,' romantic, righteous and caring.

*Seven years, brah. Married seven years to Lacey...*
*Yah, how come it feels like your honey moon?*

Billy ignored his brain. This was no time to think. Lacey
was under him, then on top, then side-saddle... *it was*
*Lacey at Whispering Beach. Lacey cleaned my head*
*wound, not Lyka.*

*There's hope for you yet, brah.*

An hour later or maybe more, neither of them were

wearing a watch or anything else. They were still curled up on the couch like two naked spoons. Billy kissed her gently on her hair and whispered in her ear.

"Thanks for finding me, Lacey."

"I'll always find you, Billy. I stayed by your bedside for days, trying to bring you out of your coma. Calling to you, singing to you. Cleaning the stitches on your head. I was so scared I might lose you."

"Coma? How long was I in a coma?"

"Five and a half days."

"Five days! Whoa! You know, I kind of remember somebody singing off key, so I decided to sleep a little longer."

Lacey poked him in his sore arm. He winced, then shut up and tried to remember anything from those five days. But there was nothing.

*How about the last seven years?*

Maybe... stuff was coming back to him, bit by bit. The living room looked more familiar. One of his guitars was leaning up against a book shelf. He was looking at its beautiful inlays when the lights went off. The hurricane winds had scored their first knockout.

Billy was sleepy as a male lion after a rough tumble with his favorite cute, skinny lioness. He wanted to roll around in the African dust, knock the lion cubs around a bit and take a long lover's nap in the sun. He pulled Lacey into a tighter spoon on the couch. They were sound asleep in less than a minute. But the lion did not sleep long tonight.

## 81  Frantic Knocking on the Door

The pounding on their door sounded like gunshots. Frantic knocks, too loud, too close together to be target practice. This was machine-gun knocking, urgent!

Billy wrapped a wet shirt around his waist and pulled open the door. The silhouette of a man was out there, waving his arms and shouting.

"Fire! The whole town is burning! Get ready to evacuate!"

Nothing in his imagination could have imagined this. Over the man's outline, the night sky, which should have been wet and black, was red with the ugly swirling colors of Hell. Flares of sparks shot up in the air trying to catch the sky on fire, then falling like incoming mortars to burn down the rest of the town. It looked like the entire southern horizon of Maui was burning. Billy threw on his shorts, Lacey pulled on a wet t-shirt. This took the captain's mind off the fire for a brief second, until she ran down the stairs. Billy chased after her. They helped knock on the rest of the condo doors to alert sleeping neighbors. He recognized some of them, but could not call them by name. Everyone gathered in the parking lot.

Suddenly he stopped. Something else was strangely wrong with this drama. *Why is there no wind?* He paused to take a feel. A sailor can sense even a cat's paw of wind. He closed his eyes and felt for direction and speed from his natural wind vanes, his unruly hair and his unshaven face... *there it was, two-miles-per hour, south by west, blowing right toward them. If the wind picks up, Lahaina will burn down. It's made of wooden structures. Their home was one of them.*

Everyone in the parking lot could see another line of

flames up on the mountain. This one was east of town. The ocean lay to the west, about a block away. Their only escape would be to drive north. He ran up the stairs. Lacey had stacked sleeping bags, emergency water, and their framed marriage license by the front door. Billy made a dozen trips to the car, his captain's eyes always on the wind. The stinking smoke was thicker now, punishing his breathing.

He conferred with his neighbors.

One woman said there were three garden hoses on this side of their building and by God, she was gonna stay and fight, to save their homes.

Billy and the others agreed. It felt like a better plan than running away. But they all knew, that if they delayed their escape, and the wind suddenly increased, they could be trapped. Their cars, were their lifeboats in this storm, but only if the roads weren't blocked by trees, down wires, or stalled traffic. It was a terrible risk to stay and fight. *Maybe we're already trapped?*

Another neighbor, a man he recognized, said, "We could all jump in the ocean with our surf boards until the flames blow past."

*It might come to that. How this happen, brah?*
*Yah, hurricanes bring flood, not fire!*
This was more dream-like to Billy than owning the White House with a Ford Thunderbird in the garage.
That seemed so real. This nightmare was surreal, utterly impossible.

"KA-BOOOOOM… BOOM!" a nearby transformer blew like two sticks of dynamite. Everyone ducked to avoid electrical shrapnel flying in all directions. Men ran to the garden hoses, to be ready when flames came to kill them.

Billy looked at their Mercedes lifeboat. He walked over to touch it on its stern. In the dark of early morning, the smooth metal felt cool to his touch. It was real. He caught his breath. Across the parking lot he saw his beautiful, chrome-grilled, nineteen-eighty-eight, Cadillac DeVille. Its white paint glowed pink, reflecting the torched, red clouds in the sky, a pink Cadillac parked in a fiery Hades.

Lacey came walking down the stairs carrying his viola and another small suitcase to the Cadillac. She looked so hot in her wet t-shirt and shorts.

"There's more to carry," she said. "We'll load both cars... save as much as we can." Billy ran up the stairs to find she had piled his all his sound equipment, mic stands and speakers just inside, ready to load. He left them stacked by the door and walked room to room seeing most things for the first time. He was still expecting to wake up any moment now, somewhere else, in some other dimension of his life, maybe in some other body. He grabbed some stuff from the refrigerator, and searched along the tops of book shelves in the living room. He found his collection of harmonicas and... his penny whistle! Music memories, good and bad, nearly knocked him over. He tossed all of it, even the memories, into a couple of Wal-Mart bags, along with some of his journals and a few photo albums.

*******

With the dim sunrise, heavy smoke covered the town like a blanket of burnt, stinking wool. Breathing was a severe challenge, but they were all still alive. They didn't have to use the garden hoses. An onshore breeze had sent the wildfire mauka (toward the mountains) burning its way up the south-east side of town where fire-fighters and a morning light rain, eventually put it out. Most of

Lahaina had dodged a flaming, thousand-acre, brush-fire-bullet *and* a hurricane all in one night. They learned later, while listening to their hand-cranked emergency radio, that sixteen homes had been destroyed. One woman was med-vac helicoptered out of town, but no one was reported missing or killed.

Lacey looked in the blue bags Billy was still carrying. In one, there were harmonicas and books. In the other bag she found four jars of olives and a small gold medal.

"This is your survival plan?" She asked. "Four jars of olives and a gold medallion?"

"I guess I value olives and gold."

Lacey took him by the hand and led him upstairs. Four-thousand-dollars-worth of professional sound stage equipment was still stacked in the living room. She shook her head in wonder; he'd saved the olives.

"Let's pray love," she said.

Then, his wife… the good wife, the one he'd prayed for ten times a day, knelt on the floor next to a jumble of amps, speakers and mic stands. Billy knelt-down next to her. He didn't think, or rationalize, he didn't doubt. He didn't hesitate.

"Thank you, thank you… Jesus," he whispered.

Lacey put her arm around his waist and prayed, "Thank you Lord, for saving us. Thank you for bringing Billy out of his coma. God speed his recovery."

Captain Billy wasn't done. "Holy Spirit-Wind of all that's Good… thank you for pushing the fire away from our town… and sending Lacey into my life. Amen."

They helped each other up.

"Race you to the shower," Billy challenged with a wink.

Lacey started running. She was cute, skinny and fast. He gave chase. She paused in a doorway and turned to let him catch her. The captain wrapped his arms around her and lifted her off the floor. She smelled like smoke from the wildfire. Lacey curled into his protective embrace, looked up at him with her beautiful, brown, Asian eyes and whispered,

"I love you my husband."

Billy believed her with all his heart.

Karma leaned back in his casino chair, shuffled his deck and of cards and smiled.

From the Author

You may wonder how much of this book really happened?

The only thing that didn't happen, is the cue-ball fight.

There is no pool table in the friendly Sly Mongoose tavern. I made that part up.

If you enjoyed this book, please return to Amazon.com and leave a review.

Mahalo,

*Oliver Gold*

Contact me at: captsails@aol.com

Made in the
USA
Columbia, SC

77410241R00191